Secret Baby for My Bossy Billionaire

An Enemies to Lovers Brother's Best Friend Romance

Lily Cross

Copyright © 2024 by Lily Cross.

All rights reserved.

No part of this publication may be reproduced, distributed, or transmitted in any form or by any means, including photocopying, recording, or other electronic or mechanical methods, without the prior written permission of the publisher, except as permitted by U.S. copyright law.

The story, all names, characters, and incidents portrayed in this production are fictitious. No identification with actual persons (living or deceased), places, buildings, and products is intended or should be inferred.

Contents

Chapter 1: Carrie — 1

Chapter 2: Stern — 15

Chapter 3: Carrie — 28

Chapter 4: Stern — 42

Chapter 5: Carrie — 55

Chapter 6: Stern — 67

Chapter 7: Carrie — 80

Chapter 8: Stern — 94

Chapter 9: Carrie — 109

Chapter 10: Stern — 121

Chapter 11: Carrie — 135

Chapter 12: Stern — 147

Chapter 13: Carrie	159
Chapter 14: Stern	170
Chapter 15: Carrie	182
Chapter 16: Stern	195
Chapter 17: Carrie	209
Chapter 18: Stern	221
Chapter 19: Carrie	233
Chapter 20: Stern	245
Chapter 21: Carrie	257
Chapter 22: Stern	270
Chapter 23: Carrie	282
Chapter 24: Carrie	294
Chapter 25: Stern	306
Chapter 26: Carrie	319
Chapter 27: Stern	334
Chapter 28: Stern	345
Chapter 29: Carrie	357
Chapter 30: Stern	369
Chapter 31: Carrie	381
Chapter 32: Stern	394

Chapter 33: Carrie	409
Chapter 34: Stern	422
Chapter 35: Carrie	434
Chapter 36: Stern	446
Chapter 37: Carrie	456
Chapter 38: Stern	471
Chapter 39: Carrie	484
Chapter 40: Family	495

Chapter 1: Carrie

"Hey, Miles, everyone to their battle stations. Here comes Bridezilla."

I am the first bridesmaid to arrive at the top of the aisle. I hear my brother's best man whispering that to him as I take my place on the bride's side of the church. The man's voice is deep and gravelly, but full of humor too. I see him nudge my brother in the side.

My brother, Miles, is too nervous to see the funny side of things. They aren't even married yet and Belinda Carson already has my brother petrified of saying or doing the wrong thing.

"Shh, Stern. She might hear." Miles shuffles and then drags his finger around the collar of his frilled shirt as if it is too tight.

Belinda insisted that all the bridesmaids wear thick pink veils over their faces during the ceremony. I think I look like a pink flower pot with big fake flowers growing out of the top.

Over the sound of the organ playing, I tease my brother. I am anonymous under the thick veil anyway.

"Miles, you're all red in the face. It's clashing with my dress."

As I go to stand on the bride's side of the aisle, I see the best man craning his neck to try and see who cracked the joke. "I didn't know Belinda had a comedian in her bevy of bridesmaids."

I like him already. "I am not a comedian. I have something called 'good taste.' I think Miles is going to miss that pretty soon."

The best man tries to stifle his laughter because the reverend minister is glaring at us. "What's the hold up with the bride? I'm starting to get a cramp in my butt from standing to attention for so long." The best man sounds kind of hopeful as if he wants Belinda to do a U-turn and head back to the hotel.

"Belinda accidentally stepped on the back of her train," I try explaining, "so the wedding planner is pinning the rip."

"It's more like RIP for my buddy here." The cute best man laughs. I give one of those snorts of suppressed mirth that sound like I am blowing a raspberry.

The reverend has had enough. "If you two don't mind, can we treat this solemn occasion with a little more dignity, please?"

Darn it. Just when I was getting ready to have my first flirtation with my brother's hot best man.

I see the best man grimace and then fall back into line. Was he just trying to get a better look at me? I hope not. I feel hideous in this outfit.

Poor Miles. He has been desperate to start a family since my parents started asking for grandchildren. That was the driving reason why he asked Belinda Carson—aka Bridezilla—to marry him.

But that is not what I am thinking about right now. I can't take my eyes off my brother's best man. He is gorgeous—and I haven't even seen his face yet.

It is not the impeccable fit of the custom-made bolero pulling across his broad shoulders that catches my eye. Or the way I can see the deltoids, lats, and trapezius muscles flexing under the thin satin material as he turns back to face front. It is the slightly dangerous way he is posed as if he is ready to pounce on something… or someone.

Oh, and yes, his ass is amazing too, encased in the tight-fitting high-waisted trousers of a flamenco dancer's partner. As if he is aware of my gaze, he flexes his shoulders and loosens his neck by stretching it to one side and then to the other. I hear the tendons crack as he eases the tension in them—the guy is seriously jacked, but more like a prowling jungle cat than a gorilla.

He is wearing the same outfit as my brother but with a completely different attitude and build. Miles looks like a slender dancer in his clothes, while his best man looks like a mountain man in disguise!

The man's build is mesmerizingly perfect, from his blond hair down to his lean, muscular legs. He has tawny blond hair—the color hairstylists call "dirty blond."

I've never had a crush before. But if I were to get one, this is what he would look like. That is what flashes through my mind as I stand beneath the dais and look up at the bridal party, before even seeing what he looks like from the front.

If he were to see me without my veil, he would be disappointed. I am wearing a calf-length fuchsia pink flamenco dress. The same as the other eleven bridesmaids who are following behind me. Belinda's bridal theme is Spanish flamenco dancers, so we are all decked out with castanets tied to our thumbs and fake silk flowers in our hair.

The pink clashes with my bright red hair, but my mom told me not to complain about it because a wedding day is all about the bride.

Belinda arrives and I step back as she and Mr. Carson, her father, mount the dais together. This is her moment in the spotlight. Her sister, Samantha, is the head bridesmaid. She can't be the matron of honor because she's not married yet.

I see her grab Belinda's bouquet and then go stand next to my brother's hot best man as the ceremony starts. I must say that I don't blame Samantha one bit as she rubs her shoulders against the best man and then twinkles her eyes up at him.

It's too bad that Samantha is having to wear the pink bridesmaid dress instead of her usual revealing plunging necklines. Both Carson girls prefer sexy clothing. At least that is what they always wear in the photos my brother occasionally sends me.

But today, Belinda made sure that she is the only woman in the bridal retinue with an alluring outfit so that she steals the limelight. She hates competition.

As the minister turns to fetch his notebook from the altar, I see the best man nudge my brother again. I am standing right behind them, so I can hear. "When he asks if anyone has an objection, can I raise my hand?"

A smile flickers over my brother's face, but he ignores his friend and turns to face Belinda and takes her hand. Mr. Dirty Blond Hair murmurs to Samantha instead. "Hey, I tried."

Samantha is all fluttering eyelashes and pursed lips as she whispers back. "Ooh, Stern, you are so naughty."

The ceremony doesn't take long. My brother's voice is soft and earnest when he answers the minister's questions. When he says "I will," my mom sobs and blows her nose as he slides the ring on Belinda's finger. When the best man steps forward with the ring, he looks over at me and gives me a wink. My tummy does a flip of happiness. I have never felt this way about a man before.

I'm my parents' youngest child and I'm eighteen. Until my two eldest brothers start a family, there will be no more young children in their house. My brother, Brody, and his wife, Alma, are pregnant and oh-so happy about that.

Brody and Alma are stuck at home looking after my parents' bed and breakfast accommodation facilities in South Africa. I am kind of envious of him not having to go through all of this hoopla, but at least I get to see a bit of New York by agreeing to be a bridesmaid.

I move back as the Reverend Minister proclaims the happy couple husband and wife. I have to watch my step so that I don't accidentally tread on the back of Belinda's train. It's very long and made of expensive imported lace.

Miles looks so happy as he walks past me, but I have to pick up Belinda's train so I miss out on congratulating him. He even manages to say something funny to his best man. "Thanks, Stern. Now remember—you are not allowed to change out of your outfit until the wedding photographs have been taken."

The gorgeous man with dirty blond hair has to walk behind the wedded couple with Samantha hanging from his arm. I hear him growl to Miles. "One photograph and then I am out of there!"

I can't say I blame him. My fuchsia pink satin flamenco dress has so much tulle in it that my skin is starting to prickle. My imagination is running overtime as I imagine what the best man might look like underneath those skintight, high-waisted Spanish pants of his.

The photographer is waiting next to the bridal car. "Come on, lovebirds. Next stop, Central Park!"

The wedding reception is at the Plaza Hotel, but the wedding retinue is going to Central Park to have the photographs taken there.

Samantha tugs the lace train out of my hand as if I am too clumsy to fold it into the limousine. "Go get into one of the other vehicles, Carrie! I'm the head bridesmaid, remember? This is for important bridal attendants only!"

We have a lot of limousines in the procession. The bridal vehicle is white with pink ribbons. Everyone else's are black with white ribbons.

I see my mom and dad cramming themselves into the back of a limousine with Belinda's parents and half a dozen bridesmaids and ushers.

"Carrie! Follow us to the park! Get into the other limo—!"

Her voice gets cut off as the driver closes the door. The bridal procession heads off to the park, leaving me on the sidewalk. I don't mind. My dress is itchy and I want to change it for the reception. If that hot blond guy from the wedding can do it then so can I.

There are lots of wedding guests heading to the Plaza. "Oh, dear." One of the Carson guests smiles at me when she sees me standing in my bright pink dress. "Did they forget you?"

Smiling, I nod. "Yeah. But honestly, I don't understand how anyone could be forgotten while they are wearing this color!"

The lady laughs. "Yes. It is very bright, isn't it? Can we give you a lift to the park?" I shake my head. "I'm sure it will be fine if I just go straight to the reception."

"That's where we are heading," the lady points to herself and then to her partner. "When our driver arrives, we can give you a lift to the Plaza."

The kind couple asks me where I am from when I get into the car with them. I don't sound like I'm from South Africa or Texas, but somewhere in between. My parents still speak with strong Texan accents, but I have picked up a lot of South African expressions growing up there.

"I'm Miles's little sister," I explain as we pull up outside the Plaza. "South Africa produces some of the top security experts in the world. The only other country to match it is Israel. That's why Miles works here now. He's in security."

Thanking them for the lift, I leave the couple to enter the ballroom for the reception while I run to the reception desk. I have my passport, bank card, and cell phone in the lace purse hanging from one wrist. Pushing my passport across the desk, I begin to explain.

"Hey there. I need to use the bridal—"

Seeing my fancy pink satin dress and looking at my passport, the receptionist puts two and two together. "The Maitland bridal party. Of course. Let me get you a key card." I don't have permission to use the suite, but I have the same surname as my brother, so I use that to gain access. I am staying with my mom and dad in Miles's Greenwich Village loft apartment.

Five minutes later, I am sitting in the Maitland honeymoon suite and texting my mom and my brother.

I caught a lift to the hotel so please don't worry about me. Was feeling sick. See you at the reception. Love, Carrie.

One of them is bound to get the message when they see that they are one vivid pink bridesmaid short for the photographs. I am not feeling sick, but the last thing I need right now is for my mom to make everyone wait while she comes to fetch me. Bright pink satin with red hair is not an image I want to keep as a souvenir of this day!

Unknown to anyone else, I have a surprise hiding underneath my hideous dress: a short white summer dress with spaghetti straps. It looks amazing with the hot pink stilettos I am wearing. All I have to do is tear off my outer dress, and voilà! My "petticoat" turns into a cute little dress.

My sexy reveal didn't go as smoothly as I hoped for. One of the spaghetti straps has broken. Removing the dress, I walk over to the bedroom and search for a sewing kit. This is the Plaza, after all. It has everything.

I catch a glimpse of myself in the floor-length mirror. I look coltish and wild, with my long red hair tumbling down my back now that it is free of the fake flower hair clips; my legs are elegantly enhanced by the four-inch stilettos. I chose my lingerie specifically so that I could wear my summer dress to the reception. Strapless white lace bra and teeny tiny white lace panties. No undergarment lines to ruin the sleek appearance of my dress.

After finding the sewing kit, I walk back into the sitting room and stand by the window. I need to use the sunlight to sew the strap back into place.

I am halfway through fixing the strap when a thought crosses my mind: Did I remember to close the door when I came in?

Chapter 2: Stern

"Ooh, Stern, you are so tall. Go stand next to my sister. You're blocking my light." The bride waves her enormous bouquet at me as if I'm a bee that is bothering her.

Belinda Carson has been running the Human Resources division at Sterns & Co. for almost five years. She tries to run everyone's life at the company too. But I am the boss, so I don't have a problem cutting her off.

"Let the photographer tell me where to stand, Belinda. He's a professional." I'm feeling pretty grumpy. These black stretch satin pants are hugging my ass so tight I had to wear one of those athletic jock straps instead of underpants. I feel like a fool, but I keep my eye on the prize—this wedding is making my best friend happy.

And I can't deny that I had a very pleasant flirtation with that one bridesmaid at the altar. Even though I could not see her face, there was a spark she had that connected with me. I will definitely be going to the reception to see what she looks like without the veil.

Miles shoots me a look, but I give him a small wink to say I am sorry. Some people bring out the worst in me and Belinda Carson is one of them.

I allow her to run the HR division because I can't be bothered to deal with hiring. She is that perfect blend of bitchy and bossy that spells disaster for any hire who does not fulfill their work parameters during the ninety-day trial period.

One of the rules at Sterns prohibits dating within the company's worker pool. I waived that rule for Miles and Belinda.

Miles Maitland has been my best friend ever since I chose him out of all the other applicants when I started my security company. He runs the logistics side of operations, while I handle the interface. Sterns & Co. will be three years old in December and is widely considered to be one of the best new private security companies in the world.

When Miles approached me six months ago to ask permission before taking Belinda out on a date, I was in two minds about it.

"I don't know, Miles. Is she really your type?"

Not only is the groom my best friend and work buddy, but we had a long history of picking up girls. Any wine bar, gym juice bar, or art exhibition would find Miles and me shooting the breeze, on the make for a date to take home.

Miles and I would sometimes go out drinking together on the weekends. It was the same routine every time: sit at a table for four and wait for a couple of women to sit down next to us.

We would buy two rounds of drinks and chat with the ladies to make sure they were single, sober, and sweet-natured. Then we would move onto the next stage if they asked us, which was always to go back with them to their apartments.

It was a flawless format that always worked. If the lady I ended up with was nice, I would maybe take her out a few more times until she gave me the "let's take this relationship to the next level" speech. That was always my cue to give her a little speech of my own, starting with "good" and ending with "bye."

I'm not cruel or mean-natured. It's just that I never saw myself settling down at the age of thirty. The world is my oyster and I want to sample a little bit of everything before making my mind up.

And things went the same on Miles's side as well.

Until a few months back when my best friend hooked up with Belinda at the annual Christmas party.

"This time it's different, Bru," Miles always calls me "Bru." It is the South African slang word for "brother." Miles has lived in South Africa since he was a kid after his parents moved there to run a guesthouse by the sea.

Finding it hard to understand, I asked Miles what was so different this time around. He was very forthcoming. "It's time for me to settle down. New York can be a lonely place. My folks aren't getting any younger and they want grandkids. Belinda is a special lady."

I wanted to warn him to pump the brakes, but it was too late. Belinda was behind the steering wheel and in control. She wanted her white wedding, dream venue, and five-star reception—the whole nine yards. The Carson family is wealthy, Hamptons-based, and highly influential in Art Investment circles.

After only two months of dating, the invites were sent out. I hardly got to see my best friend after that. Belinda pouted until Miles put down a deposit on a brownstone on the Upper East Side, leaving his old loft in the Village echoing and empty.

And now here we are, standing like a couple of flamenco-dancing goofballs in Central Park, waiting for the photographer to set up his gear.

I don't move. I'd rather wait for the photographer's assistant to tell me where to stand. Samantha takes the opportunity to run her hand down my back slowly. "Isn't it so crazy that I'm the best bridesmaid and you're the best man, Stern? Isn't there some sort of a wedding tradition that says we have to spend the night together after a few bottles of champagne?"

Her hand reaches the hollow of my back and then carries on going. I already feel naked in these tight pants without Samantha groping me too.

"Sam, you know that is never going to happen," I growl in a low voice, keeping my eye on her parents as they grin for the camera. "I value your sister as a work colleague too much to take advantage of you during her wedding."

Samantha Carson is having none of this. She's ravenous when it comes to seeing something she wants and then going for it. Whispering, she pats my ass—she can't pinch it because the pants fabric is too tight.

"No one has to know, Stern. It can just be our dirty little secret."

I plaster a fake smile on my face as the flashbulbs go off. The moment I hear the photographer saying, "Okay, now just the pretty ladies, please," I make my escape.

"I'm out of here, Miles. See you back at the reception."

He sees the dark scowl on my face. My buddy knows when I have reached my limit. He waves me goodbye with a cheerful grin. "Have a cold glass of champagne waiting for me when I get there, Bru!"

Pulling my phone out of the tiny bolero jacket's inside pocket, I call my driver. I have him on standby circling the park. Gerry is poker-faced when he opens the door for me to climb in.

"I know what you're thinking, Ger," I say, calling him out on it, letting my driver know I can see the funny side of things. "You are wondering what people were thinking as they watched me sprint through the park in this crazy getup!"

Gerry has been my driver for as long as the company has been going. He is relaxed enough with me to tell it to me straight. "This is New York, Mr. Sterns. No one would be surprised seeing a flamenco dancer racing through the park in black satin pants and bolero."

I have to agree with my driver on that one. "Get me back to the Plaza ASAP, please, Ger. It's the tail end of summer. You do not want to know how hot I am inside these pants!"

Gerry calls ahead to let the hotel know I am coming. The butler is waiting outside the entrance doors for me. He has a porter with him. "Welcome back, Mr. Sterns. Can we bring anything up to your suite for you?"

I have hired the Royal Suite at the Plaza for the duration of the wedding. It has its own elevator and staff. After spending the first ten years of my adult life in the Marines, training to become one of the most lethal hand-to-hand combatants in the SEAL division, I can stand to spoil myself occasionally with some luxury.

I wave the staff away. "I'm shower-bound, thanks. I'll ring if I need something." Raising my right hand to my eyebrow in a casual salute, I step into the elevator and wait for the doors to slide shut.

There are mirrors in all the right places in the Royal Suite at the Plaza. And while that would be fine and dandy if I happened to be making love to a beautiful woman standing up, the last thing I want right now is a full view of myself in this ridiculous outfit.

Five minutes later, the flamenco dancing clothes are on the bathroom floor and I am naked in the shower. Fifteen minutes after that, I am in a black custom-tailored tuxedo, but without the cummerbund and bow tie. As a nod to formality, I drape an untied black bow tie under the collar.

I forgot to pack a change of underpants, so I used the jockstrap again. No one is going to see it anyway. I am not about to try and get laid at my best friend's wedding.

I don't ever want to see the bright pink frilly shirt ever again and kick it across the bedroom floor. My phone rings. Checking my reflection in one of the mirrors, I read the text.

Don't forget the special vintage champagne in the bridal suite. It has to go on ice. M.

Good old Miles. He's knee-deep in posing for his wedding photographs, but he hasn't taken his eye off the ball. This means I have to go all the way back down to the hotel lobby, but I am the best man after all.

Smoothing my eyebrows with one finger and giving myself one last look in the mirror, I head out. I'm not a vain man, but there are certain things I do take pride in. Working out, health, fitness, business sense, problem-solving, and playing fair—all of these things are important to me.

I play fair in love, but not in war. Not that I have ever been in love, but I can always see when the person I am dating starts to develop feelings for me. I always try to pull the plug before it can happen, though.

I'm not ready for a long-term commitment. I wish you all the best in your life. Thank you for a wonderful time. Stern.

That's it. Short and sweet. In and out. And then I use my staff to block them if they try to contact me again.

When it comes to war, I take the Chesty Puller approach. Lt. General Lewis Puller, aka "Chesty" to every Marine in the Navy, was the meanest son of a bitch the Marine Corps had ever seen.

His most famous quote—"Hit hard, hit fast, and hit often"—is the motto for Sterns & Co. too.

I think I should add another motto to my list after this: no bolero and tight pants ever again.

Champagne, bridal suite. Got it. Stepping into a different elevator, I get up to the top floor and jog-trot to the bridal suite. Miles gave me his room key card this morning to use.

The door is slightly open. That's impossible because I know that Miles and Belinda are still trapped with the photographer at the park. I know the security at the Plaza is way too good for someone to jimmy the lock. And all the wedding presents are under lock and key in one of the downstairs reception rooms, waiting for Belinda to get around to opening them.

I listen before I make a move. I can hear a soft feminine voice humming a tune. Pushing the door wide open, I see the prettiest young woman standing by the window sewing something white. The sunlight is streaming over her head, setting the cascading red hair on fire.

She is like a work of art, the silhouette of youth, elegance, and beauty. Her skin is so pale I can see the outline of her blue veins threading underneath it. It's at that moment when all those vampire movies begin to make sense to me because I want to catch this perfect creature in my arms and bite her soft flesh, just enough to make her moan from the gentle pressure.

The young woman makes me feel hungry and horny, all at the same time. I want to touch her and lick her, taste all those hidden parts of her body, and appreciate her subtle perfume. Her long legs are slender and shapely, but almost as pale as powdered sugar.

I can't make it out at first, but she is not completely naked. Blending into her skin tone are two items of lingerie. A lacy strapless bra and what looks like a thin wisp of lace wrapped around her pert buttocks. The lingerie is so diaphanous that I can see right through it.

My heart skips a beat and then begins pumping again, only this time it's a bit faster because I am aroused. The blood rushes to my cock, free from the restricting tightness of the satin pants I was wearing earlier.

She has not even finished her task when she stops and looks up. Her eyes are silver-gray and set wide apart. Her lips curl up at the end, making it look like she is secretly smiling.

Our eyes connect and it feels as if the world stands still.

I think I am in love.

Chapter 3: Carrie

It's the first time I get to see my brother's best man's face clearly. Oh boy, he is even better from the front than he is from the back, and that is saying something.

He doesn't recognize me without the hideous pink fake flowers jammed on my head and the bridesmaid dress. I know I should cover my breasts and crotch with my hands and scream, but this is real life and not some sitcom cliché. So all I do is watch him as he watches me—I feel like a deer caught in headlights.

He is mesmerizingly good-looking now that I have the pleasure and privilege of seeing him up close. Every single one of his features is slightly exaggerated, taking them from so-so to wow in just the right degree.

His eyes are narrowed against the glare of the sun, giving him a kind of rangy, outdoors appearance, like a gunslinger who has gotten off his horse and is moseying into the saloon. I can see from the way his blond hair flops to one side that he likes to run his hand through it when it falls over his face.

The high bridge of his nose is almost savage in the way it masculinizes his profile. It gives him a regal look, like a barbarian chieftain from Scandinavia.

He's a really big guy. The firm set of his mouth suits the clean cut of his jawline, but his neck is seriously bulked where it joins the wide spread of his deltoid muscles. Everything about this man radiates positive energy, power, and control.

Seeing him up close and in the flesh gives me this strange melting feeling between my legs. I am having my first physical reaction to someone, and it feels so good.

Pulling the loose black bowtie out from under his collar, the best man sticks the bottle of champagne he is carrying in one hand between his thighs. Then he leans against the door frame and grins at me as he pulls the black tie through his strong fingers.

"I think you have the wrong bridal suite, sweetheart."

I don't know what to do. I have to finish sewing the strap before I can put the dress on.

"I'm not a bride." I don't want this sexy man to think of me as Miles's little sister. I need him to see me for myself and not part of my family unit. "I'm meant to be down at the reception." I hold the dress and sewing needle up for him to see. "But I had an ensemble emergency."

He steps into the room and closes the door behind him. He lopes around the living room looking for somewhere to put the bottle. Taking the dress out of my hands, he looks at me. "May I?"

I shrug and then frown as he inspects the delicate dress closely. It gives me a chance to see his eyes are dark blue and he is freshly shaved.

He smells of some expensive shower gel, like sandalwood and incense. God, he is divine. It thrills me to be near him.

"If this dress is for you, why are you wearing white?" my brother's best man asks me. I am confused. "Why can't I wear white? Is it because I'm a redhead?"

He is so close to me now that if I lean forward an inch, my face would brush against his chest. I stand five feet, seven inches in my bare feet, but this man is close to a foot taller than me. But he is absolutely in proportion: broad shoulders, bulging arm muscles under his tux jacket, and powerful thighs.

The proximity forces me to look up into his face. Immediately, I know that is what he wants me to do. Taking a handful of my long, red hair in his hand, he lifts it to his mouth and inhales. Then he sniffs. Again, I am reminded of an almost feral quality in this man.

"You can't wear white to a wedding or a wedding reception, sweetheart," he tells me, "only the bride is allowed to wear white to her wedding."

Inhaling sharply, I try to stop my upset from showing. The man continues. "And because you look amazingly beautiful in your white lingerie, I can only guess how sexy you will look in your little white dress, but I don't advise you to wear it. Do you know Belinda Carson?"

I smile sadly. "Yes. I'm friends with Belinda. But it was either this or a butt ugly pink dress."

Again, our eyes connect and we feel the same feelings. Grabbing my upper arms and giving me a small squeeze, he bends his head to let me know how much he agrees with me. "Yes! Oh my God, why would anyone choose such a vile color as their bridal theme, right? I just got out of the horrendous monkey suit all the men were forced to wear."

Suddenly, we are hugging and laughing. Breaking apart for a moment, the next thing I know, the man has bent down and is planting a sweet kiss on my lips. "You poor darling. How can I help?"

He brings me back down to earth with a bang. I am close to tears at the thought of having to wear the ruched pink flamenco to the reception. "I better finish sewing this and then put the pink dress back on."

The man shakes his head. "I have a better idea. Come up to my suite and I'll ask my driver to pick up something in your size from a boutique. Would you like that?"

Yes, the hot blond guy from my brother's wedding, I would most definitely like that. "I... I will just go into the bridal bedroom and get my st-stuff." I'm stuttering and overwhelmed, but there is no way I will pass up the chance to spend some more time with this man.

Backing away from him like I'm scared he might disappear in a puff of smoke if I close my eyes, I duck into the bedroom. Grabbing the bridesmaid dress, I find an empty drawer in the dresser and cram it inside.

Ever since I turned sixteen, I've been nagging my mom and dad to let me go on dates and go clubbing with my friends, but they have always said no. There is a very valid reason for them being so strict, and it has nothing to do with their traditional family values.

Sixteen years ago, my parents sold up everything they had in their small hometown of Marfa in Texas and moved to South Africa. The country had become a member of the international community ten years before and property was still cheap. Living by the sea and running an elegant guesthouse was too tempting for them after the heat and dry dust of Marfa.

My parents plowed all their cash into buying a bed and breakfast holiday accommodation facility in the small naval town of Simon's Town. But by the time I was a teenager, crime, and gang warfare had become so bad in most parts of South Africa that no one in a nice car was safe to travel from one city to the other without an armed escort.

In South Africa, stepping outside the front door can expose folks to all kinds of dangers. Snakes and hyenas in the wild, or carjackers and muggers in the city! Take your pick. To say that my parents were worried about me getting into trouble if I went out alone is an understatement.

That was why Miles moved to the United States to work in New York. He specializes in security logistics and the place where he works involves private security contracts.

We always knew that he would end up living in the United States. My brother hates crime and loves finding ways to wipe it out. Kind of like a South African Batman.

And now here I am in my brother's bridal suite, making plans to let his best man seduce me.

Adding one or two more stitches on the strap with feverish haste, I pull on the short white dress, lift my hair out of the back of the garment, and then go back out to the sitting room.

"See?" I do a little twirl for him, spinning around in my pink stilettos. "This is what I wanted to wear."

His eyes are locked on my body as if the spinning dance I am doing has the power to hypnotize him.

Shrugging out of his jacket, he drapes it over my shoulders, grabs the champagne bottle, and guides me toward the door. "Who advised you to wear such a... a daring creation?"

There is no way that I am going to confess the bait-and-switch plan I made for my bridesmaid dress! In an airy, sophisticated voice, I make a circling wave with my wrist as if a man couldn't possibly understand. "Oh, it's summer. There's nothing better than dancing in a dress that allows the skin to breathe."

"Where are you from?" The best man wants to know. "Your accent... I can't place it."

Every South African I know hates telling people where they are from because it turns a perfectly normal conversation into a debate. "Belgium." When I hear the lie coming from my mouth, I know there's no turning back now. "You know, Flemish, French, Dutch. The city of Brussels."

Grabbing the bottle of champagne from the side table, he confesses. "Actually, I don't know, but I am dying to find out."

With his hand in the small hollow of my back, the man propels me from one elevator to another with a confident forward motion. It's like he knows how much I want this.

When the doors slide shut, he turns to look at me. There are countless images of me and the handsome blond man reflected in the elevator mirrors all around us.

"Do you like dancing?" The way he says it makes me feel as if the air is being sucked out of the space.

"I... I like my skin to breathe... when I exercise... and yes, I love dancing." I am so not going to tell him that the only time I get to dance is when I am all alone in my bedroom! "And it gets so hot sometimes."

He is so close, I can feel his mouth moving against my lip when he replies. "Well, then, sweetheart, you are going to have to save a few dances for me then, aren't you?"

I would save my whole life for this man if he asked me to. He kisses me, lightly and lingers. The elevator door hisses open, interrupting our kiss. It's quite a shock to see the entire floor is a hotel suite as we walk to the left. On the right is a dining room, big enough to seat twelve people, and a formal living room too.

But the next door we come to leads somewhere I have dreamed about seeing since first laying eyes on my brother's best man. It is the bedroom. I see the clothes he was wearing for the wedding lying on the floor. He sees me staring at them and laughs.

"Can you believe it cost hundreds of dollars for them to custom fit that suit for me? And it's going straight into the bin after this." Picking up the hotel phone, he looks over at me. "What's your name? So that the boutique manager can ask for you at reception."

Thinking quickly, I tell him my name is Caron Leslie as I go and sit on the bed next to him.

He gives me a quirky look. "Like the movie star? No wonder you like dancing."

I don't say anything back. We are both waiting for the other shoe to drop. That kiss in the elevator hangs heavy in the air.

Taking my fate in both hands, I lie back on the bed very slowly, propping myself up on my elbows, never breaking eye contact with him. I can't say the words, but I don't think I need to. He knows….

He doesn't lie down beside me. He stays standing and my heart sinks down to my pink shoes.

I think he is going to reject my very obvious invitation. But when he slowly starts to unbutton his shirt, I realize my wish is about to come true.

"Shall we forget about the new dress? Clothes will only get in the way, won't they?" He wants me as much as I want him. The heat between us is tangible.

"If you have anyone waiting for you downstairs, sweetheart," he growls in his deep voice, and I know I must not disobey him, "I suggest you pull that phone out of your little purse right now and let them know you're going to be late coming to the reception—very late."

I do it quickly, never taking my eyes off him as he removes his shirt, shoes, and socks.

Hi, Mom. Sorry. I feel sick and can't make the reception. The hotel is looking after me. Don't worry about me. They've given me a room to rest in. Love, C.

Throwing the phone down, I watch riveted as the blond man starts to unzip his pants. "What's your name?" I want to know the name of the man I am about to give my V-card to.

"Simon." It's not the name I heard my brother call him at the church, but I'm too overwrought with desire to think about it too much.

"Simon. Pleased to meet you."

I give a nervous giggle. I think he finds that cute because he lies down next to me, which gives me the perfect chance to look at him—all of him.

It takes a moment for me to realize he is wearing sports gear—a jockstrap. Whatever he is hiding in the tight pouch of his jockstrap is absolutely huge, but like I said, he's a big man, so it's proportionate to his size.

He's fully erect. His cock is fighting and straining against the pouch as it tries to rear up against his hard belly. Just looking at him turns me on, and that flooding-melting feeling throbs inside my panties again.

Moving closer to me, Simon lifts my hand and holds it against his chest. This is the first time I have touched a man intimately. Running my hand over his pecs and taut stomach is enough to make me get so wet in my white lace panties that the cotton is soaked.

"You're so hard," I marvel as I rub the rigid washboard that is his stomach. He grabs my hand and presses it against the rampant outline of his cock. "Yes, Caron, I most definitely am. Can you blame me? I got rock hard the first time I saw you standing in your lingerie."

Hooking the straps off my shoulders, he tugs my dress down to expose my breasts. It thrills me when he traces the shadow of my nipples under the lacy bra. "I gave you a show when I got undressed, sweetheart," he says, giving me a devilish smile as he lies back against the pillows. "Now it's your turn to show me your moves."

He is in no hurry to rush into this, which is a good thing. I am a virgin, and he is so big. I have a feeling that it might hurt.

Chapter 4: Stern

She is so shy but so gorgeous, I can't seem to find the words to tell her how knocked out I am by her lithe body and pretty face. Her hair smacks me in the face with its vibrant color. Her silver-gray eyes with lashes heavily coated in black mascara, her generously wide mouth that is so quick to break into a smile, and her heart-shaped face: I love all of it.

I smile at her to encourage her. If she knew how amazing she is, Caron would have no trouble giving me the show of my life. But I adore how shy she is and would not have it any other way.

Standing at the side of the bed, she removes her dress and gives it a little kick with her foot.

The dress flies across the room where it settles on the floor next to the satin monkey suit I wore to the wedding. She gives a little giggle before walking over to it and hanging the dress over the dresser.

"I have to keep it from wrinkling. I have to wear it back home afterward," she tells me with her sweet smile. I want to tell her that there will be no going home if I have anything to do with it. I want this little beauty to leave here and go straight to my penthouse apartment a few blocks down from here. The thought of her leaving me does not sit well in my mind.

"You are stunning, you know that?" I can't tear my eyes off her as she walks around the bedroom in her pink stilettos and white lingerie. "But as hot as you look right now, I think you will look even hotter when you are naked."

She points at my underwear. "No fair! You still have yours."

I move to slide the jockstrap off, but Caron jumps on the bed to stop me. "No! Leave them on for now, Simon. Like Christmas morning, I want to wait."

Flicking the end of her nose, I pull her close to me. "You're cute, you know that? That has to be the first time my cock has been compared to a gift-wrapped present."

Smiling up at me, she kisses the edge of my jawline. "Then you, Mister, have been sleeping with the wrong women! I am so excited right now, it's like all my Christmases have come at once."

Our kisses become deeper and deeper as I unclip her bra and hook off her panties. I love the way she gives a soft sigh whenever I touch her intimately.

The cotton crotch of her panties is soaking and when I slide my fingers between her thighs they get glistening wet. I use the wetness as I start massaging her clit with my thumb as my fingers burrow inside her tight snatch.

First, she goes rigid and then relaxes as her body gets used to it. I take her hand and rub it against my thick shaft. Caron gasps as she caresses the outline of my cock. I am bursting to break free of the jockstrap.

"Pull it out." My voice rumbles with suppressed frustration as her fingertips brush against my knob. Her hands seem to shake as she releases my cock from the pouch. I can hardly stop myself from coming as she grips my shaft and pumps it. Her hand can't even reach around the girth, the veins are thick and pulsing.

I have never been this excited in my whole life. I can tell that she is dripping wet. As I finger her tight hole and imagine my cock sliding into her warm slit, I nearly come right then and there.

"Are you ready for me, sweetheart?" After flipping her onto her back, I kneel between her thighs and prime my cock, getting ready to drive it into her. Her eyes are so wide, she reminds me of some wild animals, the ones that want to run away but can't because they are hypnotized by the light.

"Is it going to hurt?" She wants to know. I'm kind of used to women asking me that. I'm a big man.

I kiss her and then do something nice by going down on her. I am never so eager to fuck that I can't pay a sweet snatch some loving attention.

Lapping her pussy lips with my tongue, I stop to ask a question. "Is that how you like it?"

She is too excited to give me a coherent answer. She's biting her lower lip and her eyes are tightly closed as she focuses on the sensation. "Mmm," she moans, "so good...."

Lapping her pussy and giving her clit a flick with the tip of my tongue, I wait for her thighs to unclench as her hips start to rock up and down. That is my clue. Her body is starting to take control, shutting out her mind and the worry about it hurting.

I want her to be swept away with how badly she wants to come, rather than how bad it might hurt when I ram myself into her. I'm a real gentle lover. I have to be, because of my girth and length. I am way too confident about the size of my cock to bother measuring it, but I have it on good authority of every woman I have ever been with that it is impressive.

Using my fingers, I open up her pussy. Her breath is coming in short gasps as her need to come overrules all other thoughts. Giving her clit one last lick, I move up and kiss her on the mouth. "You taste as good as you feel, darling." I know I won't be able to hold back for much longer. The pre-cum is dripping out of my knob as I get close to shooting my load.

"I... I'm ready," Caron whispers, opening her eyes to watch as I guide my shaft into her. She is so tight, I have to rub my knob over her clit and tight pussy hole to lube up the passage again.

I know I should not have let myself get so excited like this. Too late, I feel myself beginning to come the moment her pussy grips me. Driving myself deep into her, I come hard. It's like there is a barrier that does not want me inside there. But the tightness only makes me come harder and faster.

She screams with discomfort and tries to move away from me, but I'm an expert when it comes to making a woman come. Grinding myself against her clit, I rock back and forth. It is so much easier for her now that I have come.

I feel her body relax as her clit becomes stimulated and excited again. "See, sweetheart?" I murmur into her neck as I rock gently against her soft mound, "You like that, don't you? I want you to use my cock and come hard against it. Okay? I'm not going anywhere."

Her panting gets quicker as she rubs her clit against me, writhing her hips in a circle to get the full experience of penetration and stimulation at the same time. It doesn't take long for her to start orgasm. "Oh, oh, my God. It's so good!"

She comes hard, her nails raking down my back as the orgasm rocks her. I feel a hot gush of wetness flowing around the base of my cock, but I am not ready to pull out yet. To be honest, it feels as if I belong inside this beautiful woman.

I am connected to her on a spiritual level. This is the first time it has happened to me. After I have spent myself inside someone, I can't wait to roll off her so we can chat and shoot the breeze. But I don't want that with Caron.

Running the back of my hand over her cheek, I feel her tears. I get all choked up. "Shit, sweetheart. Did I hurt you? I tried so hard to make it right."

She smiles tremulously. "No, no, don't ever say that, Simon. It was wonderful. They are tears of happiness. I have never experienced anything so amazing. If you want to know the truth, I think a cock makes orgasms a hundred times nicer."

Kissing her hard, I have to laugh. "As a man, I can only agree with you, honey. But being inside you could almost drive a man mad with desire. I don't think I have ever come so hard and fast in my life."

That makes her blush. I feel myself begin to stiffen inside her again. This is so crazy. But I have to check my messages on my phone. I know Caron will understand. She was at the same wedding.

I start to tell her this as I pull myself out of her. Our juices have mixed together, but I don't care because we are right next to the bathroom. It's kind of sticky, though....

When I lift my hand, I see blood. Sitting up, I look down at the bed cover. It's red. Caron is looking upset. Is this my fault?

"I did hurt you," I start to say, "you should have stopped me." But she shakes her head.

"N-no, Simon, I didn't say anything because I wanted you so bad… but I was a virgin."

To say my world is rocked would be putting too little emphasis on how I feel at this moment. Running to the bathroom, I grab a bunch of towels off the rack and come running back with them in my hands after wetting them with water.

"Does it hurt?" I need to know. "I feel so guilty. I'm a brute for not taking it slower, but you are so hot and I wanted you so bad."

She's all shy as she blots at the blood on her thighs. "I wanted you so bad too, Simon," she whispers in a soft voice. "I'm really happy it was you."

A tight bubble of excitement is growing inside me. My mind explodes with plans for the future. Maybe it's time I settled down. I always hated the idea of living with someone or getting married because I hadn't found the right partner. But this girl, she's special.

For the first time in my life, the thought of this woman being with another man makes my mind go red with rage. A small voice inside me growls, "She's mine, mine! I want to keep her close and treat her like a precious princess. I can't ever let her go!"

"Would you like to use the bathroom?" I am all kindness and consideration now. I don't feel guilty for taking Caron Leslie's V-card, because it is clear that she wanted this to happen as much as I did. And it is also clear that she wants me in her life as much as I want her.

I watch her go to the bathroom, and even now I can't bear to be separated from her. Leaning over the bed, I grab my phone. There is a message.

Where the fuck are you? We are waiting for the champagne! You know how Belinda gets when things are late.

It's Miles. I'm meant to be his best man, but damn! I need to be here with this amazing woman. Finding the perfect woman at my best friend's wedding is such a joke, I feel like pinching myself to make sure it's real. Looking inside my previously impenetrable heart only confirms my feelings. Caron Leslie is the one. I don't need to justify this sudden change of mind. I'm thirty years old and should be getting married and settling down. God knows I am rich and successful enough.

I'm coming. I was delayed. Tell B to wait. S.

Fuck. There is no way I am putting my best friend's wedding reception before spending time with this woman. Shrugging into a T-shirt and jeans, I pull on some sneakers.

"Stay right where you are!" I shout through the bathroom door. "I have to make a turn at the reception."

Sprinting to the elevator, I run to The Grand Ballroom, only stopping to ask the servers where the side entrance is. The wedding planner tries to stop me from accessing the room. "Excuse me, sir! Are you on the guest list? Did you even bother reading what the dress code was on the invita—oh, hey, Stern."

He recognizes me. I see his eyes run up and down my body. The wedding planner does a quick mental calculation of the guests to see which one I must have been banging. It's time for me to shoot straight.

"Do I smell of sex?" I want to know, giving him my best 'naughty boy' grin.

The wedding planner is not immune to my charm. "Ooh, you are wicked, Stern. God knows where you find these women."

Riffling in his crossbody satchel, he pulls out some cologne and sprays it into the air next to me before ordering me to stand underneath it. Then he ushers me inside. The wedding party is already seated.

Belinda fumes at my late appearance, but I don't care. "Here's the champagne. Get one of the ushers to give my speech. I don't feel well."

Samantha stops halfway from pulling the chair out next to her. "What's wrong? Can't you stay for one drink?"

Miles looks worried, but his concern is for me. "It's going around. It must have been those canapes at the rehearsal dinner. My stomach was not good last night either, remember? A few other people have reported feeling sick too."

Miles slept in the other bedroom at the Royal Suite last night. The only thing wrong with his stomach was too many cocktails. Samantha and Belinda are looking seriously pissed with me.

"Sorry, good luck. I have to go. You don't want the best man getting sick at your reception, do you?"

Belinda and Samantha have to agree with me. "Go, Stern. You look all sweaty. You look—" I run out before Belinda can say the word....

Fucked.

Chapter 5: Carrie

The door opens and the steam billows out of the shower as he comes to stand behind me.

I have washed the blood away and now only bubbles are left behind. I feel him wrap his arms around me and pull me close against him. I am in heaven because he is back.

The soapy suds are delightful as he runs his large hands over me and cups my breasts. Slowly, he brings his fingers together to softly pinch my nipples. We are beyond words, we no longer need them, but I have to know what is happening at the wedding reception.

Holding Simon's hands, I can't help but sigh. "Mm, that feels so good." I can feel him getting aroused behind me. Knowing that makes me excited too. I need to find out if my parents are not looking for me, though. "What did they say at the reception when you ducked out? Was anyone upset?"

His laugh is gruff and deep. "Bride was pissed. Groom was understanding. Apparently, a few other guests are not feeling well, but I blame that on the free booze at the rehearsal dinner last night."

I am about to open my mouth and tell him that I was not allowed to go to the rehearsal dinner last night because my parents said the event finished too late, but I manage to stop myself just in time! That could have been a disaster.

It feels a little bit as if I am drunk because I am living my life with no thought for the future. I don't care if my parents shout at me for missing the reception. Any punishment they want to give me is fine, so long as I have one night with this man.

We are both dripping wet and steamy hot as we get out of the shower and move to the bed. We don't bother drying ourselves with the towels.

I find out there is a reason for it. Simon has brought a bottle of massage oil with him. Laying me down on the bed in a way that makes me feel like a queen, he gets me to turn over onto my belly.

"Let's see if we can make this a little easier on you this time." I like the way his voice sounds when he tells me what he is going to do. He pours the oil on my back and begins to rub it in. He's too heavy to sit on top of me, so he lies next to me instead. It's very intimate and sensual as his hands move over my body.

"Tell me about yourself, Caron. Why are you a virgin? And why did you decide to lose your V-card at my best friend's wedding?"

I want to tell him the truth. I really, really do. But then he will leave, and I don't want that.

"Umm… it's complicated. I guess my old boyfriend was very conservative, so we never got around to doing it. And then I came here for the wedding and just wanted to let my freak flag fly, you know?"

I hold my breath, praying that Simon finds the story plausible.

"You came from Belgium? I didn't know the Carsons had family or friends over there." His tone is engaged and truly interested. I give a sigh of relief. "No, I was over here anyway. Keeping busy, and all that."

"What do you do?"

Oh boy, I am getting into hot water here. Time for me to change the topic of conversation. Turning onto my side, I guide his hand to slide between my legs as I flutter my lashes at him. "What does it look like I am doing here, Simon? I am doing you... and you are doing me. That's all we need."

He kisses me, giving my lower lip a little nip with his teeth. "I need to know, Caron, because I want to see you again after all this wedding madness is over."

This time, we make love at a slower pace. The night stretches in front of us like a long, dark velvet passage as we kiss and intertwine our bodies. It is so passionate, but it also feels very loving. Soon, my lies forgotten, I allow this man to send me to another level of reality when he slides that thick, juicy cock of his inside me. It no longer hurts, but it fills me up in a way I never believed was possible.

"I love that, what you are doing." My nails grip the smooth skin on his back as he thrusts himself into me slowly, giving me time to appreciate the sensation. "I can feel myself getting wetter all the time."

He grins and thrusts deeper. "All I can say is thank God for Belgium conservative gentlemen."

I laugh with complete happiness. Then we get serious again as we concentrate on coming. He is so gentle, but getting my pussy to accept all of him takes a lot of controlled breathing and relaxation.

"I'm so close," he growls, "if you start to come, I swear you are going to milk me dry."

The dirty, desperate way he says it really turns me on. I let go of my control and tilt my hips so I can rub my clit against him.

We both come hard together, spasming and groaning from the huge release.

There is more kissing and touching as we lay side by side, catching our breath. "Stay right there," Simon orders me. "I'm going to get us some champagne from the kitchen."

I shout after him. "Do they have a pony in this hotel suite too? Or a combine harvester? I mean, they have everything else!"

He comes back holding two flutes and a big bottle. "You're funny, you know that?"

I giggle. "That's what my family says, I mean, the ones in Belgium."

We clink glasses and Simon makes a toast. "To ponies and combine harvesters, Caron. And to you."

He takes a sip and then reaches for his phone. "Give me your number and the name of your hotel. I want to send a car there to pick up your stuff."

The excitement starts to drain out of me as the lies start to catch up. This man is such a force of nature, I can tell he hates being told the word no. Holding up my hand in the halt sign, I roll over the mattress and pick up my purse.

"I... I think I have that information somewhere, Simon. Um... why do you want my stuff?"

His strong arm wraps around my waist and pulls me back. "I want to know everything about you, Caron. I don't want you to go back to Belgium—ever. I need you to stay here with me, so we can give this wonderful connection that we have together a shot."

This has gone too far. He is going to hate me when he finds out. "Simon," I roll away from him again, "let's take it slow. We have all night. Let's talk about this in the morning." Snuggling closer to him, I place my hand on his chest and rub the beautiful muscles of his chest and abs. "Tell me about yourself. What do you like doing?"

He relaxes as we chat. All the time, I can't help telling more lies, but we manage to have a deep conversation despite this.

Simon tells me he went from his foster home straight into the Navy. The Corps was his family, but he never wanted to pigeonhole himself into being a jarhead all his life. After an honorable discharge, he got into security where he met Miles. Pretty straightforward.

We are lying with our heads on the same pillow. His voice gets deeper and more husky as sleep comes over him. "I used to laugh about Miles falling for Belinda," he confesses, his eyes drooping as his mouth curves up on one side as he smiles. "But now I guess I'm laughing on the other side of my face… because the same thing just happened to me."

Is he saying what I think he is saying? This is crazy! I wait for Simon to fall asleep before I tiptoe to the bathroom and look at myself in the mirror. I have to fix myself up before I can go downstairs to the reception. I look completely fucked.

I must speak to Miles and get him to back up my cover story. I can't have Simon thinking I am full of shit so early on in our relationship. That would spell disaster for us.

Brushing my hair and piling on the lip gloss, I begin to look a bit more normal. Pulling my short white shift dress down as far as it will go and taking my purse with me, I sneak out to the elevator holding my shoes in my hand. It's a long walk to the Grand Ballroom, but I can't run in my pink high-heeled shoes.

The wedding planner is lurking outside the main entrance. He doesn't even recognize me from the bridal retinue. Holding out his hand, he stops me.

"Hey, girlfriend, you can't come in, I'm afraid. There is a wedding going on in there."

I am so used to lying now it comes naturally. "No, it's okay. I'm one of the bridesmaids."

He looks me up and down with one eyebrow raised. "I don't think so, sweetie."

I point to my shoes. "See? I am one of Belinda's bridesmaids. I... I was running late because I went home to get changed. I have to speak to my brother, Miles."

Speaking into his walkie-talkie, the wedding planner calls one of his minions over. "Dale, go to the head table and ask the groom if he is missing one of his entourage. A young lady with long red hair."

Dale huffs with impatience. "Everyone at the groom's family table has red hair, Maurice!"

This is true. Both my parents register high on the red-hair spectrum and so do most of our

Texas cousins and kin who accepted invitations to the wedding. Blame it on our Scottish and Irish heritage.

Maurice huffs right back. "Go do it! Just ask any of them if a young girl with long red hair is missing from the party!"

As Dale hustles off, Maurice gets chatty. "You can't blame me, darling. I am paid to keep wedding crashers away. They always try and steal the gifts."

I can hear the muffled thump of music inside. The reception must be in full swing by now. Maurice looks at my dress. "Listen, even if Miles does vouch for you, you can't go in dressed like that." He points at my white dress. "Don't worry. You are not the first of my guests today who have dropped out of the reception for a shag."

Bringing a slender bottle out of his pocket, Maurice spritzes lots of cologne over my skin. It falls on me like a cold mist.

"Can you call Miles out for me then, please?" I'm begging now. I know this is my brother's big day, but I don't want to mess things up with Simon. I have most definitely bitten off more than I can chew and all my lying chickens are coming home to roost!

But it isn't Miles who comes out of the ballroom. It's my mom.

"I thought you said you were feeling sick? Why are you dressed like that? Where is that gorgeous bridesmaid dress we gave you?"

I shrink back under the barrage of questions. "I felt better... so I came back down."

Mom grabs my arm tightly and frog marches me through the lobby. "You are wearing what looks like a petticoat, Carrie! It's disgusting—and it is white! You can't wear white to a wedding unless you are the bride! Do you want to look like an attention-seeking wannabe in front of your new sister-in-law?"

"W-where are we going?" I shoot a desperate look over my shoulder, trying to get Maurice's attention, but he is talking to Dale.

My mom hustles me out of the hotel entrance and asks the concierge to call us a town car. "We, Carrie Maitland, are going back to your brother's old apartment in the Village. If you think I am going to let our conservative guests see you dressed like that, you must be joking!"

As the car pulls away from the hotel entrance, I turn my head back, praying for Simon to come chasing after us.

He is going to think I am a lying bitch who ran out on him without telling him one shred of truth about herself.

Inside, I think I want to die with unhappiness. Will I ever see my gorgeous best man again?

# Chapter 6: Stern

Five Years Later

Miles is leaning in the doorway of my office. He's been hanging out a lot on my floor level since Belinda started divorce proceedings against him. He's moved back into his old loft apartment in the Village and has started eating takeout and microwave meals.

My friend is officially a paid-up member of the soon-to-be-divorced men's club.

"You have become a complete grump since the day I got married, Stern," Miles says, lecturing me on my bad mood. "You've changed—and it's not for the better."

Tapping the keyboard with loud, hard strokes, I try ignoring my best friend. Miles takes this as a sign to continue lecturing me.

"You were full of jokes at my wedding, Stern, and I can't forget how you warned me about Belinda. You were right—so it's me who should be in the permanent bad mood, not you."

Slamming the lid of my laptop closed, I try answering him politely. "Hey, what can I say, buddy? I tried my best to stop that stupid wedding from happening, but you didn't listen."

Miles's wedding was the last time I was truly happy. That night, when I woke up in the Royal Suite on my own, it felt like the sky had fallen on my head when I saw that Caron had gone. That woman sure did pull the wool over my eyes.

By the time I had gotten dressed and gone down to the ballroom, only a bunch of drunken ushers and bridesmaids were left shuffling around the dance floor while a few tired servers were left to clear away the tables.

I ran over to Samantha when I recognized her making out with one of the groomsmen. "Hey,

Samantha. Where are Miles and Belinda? I need to ask them about the guest list."

Perking up as she set her décolletage straight, Samantha slurred at me, "There were four hundred guests, Stern. And as for Belinda and Miles, it's their honeymoon night. Good luck getting hold of them."

I was kind of frantic at that point. "Can you help me, please, Samantha? I'm looking for a pretty young woman with crazy silver eyes and long red hair. Her name is Caron Leslie. From Belgium."

"You're going to have to do better than that, schweetie," Samantha slurred, winking at the guy she had been making out with. "All of the Maitland extended family looks like that... like a bunch of Ronald McDonald clowns...."

She was so toasted, I knew I wasn't going to get any sense out of her. Going back out to the lobby, I dialed the wedding planner. Maurice picked up on the first ring. "Don't hang up, Maurice!" He was my last hope. "Do you have a copy of the guest list with you? It's me, Stern."

Ever the professional, Maurice calmed me down. "I knew it was you, darling. Such an authoritative tone your voice has. Did you learn that in the Army?"

I'm too focused to bother telling him I was a Navy SEAL. I hear Maurice dicking around with his tablet, so I wait.

"Mmm, here it is. Whose contact deets do you want?"

Trying hard to concentrate, I take a deep breath. "Caron Leslie. That is C-A-R-O-N. Young lady. Long red hair. Slim, long legs. Silvery eyes. Bruxelloise." Suddenly, I remember what Caron told me she was wearing before she changed. "She was part of Belinda's side of the family, I think because she was wearing one of those pink bridesmaid dresses, but I'm not certain about that." Belinda had asked all of her relatives to add something pink to their outfits.

"Bruxella-what?!" The wedding planner is confused.

Trying hard to keep my patience, I explain. "She's from the city of Brussels in Belgium, Europe. Like the waffles."

After letting me know he understood. Maurice filled me in on his guest list categories. "Everyone is alphabetized, Stern. She's not here. Are you sure she's not yanking your chain? Caron Leslie, I mean, come on."

I think back to the wonderful time I spent with my sweet little virgin princess. She couldn't possibly have been yanking my chain… could she?

"Maurice, I'm begging you, start asking around. Someone must have seen her. Long, red hair."

I got the same old story from the wedding planner as I did from Samantha. "Hey, all of Miles's side of the family looks like an extra from that Braveheart movie, Stern. Relax. She'll turn up later this morning."

But the only chance I had left to find out where Caron lived was to wait for Belinda and Miles to come back from their honeymoon. I didn't think how awkward that conversation with my best friend was going to be.

Miles waltzed into the office boardroom two weeks later, looking suntanned and dapper. I hated him for being so blissful when the last two weeks had been hellish for me. I thought

I had all the time in the world to get Caron's number and organize for her to stay with me, but that was before I could imagine her sneaking away from me in the middle of the night.

Pouncing on him, I dragged him to the head of the conference table. "You took your sweet time turning your phone back on!" I growled in an almost threatening way.

Miles looked concerned. I didn't blame him. I can be very intimidating when I want to be. Patting his shoulder, I tried to laugh. "Sorry, Miles. I've been trying to locate one of the wedding guests. Caron Leslie. Red hair—"

Miles pulled away from me, scowling. "Stern, I love you, man, and you are my best friend, but if I ever find out that you pulled a move on one of my family, our friendship is over."

I froze. "I think she was one of Belinda's family...."

Miles doesn't let up. "Belinda is part of my family now too, Stern! Please don't tell me that you ghosted your duties as my best man so that you could go cathousing around with some random woman!"

It was then that a black cloud of disappointment descended over me. Caron had dumped me and split. And I could never go looking for her to find out the reason why without offending my friend. And that is how the last five years of my life have gone down for me.

It's like I'm stuck in some kind of sexual limbo. Too full of regrets to move on. Too empty inside to pursue anything but countless one-night stand encounters with wealthy socialites and bored divorcées.

But I feel a little bit of hope now because Miles and Belinda are getting a divorce. Even if it is too late for me to find Caron, I still get my wingman back now that Miles is free.

Miles sighs as he mooches further into the office. "We were both so happy at that wedding, Stern. I think it was the last time you and I managed to crack a joke without Belinda scolding us. My sister is a real comedian when it comes to humor. The two of you got on like a house on fire with that comedy routine of yours."

All I can remember is that night with Caron. The rest of the ceremony is a blur. After all, it happened five years ago.

"Sister?" Miles only has one sister, and I know she hates me for some unfathomable reason. She's always texting her brother with some bitter comment about Sterns & Co. "Was she the one making me laugh? There were so many pink bridesmaids, it was hard to keep up."

Miles nods sadly. "Yep. I don't know what you did to upset her, but she only has bad things to say about you now. But a lot of my family were pissed when you ducked out of giving a speech at the reception. Still, that is all water under the bridge now."

"Yeah." I have to agree. Our lives did not pan out the way I wanted it to. "How about scoring a drink with me after work? Maybe pick up some friendly ladies?"

Shaking his head, Miles sighs again. "It's too soon for me. And aren't you a little bit old for the wine bar scene now? What are you, Stern? Thirty-five?"

That makes me mad. "Please tell me how I am to meet someone if it is not at a wine bar, Miles! I certainly won't be dating someone from work, because we all know how crap that worked out for you!"

My friend sees I am pissed. "Hey, sorry! But you've been in a kind of one-night dating hell ever since I got married, Stern. It's not natural."

"I will tell you what is not natural, Miles!" I'm really grouchy now and have no trouble showing it. "It's not natural for a woman to hop into bed with a man and then disappear before he has time to get her phone number! So, if that's the game women want to play, then I will play it harder, tougher, and a damn sight better than they ever can!"

Miles changes the subject. "I was thinking about whether we should implement some changes to the employment policy. We have lots of female employees now, Stern. We should start to factor in things like maternity leave."

I hate disappointing my friend like this. He was desperate to have kids with Belinda, but she decided she wanted to put her career first.

He's been very considerate in making sure the women in our company with young children in their families feel comfortable.

"I told Belinda about your suggestion, buddy, but she still doesn't want kids. You have to accept that and move on with your life."

We hug it out and Miles goes to get himself a bottle of water out of the glass-fronted fridge next door. It gives him time to wipe the tears out of his eyes. My friend is like me when it comes to tackling our problems—we take defeat hard.

Coming back into the room, he perches on the edge of my desk. "It was my parents' dream for some grandkids to come down the shoot just as soon as we were able to have 'em."

Honestly, this is the kind of conversation I want to have with a glass of whisky in my hands. After taking the bottle of water out of Miles's hand, I go to the bar hidden inside the mirror and pour us each a hefty tot. I don't often drink, but when I do it's always Scotch when there's nothing to celebrate with champagne.

"Didn't your brother Brody beat you to it? Surely that's got to take some of the pressure off you?" Downing the burning liquor, I place the cut-glass crystal down gently. Well-trained by Belinda, Miles lifts my glass and puts a coaster underneath it.

"Yeah, he did. They have two little kids now, both redheads if you can believe it! But it doesn't stop me from feeling like a failure. It's lonely living the corporate life. I want a warm home full of babies bustling around my ankles at the end of the day—not some showpiece house that looks like it's permanently waiting for AD to knock on the door."

Draining his glass, my friend places it on the coaster and looks miserable. I don't know what to do. I've never been good at this type of thing. "Maybe you should come out drinking with me tonight, Miles? Get laid, get drunk, all those good things."

He shoots me a look that lets me know that he doesn't find my suggestion even remotely tempting. "Nope. My mom says she has a surprise delivery coming for me later on." Glancing at his watch, Miles dusts down the front of his pants and stands up. "Actually, she said it would be arriving right about now. I think I know what it is—or rather I should say, who it is."

I am intrigued. "Someone is coming from South Africa?"

"I think it's someone from my family. Either Brody and Alma or Carrie. They want to be with me when the divorce goes through. Make sure I don't fall into a depression or something."

I get that sinking feeling in my stomach. "Oh God, please don't let it be Carrie. I know she's your little sister, Miles, but she is such a pill."

"She hates your employment contracts, Stern. That's all. She says the work environment at the company is toxic and male-centric... and she thinks you're a dick. But she's a good kid underneath it all, I promise you."

"Fine! No need to rub it in! What happened to her being all sunny and joking like you told me she was at the wedding?" I know Carrie Maitland hates me. Miles told me that his sister emails him all the time, advising him to get another job and move away from my poisonous influence.

"I dunno." Miles shrugs. "There must have been something in the wedding cake five years ago, Bru, because we have all changed since I got married, and it's not for the better!"

I walk with him to the balcony. My office is on the mezzanine level of the building. I like it there because I can hear the water trickling over the rocks from the water feature in the lobby below.

Watching Miles walk downstairs, I lean on the wall and watch him move over to the entrance. He speaks with our security at the desk and then the doorman. He must be organizing a barcode card for his visitor.

Miles gives a shout of happiness as a young woman with long, red hair comes in the entrance and moves to hug him.

It's Caron Leslie.

Chapter 7: Carrie

I give my brother a big hug. "I'm so sorry this is happening to you, Miles." My eyes mist over with tears because I know whom to blame for this. "But what did you expect after working here for so long? How many times have I warned you about how anti-family Sterns & Co. is?"

My brother pats me on the back. "It's not what you think, Sis. The new contracts have very generous maternity leave. There is even talk about setting up a nursery center at HQ. So many of the guys are getting divorced now, they have nowhere to leave the kids when it's their weekend visit and they have to work."

Warming to my subject, I follow my brother outside. I am staying with him at the loft for now.

He's subdivided it into two-bedroom cubicles close to the bathroom side of the loft. "But that's just what I'm talking about! There wouldn't be so many of your staff getting divorced if your pigheaded boss was more reasonable. And who comes in to work over the weekends anyway?"

Miles shoots me a look of disbelief. "You have never even been formally introduced to Stern, Sis. He's a very reasonable guy, but he is driven by success." He leans forward to give the driver the address.

Simon Sterns. My brother's boss and the man who changed the course of my life forever. All I can say is, "Reasonable guy, my ass. I don't care how you try to justify his toxic behavior, it won't stop me from hating him." My mom is not here to tell me off for using bad language and knowing that Simon Sterns is close by gives me a good opportunity to swear and cuss to my heart's content!

Hating Simon always brings me down, because it makes me remember how much I have to blame myself for the mess I got myself into. During the last five years since he swept me into his arms and made me forget myself, I've had a lot of time for self-reflection.

And like a flagellant who whips their back for past sins, the memory of our lovemaking and its aftermath never fails to make me hate myself as much as I hate him. Maybe I could forgive myself if I tried to initiate contact with him again now that I am an adult, but my sister-in-law, Alma, made me swear on the Bible that I would never give Simon the benefit of the doubt.

She is a firm believer in "once bitten, twice shy", but there is this nagging doubt in my mind that Simon Sterns and I have unfinished business together. At least once a week I wish I had not made that promise to Alma, but now that I have, I can't take it back.

It feels so weird being back in New York. Last time I was here—no. I don't want to remember. It hurts too much. I must be strong and keep my eye firmly on the future.

Miles slumps down in the back seat. I can see he is taking the divorce hard. "I never thought I would be living in the loft full-time again."

Rubbing his face with his hands, my brother looks really beat up. "It's bleak there. I'm glad you're here, Sis. Bless Mom for allowing you to come. The place needs a woman's touch."

I have to ask. "Why did you give Belinda the brownstone? It's not like she has any kids that have to stay in their school zone."

Wrong thing to say! Miles covers his face again before replying in a muffled voice. "The house is on the market, Sis. Belinda is only staying there until it sells. Then she's moving to an apartment once it's off our hands. All my beautiful renovations will belong to someone else. The water feature. The herb garden. The glass dome spotlight!"

All I can do is pat his shoulder until the driver drops us off at the loft. There is a coffee shop below, and lots of customers are getting their fix of java to stave off the afternoon siesta slump.

I feel envious of those happy, carefree people standing next to their perch counters and sipping their coffee with the bags and satchels nearby. If that was South Africa, all those people would have been mugged by now.

That is why I agreed to come here. I want to leave South Africa and get a job in New York. I am lucky enough to have an American passport, so I might as well use it to escape all the crime and corruption. South Africa is a beautiful country, but it has a lot of problems.

I also want to be here to comfort my brother. When we get to the loft, I have to hold back my gasp of horror. The place is a dump! Literally, a dump. Piles of cardboard boxes spilling contents of crap everywhere. Suitcases full of wrinkled clothes lying on the floor. Dust and grime everywhere.

Miles seems to think it is normal because all he does is drop my suitcase on the floor and step inside.

I try to be gentle. "Hmm, who was renting this place from you? They seem to have been a bit lax when it came to housework."

Miles shrugs, crab-walking through the boxes and cases to reach the kitchen. After rattling the kettle, he fills it with water and sets it on the stovetop. "A friend of Samantha's was using it to show her art collection. I guess she can't do that anymore with all my shit in here."

I didn't see any art, so I guessed the friend was longer in the picture. "I could do with a nice cup of coffee, thanks, Miles. I'm still trying to fight off the jet lag."

Bending down, I start opening suitcases and taking out clothes. It makes me sad when I see all my brother's old sweats from university in there. He attended college in Cape Town before all the rioting and wild forest fires destroyed a large section of the university.

I see my brother heading for the door. "Where are you going?" I want to know. "I hope you're not expecting me to do all of this unpacking on my own!"

Waving goodbye, Miles tells me to hell with trying to find teaspoons, and that he is going to get coffee from downstairs. Giving up, I let him go. I know he's going to spend the next few hours sipping espresso and texting. My brother always keeps busy with work.

He runs the logistics operations for Sterns & Co. The position is no small shakes; he has to monitor every single shift, every single hour of the day, around the clock, all over the world! It is a huge undertaking, especially considering how many personnel call in sick or want to take vacations.

I blame Simon for my brother's crazy workload. No—from now on, I will refer to him as Mr. Sterns. That man has a stone-cold heart with zero forgiveness. He will never be Simon to me again.

Feeling restless, I pull a case into my brother's room and start unpacking the contents into the bureau. The furniture in the loft is all eclectic and mismatched, a bit like my brother's marriage.

My heart spasms as I remember how Mr. Sterns and I made jokes before the wedding together. If only I had known then what a bastard my brother's best man was.

My back hurts after so much bending and folding. But I manage to get two of Mile's suitcases unpacked and my own as well. I don't really like the loft space, but it is better than staying at a backpacker's place.

I am unemployed, but full of hope. My portfolio is sitting on the dresser and I know I have what it takes to break into interior design. I specialize in large-scale murals and installations. All I need is one project to put on my resume, and I'll be set.

In the meantime, I have to put up with these thin plywood boards that pass for walls in the loft. I hope that loud snoring wasn't one of the reasons why Belinda started divorce proceedings against my brother!

Pushing my suitcase into the corner with my foot, I go and clean the bathroom and kitchen. My phone pings and I reach for it after carefully wiping my hands on my jeans. Maybe it's finally my brother telling me he's sorry for abandoning me here without coffee.

It's a number I don't recognize. "Hello? Carrie speaking."

"Hello, Ms. Maitland. This is Phyllis from the Apollo on First Avenue. You sent us a few prints from your portfolio. Did you arrive in Manhattan safely?"

I reel back my memory, trying to think of all the places where I applied for jobs. Miles sent me links to all the best work placement websites when I was still in South Africa. I must have applied to over twenty interior design and art projects in Manhattan.

I realize I'm leaving empty air on the phone, so I start talking quickly. "Oh, yes. Hi. It's me. That's me, I mean. Yes."

Phyllis seems to be understanding of my excitement. "We are so pleased you sent over your resume to us Ms. Maitland. Is there any way you could come in for an interview sometime? No rush, get over your jet lag first."

Gosh, she sounds so nice. I have struck gold. "Please, call me Carrie. We're super casual over in South Africa."

Phyllis's tone gets more confidential as she lowers her voice. "Well, to be honest, your brother does our security for us so we recognized your surname. You sent in a very comprehensive resume. We like that. Your brother is such a nice man, although we have never met personally. Mr. Maitland is really on the ball when one of our floor guards calls in sick."

"That's my brother!" I say with pride. Who would have thought Miles's relentless work ethic would pay off for me? "Can I come over on Thursday, please? Three days should be enough for me to get in sync."

"Shall we make it for eleven in the morning? Give you enough time to find your way here. Or would you like us to send a town car?"

I never knew that the job application process in Manhattan was so nice! "No, it's okay, thank you, Phyllis. I will find my own way there. I would like to see a bit of the city."

"Don't forget your portfolio on the subway or the cab, Carrie. See you on Thursday. Bye!"

***

Three days later, I wish I accepted Phyllis's offer of a town car. I woke up late because I am nowhere near getting over my jet lag. Then I got all paranoid about my portfolio being left in the back of the cab.

Somehow, the loft is a big mess once again and I still haven't worked out what I want to wear. I thought of an outfit last night, but when I took it off the rack this morning—Miles uses racks in the loft because he doesn't like wardrobes—the clothes are still so wrinkled from being folded up in my suitcase there is no way I can wear it to a job interview.

Dithering around in circles, I head over to the bathroom where the only mirror in the loft is. "Keep cool, girl," I say to my reflection. "Your whole lives depend on getting this job." Using my hairbrush as a microphone, I yell into the handle. "Failure is not an option!"

I keep my makeup light: just a slick of tinted sunscreen, mascara, and petroleum jelly on my lips. I know better than to wear lipstick or lip gloss while using public transport. That is asking for a white line of old lip product to collect on my lower lip without me being able to see it.

Then it's back to the subdivided bedroom to forage for some clothes. There's nothing else for me to do. I have to wear a dress. It might work. I am an artist after all. Maybe I can rock the Bohemian chick look without looking like a crusty old hippie.

Pulling a polycotton mix sundress over my head, I stand on tiptoe, trying to see my reflection full length. The dress is pretty in a peasant girl sort of way. Puffed sleeves that fall off the shoulder and a flounced skirt with wide panels that sit halfway down my calves. The fabric is white with little points of flowers in blue and green dotted on it.

After doing a quick check—portfolio, purse, and phone—I head out the door. Bless Miles's heart. When I exit next to the coffee shop, a town car and driver are waiting for me.

"Carrie?" the man confirms as he opens the door for me. "Yes, did Miles send you from Sterns & Co.?"

He nods. "Yes, I'm from Sterns. Do you know where you are going?"

I give him the address. The Apollo on First Avenue, and the car pulls out slowly to join the traffic. Manhattan is so confusing and busy after the quiet little coastal town of Simon's Town. Yes, I hate the name of where I am from because it reminds me of him, but soon I will be able to say I live and work in Manhattan, and then I will never have to say the name of my brother's boss again!

The car drops me off and I am early. That has to count for something. Presenting myself at the desk in the lobby, I tell the security guard I am here to see Phyllis for a job interview. He issues me a pass, all very official and professional, and then tells me to take the elevator up to the top floor.

Yikes. I have to admit the nerves are starting to get to me as the elevator climbs to the top floor. Pulling my dress down and using my phone to check my face, I flick my hair back and pull up the puff sleeves.

The elevator doors slide open and I hold my portfolio in front of me like a shield.

There is no passageway or corridor. Just one spacious room with walls of glass and a few choice items of tasteful furniture.

Sitting behind the desk is Simon Sterns.

Chapter 8: Stern

When Carrie sees me sitting there, she pivots on her toes like a ballerina and tries to walk back into the elevator, but the doors are already sliding shut.

I can see her debate with herself whether to stick her portfolio through the door to try and get them to reopen or have it out with me here and now. After the door hisses closed, she turns to face me. The contents of her portfolio must be too important for her to risk using it as a doorstop.

We stand staring at one another for what seems like a long while. My mind is fighting with two different memories: the wonderful day this woman and I spent together at the wedding, and how she sneaked out on me without so much as stopping to say goodbye.

"Let me out."

When she was trying to exit, Carrie must have noticed that there was no "down" button next to the elevator, only one button to open and close the doors. Everything else is automatic.

Steepling my fingers as I lean forward and place my elbows on the desk, I explain the situation to her. "The doors only open when the system recognizes a registered fingerprint, Carrie. Please sit down. Did you like the town car I sent to pick you up?"

If looks could kill, I would be dead right now. Staying where she is by the elevator, Carrie raises her voice. "You could have just asked my brother to set a meeting, Mr. Sterns. There was no need for all this cloak and dagger stuff."

"Please sit down, Carrie. You might have been only eighteen years old when you told me all those lies about yourself, but I would like to think that we have moved on from that level of immaturity, no?"

The moment I saw Miles greeting the woman I knew as Caron Leslie in the lobby, my need to know more about her kicked into high gear. Sprinting back into my office, I started tapping into Miles's personnel file.

We have never been the kind of friends to show one another family photographs and chitchat about our relations. Firstly, because that is lame, and secondly, because I don't have a family. Miles has always been sensitive to that fact.

Miles is the same age as I am, thirty-five. Raised in the small South African Cape Peninsula naval village of Simon's Town—I have to admit that created a smile on my face—to American parents with dual citizenship. Running my finger down the screen, I got to his family.

One younger brother, Brody Maitland, married with children. But I already knew that. And one younger sister... Carrie Maitland. Typing with feverish excitement, like a bloodhound on the trail of something big, I changed the search engine over to South Africa and tapped in that name.

A few headlines popped up. "Carrie Maitland (18), causes a stir in the South African art world!" And then the article went on to report how Carrie had to hand back the scholarship she had won so that it could go to someone who needed the money more than she did.

When I checked the article, my heart froze. It was the same year Belinda and Miles got married. Things were slowly starting to fall into place.

I had walked in on Miles's eighteen-year-old sister changing out of her bridesmaid dress. She had lied to me from the start. Her name, her country of origin, her connection to my best friend. No wonder I could never find her.

And it wasn't just because I was shaking all the wrong trees; Miles had gone ballistic at the thought of me screwing one of the strictly off-limits female wedding guests instead of fulfilling my duties as the best man!

But my laptop wasn't finished supplying me with information. The internal Sterns & Co. software sent me an alert. A Carrie Maitland had been flagged in the company data.

Clicking on the popup window, I read the file. Carrie Maitland had applied to HR for a job. She wanted to be considered as a candidate for the mural I have commissioned to be created in the lobby at Apollo on First.

How did I not know about this? The Apollo is set to be the new headquarters of Sterns & Co. One phone call to Phyllis Burroughs later, and laying my hands on my best friend's sister was within my sights once again....

And now, this young woman sitting in front of me, a scornful look on her face, broke my heart. And I want her to apologize.

She sits in silence, trying to keep her face neutral. A few twitches of nerves tell me that she is nervous. I try to coax an apology out of her. "I love your body of work, Carrie. You can have the job if you say you are sorry for all the lies you told me five years ago."

As beautiful as she is, Carrie's face morphs into a Valkyrie of wrath when I say that. "Activate that fucking elevator with your fingerprint now, Mr. Sterns! I would rather die than say sorry to you!"

I am unmoved by her outburst. "I am going to pretend you didn't say that, Carrie. I know you need this job. Bend the fucking knee, say you are sorry, and let's move on from there, shall we?"

It's Clash of the Titans in this spacious room. I have never felt such an enormous battle of wills before, but I am determined to win.

Using a classic interrogation technique, I switch tactics. Getting out of my chair, I move around to her side of the desk and sit on the edge, facing her. Reaching out my hand, I wait for her to place the portfolio into it, which she does after a slight pause.

Paging through the large black folder, I take a lot of pleasure from looking at her work. "What made you change from paintings to murals?"

Carrie glares at me, sensing a trick question. I just wait for her to open up to me. Eventually, she replies. "I helped a friend install a mosaic in an indoor swimming pool at a condominium estate in Cape Town. I liked the scope a wall offers an artist."

Settling myself on the edge of the desk, I counter her statement. "Mosaics are not art. It's more like a hobby, don't you think? Finding an outline you like and then blowing it up on an overhead projector to show you where to place the colors."

Like a frightened colt, I see Carrie drop her guard as she begins to trust me. She forgets our difficult circumstances and relaxes as she talks about her passion for art.

"My mosaics are done freehand, using the same techniques they did in Ancient Rome. My murals are mostly frescoes. I would like to see you tell artists like Michelangelo and Diego Rivera that their art is a hobby to their faces."

Placing her portfolio down on the desk, I walk back to sit in my chair. "Phyllis tells me that your concept for the lobby is outstanding. I agree with her. Would you like to see the architectural blueprints in 3D?"

Jerking my thumb to the right, I indicate towards the long trestle table where a white 3D-printed miniature of the Apollo has been set up. Reluctantly, Carrie follows me there. When she is standing beside me, I crouch over, pointing to the miniaturized lobby entrance.

"I've extended the lobby and entrance out from the main building. I got the idea from the Guggenheim. But I think their lobby is too sterile—I know it has to be so that the art stands out, but I want Apollo on First to make a statement from the time people walk through the doors. I want the mural to be so riveting that it makes everyone forget why they came inside in the first place."

Watching her closely, I can see the enthusiasm building in Carrie's eyes. "Yes, that is such a good idea," she agrees with me. "For too long, architects and interior designers have been sidelining lobbies, fobbing off the area with planters or marble."

Time for me to drop the carrot in front of her. "I have Architectural Digest interested in showcasing the building…. The artist who gets this commission will be the hot name on every architect and designer's lips for a long time."

She is standing close to me now, staring at the lobby miniature with excited eyes. From the way Carrie licks her lips, I know she wants this more than anything else—at least as far as her career is concerned. I know from personal experience that Carrie once wanted me more than anything else in the world too.

Until she decided to duck out on me.

Taking her hand, I hold it tightly as she struggles to pull away. "Like I said, Carrie, the project is yours. All you have to do is say sorry for—" I can't say the words. I won't give her the satisfaction of knowing how deeply she hurt me.

She stops struggling and goes still. We are so close now that I can smell the familiar scent of shampoo she uses. It brings back floods of memories for me, all of them good and positive ones. I can't let her go, but she has to apologize!

Pinching her chin, I lift her face to look at me. "Carrie. Please make me understand why you were so cruel to me. Your lies turned me into the biggest grump. For five years, I've carried around a grudge against you."

"Let me go! You have punished me enough!" Her silver-gray eyes glitter with unshed tears as she goes limp, tired of fighting.

For some reason, her admission just makes me angry. "If you ask me, I haven't punished you enough at all! Why the lies? It would have been so easy for you to walk away from us before I made a fool of myself."

The tears are falling freely down her cheeks now. "Who would want me without the lies? Please tell me that. It was sophisticated, sexy Caron Leslie who attracted you, not little Carrie Maitland!"

Nice comeback, but I wasn't having it. "You blame me for not wanting to take my best friend's eighteen-year-old sister's V-card on his wedding day. Are you insane? Of course, I wouldn't have done that! It would have been nice to have all the facts so that I could have walked away."

Sniffing and wiping her cheeks with the back of her hand, Carrie walks to the desk and grabs her portfolio off it. "Shove your job, Mister Sterns! All you ever do is walk away from things you should face up to."

I'm really exasperated now. "Put that fucking portfolio down! What are you going to do? Walk through the wall? I told you, I'm not letting you out of here until you apologize! For the lies. And for leaving."

Throwing the portfolio down and making the smooth sheets of art paper flap out like falling leaves, Carrie bunches her hands into fists. I don't care if she wants to pop me one in the face. I stand in front of her. We sweat it out, each waiting for the other to break.

"I had to leave," Carrie confesses to me in a small voice. "I went down to the wedding reception to find my brother. I wanted him to cover me for the fake backstory I gave you. But my mom saw me wearing that white dress, so she flipped out and took me home. And please don't forget that I wasn't the only one holding back all the information! You told me your name was Simon. You didn't even tell me how you were connected to my brother!"

I am blustering now. "Everyone knows who I am, Carrie. What rock were you living under? How can you not know who your brother's best man was?"

"My mom didn't let me go to the rehearsal dinner because it went on too late. I was a teenager. I had to listen to my mom!"

Suddenly, my legs feel weak. All these years of grumpiness and resentment because of a teenage girl getting scolded by her mother.

Rubbing my hands down my face, I breathe out slowly. "What were you going to say to Miles? That you were having a fuckfest with the best man in the Royal Suite under an assumed identity?"

Carrie seems to be deflated and defeated. I want to comfort her now that I know she didn't deliberately run away from me. "No, don't be stupid. Miles would have gone bananas. I wanted to ask him to pretend he knew someone called Caron Leslie from Brussels in Belgium."

I give a bark of laughter. My emotions are swinging leftfield now. "But you told me you were part of Belinda's party. Remember? That story would never fly anyway. The moment I started asking Miles about a pretty redhead woman, he turned into the Hulk, threatening me with dire reprisals if I got it on with anyone from his family. You see my problem? My hands were tied from the start."

As I watch her, I see Carrie's brain working overtime as she tries to find a flaw in my logic.

"So, was it my brother who made you not contact me, Stern, when he threatened you to stay away from anyone in his family?"

Raising my hands in the surrender sign, I nod. "You're darn tootin'. His words were, and I quote, 'I love you; you are my best friend, but if I ever find out that you pulled a move on one of my family, our friendship is over.' End quote. Miles might have said that to me five years ago, but it is still etched in my memory."

Carrie's beautiful eyes lock on mine. "So, you put your friendship with my brother above us?"

I wasn't having any of that. "Don't forget you ducked out on me. You fed me a bunch of bullshit about your identity. And then you failed to give me your contact deets. As far as I was concerned when I found out the truth, Carrie, you made your bed of lies, and you could lie on it… alone."

She blinks and swallows. My words have hurt her deeply. But I can see her making her mind up. "Fine. We'll call it a truce. I think we have punished one another enough, don't you?"

It breaks my heart to see her so downhearted, but I have carried this resentment around with me for too long to think about it too deeply. "Yes. A truce. Will you take the assignment, Carrie? Are you okay accepting me as your boss?"

"Yes. I suppose I am... for now." Standing up briskly, she shoots me a tight smile and bends to pick up her art off the floor. I hunker down next to her to help, making sure to use the edges of my fingers so I don't make smudges.

I can't resist placing my hand on the hollow of her back as we stand up. She is as supple and deliciously svelte as before, but her body has filled out with some serious womanly curves. I feel a tug in my cold heart, coming from a place I have not used in five years.

But my pride and anger are still behind the wheel. "Come," I say, guiding her over to the elevator, "I will escort you down to the lobby. I would love to hear some of your ideas for the space."

I wanted it to be so polite and civil when we got into the close confines of the elevator together, but my body has other ideas. The moment the doors slide shut and her sweet proximity becomes more acute, I find myself getting aroused.

It's that weird love-hate barrier that gets turned on by mental aggression when two similar minds engage in combat. The adrenaline gets converted into an intense sexual urge as the easiest outlet for it.

Clearing my throat, I place my hands in front of my pants. Carrie looks down at my hands, but all she says out loud is, "You have to activate the ride with your fingers, Stern. Remember?"

But the only ride I want to activate is on her.

Chapter 9: Carrie

He leans forward to push the button but stops short of touching it. When he lifts his hand away from the front of his pants, I can see how excited Stern is. He is throbbing and completely rampant. There is no way he can hide it with just one hand.

I hate myself, but my pussy floods with excitement too. I swear that if he were to run his fingers lightly over the crotch of my panties, I would come right now. It's been too long....

The air is electric between us. There is still so much resentment, but the old fire flares up, the same as if it never really went out.

As if I am hypnotized, I reach out and caress the front of his pants. The outline of his cock rears up, straining against the thin fabric. Whipping my hand away as if I touched a snake, I start to apologize, but it is too late.

He kisses me deeply. All the longing and anguish of the last five years simmer underneath his forceful embrace. His arms are strong, almost crushing me against his chest.

I remember the tattoos he showed me all those years ago, and I can't help it—I want to see him naked again. Why am I so attracted to this beast of a man? He is brutal and mean and, oh my God, he is so hot.

His fingers run through my hair, giving the roots a small tug. It's as if he really wants to show that he is the boss and there is no point in me fighting it any longer. I let him kiss me roughly. I like the thought that his hard kisses are a kind of punishment for all my lies.

I want to hate Simon Sterns, but I can't. I feel sorry for his lonely life and grumpy exterior because I know what a wonderful man is hiding under it all. If only he had forgiven me five years ago, our lives could have been so different.

Struggling to get loose from his hold, I try to fight the wave of passion coursing through my body. "N-no, Stern. We can't—"

"Yes," he growls, "we can, and we will."

I am swept away by my desire, and do nothing when he lifts the hem of my dress to access the pulsating clit between my dripping pussy lips. When his finger slides in there, I give a loud moan. I didn't realize how close I was to coming.

He fingers my clit the way he knows I like it. There is no need for him to reach for oil this time, I am so wet all he has to do is dig his fingers into my glistening pussy hole and then use it to lube that small, pulsing nub.

I am pressed against the wall and panting as he fingers me with a quick, firm movement. I try to push him away when I feel myself coming, but he knows it is only my way of attempting to reassert my control.

As my orgasm begins to build inside me, I fumble my hand to his zipper and slide it inside once the opening is wide enough. I come hard the moment I touch his massive cock. Gripping the shaft, I pump him as I ride the wave of my pleasure.

Pushing him backward so that I can kneel in front of him, I manipulate his big prick out of the zipper so I can suck it. We don't even notice it when Stern's hand activates the elevator and we start to go down—I'm too busy going down on my new boss.

His cock is delicious. I look up at his face as I lick his knob, but Stern has his eyes closed as he bites back his groans of pleasure. When he opens his eyes, I have to admit how much I adore their blue intensity.

Reaching his hand out towards me, Stern guides my head to take as much of his cock into my mouth as possible—and then the elevator door slides open onto the first-floor lobby.

Naturally, the security guy at the desk turns to see who is coming out. For what seems like a long time, our surprised trio is locked in a staring contest. Clambering to stand up, I jump off my knees and pull down my dress because it is all tucked into my panties.

But Stern's cock is still hanging out of his pants.

"Jesus Christ!" The security guard in the lobby is taken by surprise.

Pelting to the entrance, my portfolio flapping in my hands, I toss my pass card onto the desk and run outside.

I run like the wind, sure that Stern will come after me. Ducking inside a bodega, I hide behind an aisle and wait. The clerk looks at me funny, but that is only because of my enormous portfolio. I mouth the word, sorry at her.

Fully dressed and presentable, Stern stalks past the window like a prowling jungle cat. He seems anxious, not at all embarrassed, but I am too distraught to face him.

Why, oh why did I cave into my sexual attraction to him? He treated me so badly, choosing to stay friends with my brother rather than be with me. If I ever had sex with him again, I would hate myself for being weak.

I wait. After pulling my phone out of my purse, I turn it to silent. Sure enough, it buzzes. Then a message comes through.

Where the fuck are you? Come back. I am waiting for you in the lobby.

I don't move a muscle. He is not waiting for me in the lobby. He is out here on the streets, hunting me down!

Simon Sterns still has a long way to go if he wants me to come back. My phone goes mad with another call, followed by yet another message.

That guy works for me. My employees' opinions don't matter, Carrie. Come back. Please.

Another minute or two and I see Stern walking back in the direction of the Apollo, his phone in his hand as he waits for me to respond. The man is a relentless machine! Anyone else would have given up and gone back to their nice air-conditioned office by now!

It is only my second meeting with Simon Sterns and I am starting to realize a few things about him. One, he has somehow managed to create a kind of sexual control over me—one which I am helpless to resist. And two, he doesn't care what his employees think about him.

Strangely enough, it's the second realization that worries me the most. If I accept this art project assignment, that means I am officially working for my hot billionaire boss and my brother's best friend!

***

It took hours for me to get back to the Village. I am starting to understand why everyone takes cabs and town cars everywhere. Manhattan can be a bewildering place when the high-rises block out the view and every building looks the same.

The city is always in such a constant state of flux that GPS isn't accurate, and looking at a map gives a Manhattan newbie no clue as to how long a block is when walking it in heeled shoes!

It's the middle of the afternoon when I stomp up the stairs to the loft. As usual, there is no food or drink in the kitchen. One quick look into

Miles's section of the loft shows me he had a bag of chips and a soda for breakfast.

My brother's life is spiraling out of control since he split up with Belinda. I haven't spoken to him about it too much—there is a slim chance that they still might get back together. If they do, then I will be the "bad guy" for having an opinion on the matter.

In the safety of my cordoned-off bedroom, I check my phone. There are so many missed calls and unread text alerts that I throw the phone down onto my bed and leave it there. My mind is in a whirl because I can't help feeling that I am weak and stupid for not resisting Simon Stern's mesmerizing kisses.

Looking at the clock on the wall above the stove, I curse. I missed calling South Africa because of that stupid long walk home! Slumping down on the old armchair, I text.

Hi guys! I love you so much and miss you even more! I have a job and soon I will have a place of my own. How are things there? I hope that we will see each other soon. I am going to be a world-famous fresco painter and then we can all live together. Love you lots xxx

One of Stern's messages catches my eye.

Come back. We have so much to talk about.

Huffing a long puff of air out of my lungs, I close my eyes and think. I really want the job. Stern is right, it will make me famous. And I know he chose me for it because my work is unique.

Stern is way too much of a shrewd businessman for him to hire me just so he can get control over me. Typical bossman, he wants the best of both worlds. He wants to eat his cake and have it too. Or should that be phrased to eat out my pussy and have me too? I don't know anymore.

Realizing that I am starving, I haul myself out of the armchair and go downstairs to the coffee shop. I don't want coffee, but they have a nice range of sandwiches and cakes on display.

There is a queue, but I am happy to wait. I have a lot on my mind. If I take the job, not only will it be enough for me to help my little family visit here, but it will also turn me into an art superstar. If I turn it down, though, all the other complications in my life will get so much easier.

Munching on my ham salad sandwich, I make up my mind. It's best if I wait to see if any of the other jobs get back to me first.

My phone rings. It's Miles. "Hey, Milo. You left the loft like a pigsty. Don't forget to bring back groceries if you want supper." I am still way too broke to buy groceries myself.

"Yeah, sure. What is this I am hearing about you and Stern?" Miles sounds pissed. My heart turns to ice and then begins to flutter. Am I having a stroke? Sweat breaks out on my forehead and I feel sick. Somehow, he found out about me and Stern at the wedding.

"M-Miles... I c-can explain—"

My brother butts in. "Explain nothing! He's standing here in my office, telling me that Phyllis and he picked you out of hundreds of applicants, and then you go and turn down his amazing offer. I am disappointed in you, Carrie! And if you expect me to carry your ungrateful, unemployed ass in Manhattan while you fuck around with serious job proposals, you can go back home on the next flight! I am going through a divorce—I don't need this in my life right now. Stern is my best friend!"

I am so relieved that my brother hasn't found out about me and his best friend, that is all I can think about. Stern is a masterful player, running to my brother and telling him his side of the story first. Now, it's Stern with all the face cards in his hand.

"Fine! Tell him I accept his proposal! Now will you please buy some fresh produce on the way home, Miles? Before we both get scurvy!"

"I am pleased to hear you are ready to listen to reason, Sis." Miles sniffs into the speaker, making the sound echo.

I hear the phone on the end of the line make shuffling noises as someone takes it out of my brother's hand. And then the familiar deep voice growls in my ear.

"I am so pleased to hear that you have decided to come around to my way of seeing things, Carrie. I have every confidence in you presenting me with the most beautiful artwork once you are finished."

Purring in a sexy way, I whisper. "Hold the phone close to your ear, Stern. I want to speak to you about what happened in the elevator—and I don't want my brother listening in."

The phone crackles. Stern sounds satisfied as he replies, "Yes, go on."

"Fuck you, Simon Sterns!" I hiss the words into the phone and then disconnect the call.

Chapter 10: Stern

I have to give Carrie ten out of ten for audaciousness. I don't know why, but now that I know I have her back in my sights, I feel much happier. I want to punish her for running out on me and telling me lies, but I can also understand her reasoning.

She has gained a lot of confidence over the years, which shows in the way she interacts with me. Gone is that hesitant young woman who let me lead the way in all things. Her sunny personality still manages to shine through, especially when interacting with her brother.

Miles looks at me strangely when I hand him back his phone. "What did she say to you? If

Carrie gives you any trouble, buddy, just let me know. She's always been such a good little girl. I guess she can't stay the family baby forever."

I couldn't agree more, but I want to avoid treading in dangerous waters. "I just want your sister to paint my mural, Miles." A vision of Carrie kneeling in front of me with my dick in her mouth flashes in my mind. It shocks me into reacting.

"What's wrong?" Miles puts a concerned hand on my arm. "You inhaled sharply and then kind of staggered. Low blood sugar?"

Low blood pressure more like! Because my cock gets tumescent with blood every time I think of Carrie. "Hey, no, I'm fine. I'm going to go grab something at the canteen. Want to join me?"

Miles declines my invitation and I make my getaway. My phone rings as I head to the canteen floor. It's Belinda.

"Hi, Stern." With Belinda, it's always business as usual. She knows I can't fire her just because she's dumping my best friend. "Can you please come to HR? I need to ask you something."

She is so ballsy, I hate it. There has always been a kind of smug triumphant vibe about Belinda. She has a powerful job and title, and she makes sure that everyone knows it.

But that shit does not fly with me. "I'm heading to the canteen. Come to my office on the mezzanine level in one hour." I disconnect the phone, wishing that I could disconnect Belinda from my life completely.

Belinda is looking particularly satisfied when she comes into my office later. "What is it now, Belinda? What is so important that you can't stick it in an email?"

I continue working as she stands in front of me. I have no time for her since she kicked my buddy to the curb. The man had a right to voice his discontent when he found out about her refusal to have kids. Belinda even refused to adopt, which seems a bit petty from my point of view.

"Remember when you gave permission for Miles to loop me into all the hires, Stern?"

I carry on typing. "Yeah."

"So, I noticed you and Phyllis made one without me. Can you give me an explanation?"

The blood starts to mount to my face, I am so mad. It's strange how the battle rage I experienced in the Corps is completely different from the irritation I feel when one of my subordinates at work attempts to question my authority.

But I have to play nice. Belinda is connected to all the equality groups in the state. "I can make a hire without your approval, Belinda. I. Am. The. Boss. Do I have to spell it out for you as well?"

Whipping out her notepad, Belinda smirks. "Actually, Stern, you have to keep me updated with all the hires you make Stateside. That's why you gave permission for Miles to loop me into all the new contracts in the first place."

I forgot that Belinda has the authority to dip her nose into what is going on at Apollo on First as well as back at HQ. This irks me. The last thing I need is her questioning my motives.

Belinda continues. "Your most recent hire caught my eye for several reasons, Stern. I'm sure I don't need to remind you that Sterns

& Co. must advertise every available position so that it reaches the widest demographic of applicants."

Yes. I did know that which is why I used Phyllis to set up the interview with Carrie and not Belinda. She has my attention now, but I'm not about to let that show.

"Sure, Belinda. Go ahead. Hit up the headhunters and ask them to send over all the artists on their books. All the award-winning, South African artists with an American passport. I want all the candidates' profiles and portfolios on my desk by the end of day."

I see Belinda fold her arms as she sizes me up. "I know you are only using Miles's sister as a way to siphon money over to my soon-to-be ex-husband, Stern. I won't stand for it. If he gets any fresh cash flow into his account while the divorce is still being finalized, I want my share."

A sigh of relief is slowly exhaled out of my lungs. Belinda doesn't notice. She's too fixated on screwing Miles out of every penny she can get out of him.

My relief allows me to crack one of my jokes. I haven't been in a joking mood for so long, it feels kind of nice to be back in the game.

"You can still get a share of the money, Belinda. I believe that Carrie is still unmarried. You have time. Ask her to marry you once your divorce is through. I'm sure Miles's sister will be more than happy to hand you fifty percent of her commission once the ring is on her finger. Those Maitlands, huh? There's a sucker born every minute, don't you agree?"

Belinda insisted on marrying Miles without a prenup. I want to twist the knife a little because she is taking my best friend for everything she can lay her hands on. She could not believe it when Miles drew the line in the sand when it came to starting a family.

She's not shy about this, though. Belinda is proud to be screwing Miles over. "Serves him right for being such a big baby about wanting kids. It's a woman's right to change her mind."

I have the strong suspicion that Belinda never wanted kids in the first place. She does not have a maternal bone in her body. Striding forward, she grips the edge of my desk and leans in.

"Quit shitting around, Stern. I can make life very difficult for you if I am so inclined. You love being surrounded by your Beta yes-men, but I am not one of them. I will conduct the interviews for the lobby artist and send the best candidates over to you when they are good and ready."

"Art is subjective, Belinda, and the Apollo is my project."

She gives a squeak of laughter and throws her head back. "I don't care. All Sterns & Co. hires must go through HR."

Holding up one finger, I pick up the phone and ask my assistant to put me through to the architect in charge of construction at Apollo on First. Belinda frowns and crosses her arms, waiting. I ignore her.

"Hey, Mannie. I was wondering if you could add an art installation for the lobby to your work quota. Yeah. I have to toe the line at Sterns because of HR, and there's this artist I really like. Only I can't hire her this side because—yep. You can? Thanks. I will flick her email address over to you right now. Cheers, mate."

Disconnecting the line, I sit back in my desk chair and clasp my hands behind my head. "There, Belinda. Problem sorted. You'll have to speak to Miles's lawyer directly if you want to check if the payments are being made into his account."

She storms out. Grinning to myself, I follow her to the corridor and watch her stomp across the marble floor of the lobby below.

***

It's been two days and I haven't heard back from Carrie. I can't go another day without sealing the deal with her. It has been busy for the last forty-eight hours, unlinking Belinda's system at HR from all work contract communications and name flags.

Now, the only way HR will know what names I am considering taking on as employees is by asking me directly. Belinda found out this morning, but I told her to discuss her concerns with Miles. "He's the head of company security logistics, Belinda. He can fill you in."

She hung up in a huff because she is not talking to Miles at the moment. I think she expected Miles to come crawling back to her and accept her choice, but she has no idea how badly my friend wants to start a family.

Jittery and impatient, I call Phyllis. She picks up on the first ring. "Yes, sir?" Phyllis is old-school, the last of those ladies who were proud to call themselves secretaries and not feel inferior by the word.

"Has Mannie gotten back to you yet about the hire?"

She knows to whom I am referring. Phyllis is as sharp as a knife.

"Yes, sir. Miss Maitland expressed great happiness when Mr. Milano made her the offer after the interview. She signed the contract immediately. He forwarded it through to me now. I was just going to email you."

I am confused. "Why was Carrie happy about Mannie?" It doesn't make sense. Mannie loves his pasta and hates the gym. He's the last person she would be attracted to, surely? And he's married.

Phyllis is silent on the line. "Come on, Phyllis. Spill the beans. I won't be cross."

Clearing her throat, my assistant states firmly, "Miss Maitland was under the impression that you would be heading the project, sir. When she found out Mr. Milano had final approval, she was happy. She said—and this comes from Mannie, sir, not me—'I don't want to liaise with Mr. Sterns at all. He's too bossy.'"

Gripping the phone hard, I growl down the line. "I'm the damn boss, Phyllis! How else am I meant to behave?"

We say goodbye politely because Phyllis knows my bark is worse than my bite. Drumming my fingers on the table, I grab the phone and ask for Belinda.

She is not pleased to hear from me. "What petty punishment have you and Miles got planned for me now, Stern?"

I can be very charming when I want to be. "Hey, Belinda. Listen, no harm, no foul. Okay? You are a very valued member of the Sterns team, and I would hate for you to think that we don't function better with you in charge of your department."

"Fine. Apology accepted. Why are you calling?" I can hear Belinda mellowing under the compliment.

"I want you to have a bead on the art project at the Apollo. I don't want you to feel left out just because of Miles. I'll tell you what. Send one of your staff over to First Avenue, and I'll make sure she updates you on everything, keeping you in the loop."

Belinda thinks it over, trying to see a hidden trap in the arrangement. "Just to be clear, Stern. My staff member is going to stick around and report back to me on everything relating to finances."

"Sure, just send the person over to me first. I want to share my vision with them."

Half an hour later, my assistant tells me that a Gail Patterson is waiting to see me."

"Send her in."

Gail strolls in, completely at ease. She's a large, comfortably built lady with a wide grin and bright eyes. I get up from behind my desk and walk around to shake hands with her. She beams a smile at me.

"You're even bigger in the flesh, Mr. Sterns! Pleased to meet you in person."

Gesturing for Gail to sit down, I return to my seat. "Gail, can I trust you?"

She doesn't have to think twice. "Of course you can, Mr. Sterns. Is this something to do with Mr. and Mrs. Maitland's divorce? Oh, I forgot. Belinda doesn't want people calling her that anymore."

I am picking up that Belinda is not as popular as she thinks she is. "Actually, Gail, this is something personal to me. I hired Miles's sister to do the new mural painting in the lobby at Apollo on First. We had to do the hire through the architect because it is easier that way."

Gail gives a big laugh. "Hah! Everything gets easier when HR isn't sticking its nose in everywhere!"

"Damn straight." I give a wink. Gail totally gets it. "So, would you do me a favor? I need you to become Carrie Maitland's new best friend. She's all alone in the big, bad city, and I don't want anything—or anyone—upsetting her."

Gail sits back, gazing at me shrewdly. "Sure thing, Mr. Sterns. I hear you. How much are you going to pay me? Extra."

I love this woman. She's a straight shooter, like me. "How about an all-expenses-paid expense account? Free use. So long as it's bought in a store or a restaurant. No online. No cashouts. No refunds or returns."

"Mr. Sterns! You mean I can decorate my entire apartment and dine out on your dime?!"

I nod. "I think you better start calling me Stern, Gail. Do we have a bargain?"

"I ain't no spy, Stern, but I'll look after your young protégée for you as if she were my own child!"

"Thank you, Gail. Look after Carrie for me. She's a special girl."

Chapter 11: Carrie

Something unusual happens after Miles goes to work. The buzzer rings to let me know a visitor is downstairs. It's not a delivery. My brother never orders online because his work hours mean the package gets left on the sidewalk all day.

Of course, the video intercom doesn't work, so I trot downstairs and open the door in person. A bountiful, beautiful lady is standing there, smiling at me. "Carrie? Carrie Maitland?"

I nod and she sweeps past me, stopping at the entrance to hug me. "You got the same eyes as your brother! But your hair is a lighter red. I don't know him personally, but the head honchos have got images of themselves on the company website. I'm Gail Patterson, your Sterns & Co. liaison, but I report to Mr. Mannie. He wants you to be happy, so your artistic process can flow!"

For some reason, I find myself eagerly inviting Gail upstairs. She is a force of nature of the best kind, and I am getting all kinds of positive vibes from her.

It must be because I'm dying for some female companionship. Back in South Africa, I only got to interact with my mom every day, because we ran the accommodation facility together.

"Pleased to meet you, Gail."

She doesn't answer me at once because the loft is a mess and it can be a little bit daunting to walk into such a large, but dirty, space. I see her checking out some cobwebs blowing from the fluorescent light fittings hanging from chains on the exposed steel rafters.

"Miles lives here?" Gail looks dubious.

"Hardly!" I have to giggle at her pretend critical face. "Miles lives for work. He says it keeps his mind off all his problems."

My new friend wrinkles her nose. "Carrie, this loft is a problem! Come, let's get you into some walking shoes—we have some serious shopping to do."

"Do you know the best stores? Please tell me that you're local. I find Manhattan the most bewildering place to navigate."

That's one of the things that confuses me about this city: too many choices when it comes to shopping.

Gail laughs as she rummages through one of the suitcases to find a pair of shoes for me to wear. "I'm as local as they come, Carrie. But the streets are not the only areas you will have to learn to navigate. New York has to be the rudest city in the world."

I laugh. "Don't worry, we have porn in South Africa now. I can handle it."

Propelling me out the door and downstairs, Gail chuckles. "Come on, let's go somewhere nice and have brunch. Perhaps we will meet some of those rude people I'm trying to warn you about on the way. In New York, Carrie, porn is the least of your worries. New Yorkers are the rudest people in the world. Straight up, low down, aggro, bullshit bad manners! You better toughen up to it now, girl, before you get your feelings hurt!"

Gail jumps over the puddles of discarded men's clothes Miles has left scattered around the loft before giving up and searching for house cleaning services online. "I can see you have done your best to sort out this manly mess," she explains to me, "but it's best if you concentrate on your creative process now."

When I see Gail take out a black credit card from her purse and begin speaking the numbers and security code into the phone, I try to stop her. "Gail, you're an angel, but I can't have you paying for that."

"It's done," Gail says in a no-nonsense tone. "Mr. Mannie insists you have an advance on your commission, Carrie, plus spending money. You're an artist, for God's sake. Start acting like the diva I know you can be."

That makes me giggle. "My mom would go mad if she knew I was spending recklessly."

Gail clucks her tongue. "Hell, she won't know. Live a little." Once I have changed into another summer dress and an old pair of flip-flops, we head for the sidewalk and hail a cab. It's hot and fuggy outside, but what I love about the States is the dedication to making every interior ambient and elegant.

I kind of like using Mr. Milano's advance payment for everything. Gail tells the cab driver to take us to the house-cleaning depot first, so she can sign up for the service and give them instruction in person. Then we head over to Milady's, just off Sixth Avenue, for lunch.

After scarfing down delicious burgers, Gail loops her arm through mine and we walk to Bloomingdale's together. It's really great seeing Manhattan through her eyes. She tells me all about the most important art galleries and museums and then points out the landmark buildings on the skyline.

For the first time in ages, I feel excited about my life. I guess I really needed a female friend to talk to. "This is so nice, Gail," I have to tell her. "I've been housebound for a long time. I'd forgotten how amazing it is to walk the streets."

She pats my hand. "Don't worry, girl. I'm going to show you where to walk. There are a few areas you don't want to walk alone, and a few more places you shouldn't go to at night, but otherwise, it's all good."

"In South Africa, a woman can't walk anywhere alone." I know I'm venting, but life is so hard in my home country that I need to share that. "No walking in the city streets. No hiking the trails. No strolling in the park or along the beach. Nothing."

Guiding me through the famous Bloomingdale's doors, Gail leads me to the makeup counter. The air smells of the most delicious perfumes. "Are you kidding me?" she looks skeptical, "please tell me you are yanking my chain?"

I shake my head. "Nope. It's true. Sure, there are a few places in Cape Town where women can walk the streets on their own, and the malls are relatively safe, but traveling alone as a woman is courting danger."

Gail leads me over to one of the canvas makeup artist chairs where we wait for the MUA to approach us. Her eyes are wide with shock when she hears me telling her this. "What happens if you go out alone?"

I pull a face. "Sunglasses ripped off your head. Jewelry, purse, phone—all gone. And that's just in town or if you are sitting in your car at the traffic light. If you are in the park, beach, or hiking trail, it's more likely you will get killed. It's a shit show, kept hidden from the tourists by hotel walls and security."

A balanced expression appears on Gail's face. "Carrie, are you sure your mom isn't just trying to scare you into staying at home by telling you how bad it is outside? Every city has those places where only fools and horses are going to visit on the fly. But it can't be everywhere."

"Honestly, Gail," I squeeze her hand, "that's the sanest remark I have ever heard someone say. I should get out more. Trust folks to do right by me."

We laugh together when Gail says, "Now, let's not overdo it! I'll get into big trouble if something bad happens to you!"

Bloomingdale's is like some gorgeous dream I can just walk into, only it has real flesh-and-blood people who are there to fulfill my every wish. The MUA is divine, with the most perfect skin and arched eyebrows.

They show me how to bring out my features. "The undertone of your skin is blue, and while that's great for bringing out the color of those freaky pretty eyes of yours, it's a hard color to match with foundation."

Gail agrees. "I would have thought my friend's eye color was contacts if I didn't know that her brother's eyes are the same color."

I risk talking even though the MUA has asked me to stay still. "Miles is so low maintenance, I doubt he would have time to stick contacts in his eyes every morning!"

When the MUA finishes, I look in the oval hand mirror and my mouth drops open. I look fantastic. Truly city-slicker amazing. They have managed to match my skin tone exactly by using sparkling white duster as a highlight and a soft blush of pink for color on my cheeks. "That pink has heavy blue tones, Carrie, so it looks natural.

Stay away from bronzer at all costs. Now, let's get you sorted out with a signature perfume."

I have the best time choosing an expensive designer perfume. All I used back home in South Africa was a cheap over-the-counter body spray. This is my money to spend, so I go a little mad, heading for the Givenchy counter.

Gail says when a woman decides to get serious about perfume, she will only buy Givenchy. I gravitate towards L'Interdit. The top notes are pear and bergamot, and the base notes are patchouli and vanilla.

"I don't recommend this white floral fragrance for summer because the middle notes of tuberose, jasmine, and orange blossom can be intense," the parfumier advises me. I have to smile and shake my head. "You had me at patchouli. For me, that's the best scent in the world."

Next, we move on to fashion. This is where I don't have much of an opinion. So long as I don't look like an old Victorian lady, I am happy. Gail manages to find me a personal shopper and asks her to send over a selection of clothing in my size to the loft on approval. One wave of the magic black credit card later, and it is done.

"I have to say that I am starting to love that credit card of Mannie's, Gail," I say to my friend. "Are you sure he is fine with my spending?"

Gail gives me a considerate look as if she is weighing up how to explain it to me. "Mr. Milano wants Stern to be happy, Carrie. Mr. Sterns is a very important guy, but you already know that, don't you?"

Lifting my eyes to the sky, I sigh. "Yes, yes, whatever."

"You don't like Stern?"

I don't know how to answer that, so I stay silent. Gail fills in the gap. "I've been working at Sterns & Co. since the beginning. Stern was laser-focused on providing the best security money can buy. It's not just bigwigs he looks after; Stern has made home security accessible for ordinary folks too."

"Huh. Just in time to profit from the collapse of civilization. That's not kindness, Gail, that's opportunistic."

My new friend's eyes get wider. "Wow. You really don't like Stern?"

I shrug, flicking through a rack of hangers dripping with high-priced couture gowns. "He's tolerable. Barely. I don't trust anyone who is that good-looking and single. He's probably a player."

I don't say anything about how he chose his friendship with my brother over me. I am still kicking myself because it was my lies that made that happen.

"He's changed a lot, Stern has." Gail guides me over to designer purses and starts inspecting the stitching and embossments. "Whenever Belinda spoke about her boyfriend's best friend, she would say that Miles and Stern were the biggest couple of jokers around. But after the wedding, that stopped. I heard on the grapevine that the boss got really grumpy after that."

I wonder if I had anything to do with that. It would be some comfort to know that Stern took the neglect of his responsibilities to heart, but I am not cruel enough to want him to suffer for it.

"Do you think he misses hanging out with my brother?" I ask Gail. I am really enjoying her perspective on life at Sterns & Co. after I left the hotel suite and never came back.

"Oh, they still hang out. Belinda complains about that all the time. I'm not sure why Stern had his change of personality after the wedding. Now, let's get you this Montblanc messenger bag, Carrie because I can see that you aren't taking a shine to all these fancy purses! Your notepad and pens will fit into it nicely."

I am starting to lose count of all the times Gail has swiped that black card of hers—and we still haven't gotten around to trying on the clothes back home!

Then my phone rings. Without thinking, I press green in case it comes from home.

"Carrie, when can I come and see you at the loft?"

It's Simon Sterns.

Chapter 12: Stern

Her voice is tight, but polite when Carrie replies, "I have no idea. You will have to speak to my brother."

And then she disconnects the call. Two strong emotions fight inside me. Anger that I was conned into having feelings for my best friend's baby sister. And frustration that Carrie is taking it out on me for the problem her lies caused us from the start.

How can she hold it against me? The moment I laid eyes on her—no, strike that—the moment we laid eyes on each other, it was like time stood still. Our attraction was instant, and I know it was not just physical.

Now that I think back to what Miles told me, Carrie and I bonded right from the start. When we were standing at the head of the aisle inside the church, we had a good thing going, joking and laughing together, as if we were old friends standing at the head of the aisle and not Miles.

Fumbling with my phone, I text Gail. WTF?

I suppose she doesn't get right back to me in case it looks a bit suspicious, so I head out to my private onsite gym and go work out my frustrations on the punching bag. I work out my whole body. Jumping rope, running on the treadmill, row machine, punch bag, lifting weights. I must have been there for two to three hours before I dare go back to the locker and check my phone.

Two texts from Gail. God bless that woman. The last message came in five minutes ago.

Where are you? We've been trying on clothes for the last two and a half hours, Mr. S. I'm about to head home. If you meet me downstairs in twenty minutes, I can pretend to be surprised to see you there and let you in. Make sure Miles stays busy somewhere else.

I don't waste time getting back to her.

Stay there. I can be there in thirty minutes. I'll get Miles to do a sleepover at one of the new contracts. Thank you.

There's no time for me to shower, shave, change, or call the town car to come around and pick up. Grabbing my wallet, I run down from the mezzanine level and sprint out to the sidewalk, ignoring the surprised looks from the doorman and security guys at the lobby desk.

One of the guys tries to help me. "Mr. Sterns? Can I call you a cab?" the doorman says, rushing forward to offer assistance. I can see him checking the sweat stains on my chest and armpits under my light gray gym sweater. Two elderly ladies walk a wide circle around me, darting disapproving looks at my apparel.

The doorman flags down a yellow cab for me. I'm in too much of a hurry for an Uber service or to call Gerry for the town car. I wait for the doorman to close the door before I give the driver the loft address. The driver nods and pulls away from the curb. No judgment there.

I get busy with my phone. Miles picks up on the second ring. I know why. He was checking to see if it was not Belinda first. As their divorce progresses, it seems to become more bitter.

A thought flashes across my mind. I hope I never get it so wrong when I get married. "Hey, Miles. I was going to handle the Delgardo contract walk-through, but something has come up. Can you fill in for me please?"

"Can I take the private jet?" Miles sounds keen. "I don't think I can face the red eye, even traveling First Class."

"Buddy"—I am smiling and relaxed now—"I wouldn't have it any other way."

That's where I leave it. I have never been one for overkill. If I were to mention to Miles that I would contact Carrie on his behalf and let her know her brother was flying out to California, he would immediately become suspicious.

Leaning back in the cab seat, I give a small laugh and close my eyes. How did it get like this so fast? I am sneaking around behind my best friend's back so that I can see his baby sis. It's crazy, but I feel more alive now than I have felt for the past five years.

My driver is excellent, taking us up Hudson towards the Village as quickly as the lights allow. Downtown traffic is kind, which stops me from fuming in the backseat the way New Yorkers always tend to do, muttering about how they could go faster if they got out and jogged instead of sitting in the congestion.

Pulling up outside the loft, I throw him a bill that makes his eyes widen. Despite my disheveled appearance, he can tell I'm not the kind of guy who would wait to receive change. "Th-thanks, friend!"

I already messaged Gail to tell her I was outside. I see some of the coffee shop patrons shoot looks at me. I guess it is not often a tall, muscle-bound man in sweats dares to walk the Village streets during daylight hours. But I don't care.

Gail's eyes widen when she opens the street entrance door. "Hell! That's what you look like," she whispers. "When I said to hurry, Boss, I didn't mean for you to drop your jazzercise class in the middle of doing the disco hustle and run over here."

"Oh, ha, ha." I can take a joke. I can take anything now that I know I get a chance to see Carrie again.

In a loud voice, Gail shouts up the stairs. "Oh, hey, Stern! What a coincidence! Were you jogging in the neighborhood? Come on in."

As I mount the stairs, Gail shouts even louder. "My oh my! Is that the time? I gotta be going, Carrie sweetie. Text me later. Bye!"

Carrie is at the door, looking down on me as I climb up. Her face is neutral. Do I have a chance?

"Hey, Carrie. I popped by to see how things are going. Can I come in please?"

She steps back and allows me inside. The loft is gleaming and beautifully clean, but it's such a masculine space I struggle seeing soft, feminine Carrie Maitland living here. The floor is covered with shopping bags carrying the Bloomingdale's logo.

When I turn around, I notice her face has subtle changes to it. Her lashes are dark, but so are her eyelids. A faint hint of mauve pink colors her cheeks and her lips compliment the tint. "You look beautiful." I blurt out the words before I can check my enthusiasm.

I just have to face it that I will never be laid back about Carrie's unique beauty. She hooked me in from the start and I have not been able to break free for five years.

"Thank you." Carrie is playing it cool while she decides what to do about my unexpected visit. "Would you like to use the shower?"

"Do I look that bad?" I want to know. She shakes her head, a slight smile lilting on her lips. "No, I've seen you work up a sweat before. But I've never seen you lose your cool. What happened?"

She thinks I stopped here with bad news. Behind her polite curiosity, Carrie is worried. I shake my head. "No, no, Miles is fine. He's better than fine. I...."

I decide not to divulge the part I played in her brother's absence. "Miles had to fly to LA on the company jet. A client wanted their domestic security checked out in person. The Delgardo residence is one of the largest private homes in Bel Air, so we have to treat them with kid gloves."

Carrie snorts from laughing. "All you billionaires are the same. Wanting special treatment."

That hurts. "Unlike the three generations of wealth the Delgardo family own, Carrie, I started with nothing. And I am nothing like any other man! Be he a fucking billionaire or a bum."

I thought she would be happy to have touched a nerve, but I see Carrie blush and hang her head. "I'm sorry, Stern. That was rude of me. I wish you hadn't pitched up here. If I want to run and hide from you, you should just let me."

Why does she always have this effect on me? Reaching out for her hand, I grab hold of it. "Stop hiding from me, Carrie. What good will it do us? Sooner or later we have to face facts. Miles is going to find out about us."

She goes pale and pulls her hand away. "If you think I am going to drop that bomb on my poor brother during the middle of his divorce, you have to be running mad! You should have seen his reaction when Brody told him Alma was pregnant for the second time! He was close to collapse from sorrow. Men have the right to be broody, you know!"

I don't see a connection. "Miles should toughen up, and so should you. Come and have dinner with me. Wear one of your new dresses."

It's as if I asked her to sew the buttons on my shirt. Carrie backs away, shaking her head. I get mad. "I'm your boss now, Carrie, whether you like it or not! You should start to learn to do what I say."

Carrie stands firm. "No, I don't have to obey you. Mr. Milano is my boss, not you. Trust you to jump to the wrong conclusion, Stern. You are so grumpy all the time, you didn't even bother finding out why I didn't like the idea of going to dinner with you."

"Why do you always have to complicate things!" I am boiling with annoyance. "It's my building, so you work for me! Suck it up, Carrie, and stop being a baby."

She's angry now too. "Baby? That didn't stop you from banging me when I was still in senior high!"

Starting to pace around the loft, I grab my hair by the roots with frustration. "You lied to me! Don't throw that in my face."

Carrie pouts. "You're the one throwing shade, Stern. I swear that if you throw that job in my face one more time, I'm leaving and never coming back."

"You can't leave," I am happy to remind her. "You already started spending your commission." I point at all the clothes in the bags on the floor.

Is that a glint of a smile on her pretty face? Carrie shows me the "I surrender" sign with her hands. "I have to admit, Stern. It was wonderful having my own money to spend on nice things."

This is not the time or place for me to tell her that it's my money she's spending. And I don't begrudge her one penny of it. Sucking back my bad mood, I breathe in deeply and exhale. "Fine, Carrie. Would you be so kind as to tell me why we can't go out for dinner?"

Folding her arms and nodding, Carrie smiles. "That's better. Truth is, I don't want to go out with you dressed like that. You look like the main dancer from a Step Up movie."

Walking over to the bathroom, I take a look at my reflection in the mirror. I can hear Carrie opening bags and rattling hangers on the rack behind me. She's right. I look a mess and I was way too quick to jump into aggro mode when I thought she was denying me outright.

Dodging around the bags, I go to the open-plan kitchen and sit down. "I don't look like a Step Up dancer. I'm blond. Have you noticed there aren't any blond leading men anymore? Did we do something wrong?"

Ten seconds later, Carrie and I are talking like a house on fire, debating the pros and cons of dark versus light hair. She ends the argument by telling me that the most famous star in Hollywood is a blond. "Leo DiCaprio, Stern. He's blond enough to qualify. And the guy who plays Thor."

I concede. "Sure, but Leo's not exactly Hollywood. I think he's based in Manhattan. And Thor lives in Australia. Now, about that dinner?"

She shoots me the cutest smile and our fight is forgotten. "What dress do you think I should wear?"

Chapter 13: Carrie

I never knew making-up could be this nice. Sure, I don't have any experience to know how it should go, but I feel myself blossoming under the respect and care Stern seems to want to lavish on me.

It kind of helps knowing that Miles is all the way away in California! I might hate the loft, but after the cleaning service finished tidying it up I think the space has possibilities.

"Can I see your bedroom?" Stern asks me politely. "I have never been inside a bedroom with walls and no ceiling before."

That makes me giggle. "Miles likes the deconstructed vibe a loft offers him. He's still cut up about having to sell the brownstone with all his DIY upgrades included. Our dad taught us all to be very handy when it came to projects. I guess that's why I took to producing murals and frescoes so quickly."

The words are bubbling up to my mouth as I chatter away, the feeling of elation making me breathless and high energy. I feel triumphant because this is the first time Stern and I have resolved things without throwing all of our toys out of the cot.

I always saw him as this really cool dude who was so slick he could show butter how to act smooth. But I guess I don't know him well enough to form an opinion. After he showed up here in his sports gear, all sweaty and worried that I would deny him entrance, I felt a pang of pity for him.

It makes me so happy when he jokes and smiles the way he did at my brother's wedding. It's at moments like that when I can relax and know all my lies didn't really ruin his life the same way it did mine.

Showing Stern my bedroom feels normal. That fight we had sure cleared the air. "This is my bed...." I quickly move to show him the rest of the room. "And this is the rack where I hang all my clothes. Miles doesn't like the aesthetic of a wardrobe, but he hasn't gotten around to adding walk-in closets yet."

"It looks like my friend Miles doesn't like the aesthetic of 'comfort.' Full stop." Stern ignores all my pretty dresses, skirts, and blouses on the rack. He's a man's man, so I forgive him. Secretly, I thank my lucky stars for Gail. She's my rock when it comes to dress shopping and she gives me all the approval I need when it comes to looking pretty.

"Is that it?" As if it is the most natural thing in the world, Stern flops down on my bed and stares up at the exposed steel beams twenty feet above him and the roof beyond that. "The HVAC must have to crank at maximum capacity all day and night to keep this place cool."

I feel shy with him lying on my bed. "I would think you liked being here, Stern, with the HVAC cranked so high.... At least you have stopped sweating."

Grabbing my wrist, he pulls me down to lie on the bed next to him. "You cheeky brat. I should spank you. I'll have you know that's how I always look after a workout. I skipped the shower because—"

I wait for him to tell me, but he breaks off and seems to be thinking first before he continues. "Because it was so hot outside, why bother, you know? I wanted to come past here and tell you about Miles flying west, and I knew you wouldn't answer my call."

That makes me feel even more like a brat. "Is that the impression I gave you, Stern? I... I'm sorry. Things have become so complicated between us so fast, I don't know whether I'm coming or going."

Turning onto his side, Stern gazes straight into my eyes. For the first time since I went to Bloomingdale's, I am pleased I visited the MUA. If I looked fabulous then, I must do so now. He is superstar handsome, it's not fair. Even hot and sweaty, Simon Sterns is hot enough to make me break into a sweat.

I try so hard not to be that teenage girl still in high school who sees life through rose-tinted glasses. That was when I believed in love at first sight, knights in shining armor sweeping me off my feet and into bed, and happily-ever-afters.

But Stern has a way of blanking my memory. My body can never forget how he makes me feel inside and out.

His eyes are clear blue, like the icebergs they find floating in the Atlantic Ocean. He has the face of a man who went from boyhood to manhood the tough way. This close and in the daylight, I can see the scars I missed before.

Reaching out my finger, I trace them with a light touch. One scar cleaves his left eyebrow into two sections. Another one indents his left cheekbone with a half-inch scar shaped like a crescent. He has a small hollow chicken pox scar on the right of his forehead and a thin white line cutting down the right side of his cheek.

So rugged, but those injuries must have hurt when he got them. I press the lined scar on his cheek. "Did you have a knife fight?" He looks confused. The man has so many scars that he must have forgotten half of them!

"I've had dozens," he says, trying to laugh and change the subject. "Now, where do you want to go for dinner?"

This time, it's me who grabs his wrist to stop him from leaving. "I'm not hungry... for food."

It's as if the shutters fall down on the rest of the world and only Stern and I are left lying in it. Call me weak for not sticking to my guns and staying aloof from the man I looked upon as an enemy for five long years, but my body craves him.

Shifting closer, I press my lips against his mouth, half hesitant that he might reject me. After all, we have such a complicated history together.

My stomach flips as he returns my kiss. This time, that rampant rearing lust we felt in the elevator is gone. There is no urgency or impatience. We have all the time in the world to get this done, even though I don't think we know what it is yet.

Long, lingering, delicious kisses join us in a sensual embrace. Do I get just the tiniest bit turned on by the scent of his sweat rising up from his body? Yes. This close, we notice things that fumbling to fuck in the elevator denied us.

"You smell like cookies." Stern doesn't take his mouth away from me, so I can feel him say the words as well as hear them. Secretly, I thank my perfume choice. Those vanilla and patchouli base notes are as close to eating a cookie as a man can get without literally sticking his hand in the jar.

Stern is hungry for something else, just like me. Sliding his hand up my thigh, raising the hem of my dress to my waist, he hooks his finger under my panties and pulls the crotch to one side. When the kisses on my mouth mix with his finger stroking my pussy, my excitement level ratchets up several notches.

His touch is delicate, with just a hint of what is to come by the way the tip of his finger traces the slit, searching for the hard bump of my clit and the pliant entrance of my vulva. I don't have to tell Stern that when he inserts his finger deep inside me, he'll find me dripping wet.

I have craved this for so long, trapped to live out the consequences of my web of lies on the other side of the world. The way my body reacts to him is somehow able to override how much I hate him for rejecting me when he found out the truth.

If this is grudge fucking, then sign me up! I hate the man, but love the way he makes my body feel. Moving my hand down to his hip, I lift his sweater and glide my finger around the band of his pants until I feel the hardness of his knob bulging out underneath.

Pulling back the band gently, I begin to massage his knob with my fingertips, using the pre-cum as lube. It really turns me on when I feel Stern shudder. He sits up and pulls off his sweater, giving me an eyeful of all the tattoos he picked up when he served in the military. The muscles flex as he twists around to throw the sweater onto the floor; his body is as gorgeous as ever, with no hint of softness or flab.

The way we fuck is like a beautiful dance, and I am happy for Stern to take the lead. My eyes stare as he sits on the edge of the bed to pull off his socks and sneakers. Casual Stern is just as hot as dressed for business Stern—he's one of those men who looks amazing in clothes and out of them.

Standing up and stepping out of his pants, he comes to lie down beside me. "You like what you see?"

For one moment, I am tempted to tell him that he is the only man I have ever seen naked, never mind fucked, but I don't want to remind him of my broken heart. I am no longer that young starstruck girl spinning lies to try and make herself more acceptable.

Kneeling on the bed and shifting to sit between his legs, I lick my lips. "Yes. Now more than ever. I can't stop thinking about that unfinished business in the elevator, Stern. Now, where were we?"

Unzipping my dress, I let the garment fall to my waist before I unclip my bra. After throwing it on the floor to join the rest of the clothes, I lean forward so that my nipples are brushing against his balls. Gripping his thick shaft, I lick his knob a few times before sliding the whole thing in my mouth.

It makes me feel powerful when Stern groans and closes his eyes. But he opens them again so he can watch my lips sucking and licking around his cock.

"Where did you learn how to do that?" He wants to know, but I am not about to ruin this with an overshare. "Lots of long, lonely nights dreaming of you." I don't take my mouth away when I speak. I want him to feel my lips moving.

Growling in a deeply sexy way, Stern flips me onto my back. "When I come, sweetheart, I want to be balls deep inside you. Can you handle that?"

I'm so wet, I can handle a good pounding from his massive cock. "Fuck me, Stern," I whisper, "fuck me hard."

I almost start to come when he slides into me. It's because his girth manages to cause friction on my clit when it pounds inside me. It's better than any vibrator because it's attached to Stern.

Lying with his head tucked against my neck, he goes still for a beat, letting us both relish the golden moment before we come. I adore the way he grinds his cock into me, letting me use the base of his shaft to rub my clit on. A few subtle tilts of my hips and I'm close.

We are so attuned to how our bodies work that we don't need to use words. One hard thrust and he bursts. Just the thought of him releasing his cum into me makes me come like rolling waves of exquisite pleasure. And then the silence follows as we appreciate the feeling, the relief, and that warm surge of emotion.

Have Simon Sterns and I just made love?

Chapter 14: Stern

Rolling off the woman who has just helped me have the best orgasm of my life, I am forced to stare up at the god-awful industrial nightmare of a ceiling again. I swear I can feel the tar melting off the roof tiles in the heat from the sun outside.

Sunbeams stream through the skylights and casement windows. I can see dust motes circling from the eddies of cold air blasting out of the HVAC. Do I feel happy about what just happened? Yes. Am I pissed that Carrie has to put up with living here with Miles? Absolutely.

I pull her close to kiss her cheek. "Thank you. I don't deserve your forgiveness. I should have fought harder for Miles to give me his blessing to go looking for the sexy redhead from the wedding...."

Carrie gives a little sigh. "It's a mess, but I'm glad I no longer have to clean it up. You can't lose my brother in your business or as your friend. We never should have gotten together in the first place."

"But we are together." That's what I want to say, but I don't have the courage. Navy SEAL NCO Simon Sterns, survivor of two tours and countless black ops missions, is now too scared to say what he feels.

I don't want to rock the boat. Carrie carried a grudge against me for not following up on our liaison and there is nothing I can do to turn back time and make that better.

"Hey, I don't know about you, but I could murder a steak, Carrie. How about it?"

Shooing me over to the shower after pushing a towel into my hands, she tidies the room. I hear her pushing hangers from side to side on the rack as she makes up her mind about what to wear. When I finish showering, Carrie goes into the bathroom after me. It's the only closed-off space in the loft because the plumbing is part of the wall structure.

Reaching for my phone, I see a message from my credit card provider, checking that I am still okay with deactivating the "Approve or Reject" payment alert bank service. I flick off a quick email so that they have a record, telling them that I am fully aware of the recent feminine-centric purchases made with the card.

They are so used to me buying the latest sports car or motorbike, or whatever new boy toys come on the market, it must be a real shock to the system for them to see purchases being made at the dress section at Bloomingdale's.

I have to keep on hiding behind Gail because I don't want Carrie to think I'm trying to love-bomb her. She comes back into the room with droplets of water running down her skin and instantly, I get distracted. "Are you enjoying walking around naked now that Miles is miles away?"

We are back to being our old joking selves. Not only do I feel younger since Carrie came back into my life, but I feel happier too. No, strike that. Wrong choice of words; our lives are still far too complicated for me to be truly happy.

But for now, I am content.

"I'm enjoying it, period," Carrie quips as she zips herself into a fresh dress. "I don't exactly prance around without my clothes on in Simon's Town either. Mom and Dad are so strict."

"Jesus Christ, Carrie!" I can't believe what I'm hearing. "You're twenty-three years old now. Your parents should learn to loosen the strings a little!"

Walking to the mirror, she begins smoothing cream in small dabs on her face, keeping eye contact with me by staring at my reflection. "I just finished college, Stern. I owe it to my parents to respect the huge sacrifice and concession they made for us over the last five years."

That catches my interest. "Do they have a clue how much Miles makes here? With the exchange rate, your parents would never have to work a day in their lives again. They could close that bed and breakfast of theirs and retire."

Carrie shakes her head sadly as she brushes her hair with her fingers. "Miles and my parents have a complicated relationship at the moment, Stern. I can't talk about it."

Thinking that it might have something to do with Miles's failure to produce grandchildren for the Maitlands, I keep my mouth closed. We walk down to the street after Carrie shuts off the AC and switches on the fancy security system.

Crossing over to Seventh Avenue, we catch a cab downtown. All the best steakhouses are close to the Financial District. We decide on Morton's and are seated in one of the best booths, with only the soft glow of lampshades to help us read the menu. The server helpfully turns the table so that Carrie and I can sit next to one another in the booth.

Taking great pleasure watching Carrie smile as she touches the famous Morton's sleeping pig lampstands, we order steak and plenty of sides. "I'm starving after all that exercise," I say by way of conversation.

She gives me a side smile. "Walking, or the other thing?"

I have to kiss her. "Both."

The years disappear as we go back to chatting the way we did the first time, the day of the wedding. Carrie likes to roll back the sleeve of the shirt I borrowed from Miles's side of the loft and ask me about my tattoos. Finally, we have the time to get to know one another more intimately.

"It's hard for me to remember the unique circumstances of each one," I confess, "but I promised myself when I joined the Corps that I would get a tat in each new country I visited."

Tilting her head like a bird, Carrie gives me a speculative stare. "You have way too many tattoos for you to have stuck to getting them in every port of call, Stern."

That makes me laugh. "Sure, but that's how it started. I prefer black tats, because they are the easiest to remove if I ever decided to take another route in life."

Carrie is intrigued. "What do you mean?"

I sigh, waiting for the server to set our food in front of us before I reply. "If I tell you, it will sound pretentious. In fact, I've never told anyone what I was originally trained to do."

Giving my forearm a little pinch, Carrie encourages me to confide in her. "You can't give me a taste and then deny me the full story, Stern. That's cruel."

I swallow my mouthful, shaking my head. "It's no big deal. I trained to join the Military Police, but decided against it in the end. I played around with doing black ops in foreign countries after that. That's why I got black tattoos; so they can be lasered off easily."

Carrie eats her food, but I can tell she's waiting for me to explain. "I couldn't go undercover with my skin covered in pro-America tats." Pulling the neckline of my shirt to one side, I point to the small flag tattoo on the left side of my chest. "It's a dead giveaway, having the Stars and Stripes over my heart, but no one understands how my country and my Corps are the only family I have ever known."

Carrie snorts because she is taking a sip of her martini. After blotting her mouth with the napkin, she frowns at me. "Give me a better warning next time you want to make such a heartfelt statement, Stern. However, I didn't have you down as the job-hopping type."

Raising one eyebrow, I finish my steak and push my plate away. "Job hopping?"

Throwing her hands up in the air, Carrie breaks into laughter. "Come on! Navy, Military Police, going undercover in another country, and now security. If that's not job hopping, I don't know what is."

A smile breaks on my face. "What is it that you think I did in all those jobs, Carrie?"

She sits back, also finished with her food. "Um… sailing in boats, chasing down runaway soldiers—what's it called again? Going AWOL—spying, and then securing peoples' homes so they don't get burgled. Pretty diverse resumé you got there, honey."

Trying not to be chuffed that she called me "honey," I stick to enlightening my lover. "No, no, and no. All of those first three jobs, what they have in common and what they trained me to do, is hunt, fight, and kill. The security service Sterns & Co. provides to its clients is to protect them at all cost. And my more wealthy clients would definitely want us to kill for them if they were under threat."

Carrie refuses to believe me. "I call BS, Stern! That's illegal."

Sliding my arm around the back of her shoulders, I murmur in a low voice. "I don't want us to have any secrets, Carrie, so you have to believe me. They pay me the big bucks to put the fear into anyone who is thinking about committing a crime. Haven't you noticed how you don't hear about stalkers gaining entrance to famous people's Hollywood mansions anymore? It doesn't happen because of the protection systems that people like Miles and me have developed.

"Our knowledge of the law allows us to dispatch or hurt bad people by manipulating the right legal circumstances for us to do it. And we also lobby state governments to change stalker and burglary laws too."

Her mouth is a round "O" of surprise. "Miles never told me. He said his job is to make sure there is always a security guard on duty."

I shrug. "I suppose that's one way of putting it. Most of my training involved me becoming a highly efficient killer with my body or with a weapon. Those 'runaway soldiers' you refer to are no joke, Carrie. I have to be bigger and badder to catch them. For a while, I liked the idea of black ops...."

She notices my pause. "So, why didn't you do that?"

The server brings Carrie a complimentary chocolate lava cake with ice cream. I wait for them to leave before I answer. "It was tempting, I had nothing tying me down and the excitement was guaranteed, but I was tired of my rootless existence. I wanted somewhere to call home. So I mustered out and foundered Sterns."

Carrie holds a taste of vanilla ice cream to my mouth and I lick it off. Our eyes smile at each other above the spoon. "Enough of talking about me. Would you like to come and see my apartment?" I hope she can read the need in my eyes. "It's uptown, but it's still early. We can take a cab and be there in less than half an hour."

She taps the chocolate dessert with the spoon like a drum. We are full, but chocolate lava cake and ice cream can tempt anyone.

"You still reek of the Corps, Stern." It's not a criticism, just an observation. Carrie continues. "And I'm not just talking about your killer instincts. You might have a home now, but I bet you get up every morning as if a bugle is blowing reveille. I bet your bed is made so tight a penny would bounce off it. And I have no doubt the shelves of your closet are neater than the GAP's."

I hold out my hand. "Want to bet?"

Carrie laughs. She knows a lure when she hears it. "Meaning you want me to come back with you to your apartment?"

"Yep." I am shameless when it comes to getting what I want. Tapping the side of the plate with her spoon, Carrie agrees. "But I want you to give me your phone right now—and make sure the ringer is off—so that I can be sure you aren't secretly texting your butler to rough up the bedroom for you."

No hesitation, I hand her my phone. "What are you going to wager?" I want to know. "As much as I love the idea of lording it over you when you see that my place is untidier than Miles's loft, I would like a sweetener."

Carrie watches me add the tip in cash to the check before she winks and smiles. "Oh, don't you worry, Mr. Sterns. I'll make it sweet for you."

Chapter 15: Carrie

It's like we were never separated at all. We have been able to mesh our lives back together again as if the bitterness I felt towards him never happened.

I no longer feel weak and jilted for the way Stern rejected the thought of staying in contact with me because I am starting to get a better idea of how much my brother is part of his life.

In the cab, he takes my hand, sliding his fingers between mine. I can feel the strength in those hands and wonder why such a nice guy would choose such a bloodthirsty vocation in life. Jokes aside, can I see Simon Stern as a ruthless, weaponized bodyguard for hire?

He sees me eyeing him sideways. "What?" he wants to know.

"Nothing." I don't engage because the cab driver might be listening. "It's just that after what you told me, besides the merciless style of your haircut, I can't see you as someone dangerous, Stern. I just can't."

Grinning, he runs one hand over his hair. "You don't like it? You want me to grow it out? Do I look like a jarhead?"

Pinching my fingers together to show a tiny gap, I smile. "Just a bit."

We laugh all the way back to his apartment building, where Stern sticks a hand in his pocket and pays the driver cash. The doorman ushers us inside and pushes the penthouse elevator for us.

"Why do you pay cash for some things?" I ask Stern as the elevator hisses upwards at a fast speed.

"I always keep cash on hand. It's easier for me to show my gratitude for service. That way, I know my guy can just skim his tip off the top without his employer or the taxman taking a cut."

It's at moments like this when I think that Stern has way more substance in his character than I give him credit for. He's not some brute with a billion-dollar business; he's a thoughtful, caring guy.

The penthouse is dark and feels empty when we step inside. Taking his phone out of my purse, I show him that I am putting it on the side table as we enter the living room.

A soft glow is coming from the tall lamp next to the sliding doors leading out to the patio balcony. I wonder if he accidentally left it on when he headed out for work this morning. Suddenly, my busy day seems to catch up with me.

His apartment is astonishingly modern. Every room has ceiling-to-floor windows overlooking the cityscape. Lights twinkle in the buildings opposite us like bright yellow stars. The kitchen and living room areas flow together, joined by a gas hob island with pendulum lampshades and a utensil rack hanging from the tall ceiling.

I'm tired as I look around the silk-covered walls and vaulted roofs. And the entire apartment is immaculate, just like I said it would be. "You cheat," I tell him as he follows me into the bedroom. "You lied."

"Hey, you can't blame me." Stern seems to be really happy that I am here. He takes a coin out of his pants pocket and bounces it on the bed. But then he ruins the joke by saying something that totally turns me on. "Nice and tight. Just the way I like it."

My tiredness is gone in an instant. I can feel myself getting wet at the thought of his lovely cock sliding into me. Reaching out his hand for me, Stern wants to show me the place before we do what we are so desperate to do in the bedroom.

"Come outside to the balcony. It's the best place to be on a hot summer's night." He is right about that. The balcony is really high-tech tech too, with automated sliding doors that close off the space in winter so that the heated tether pool can still be used.

"That pool has my name on it." I start to strip off my clothes, giving Stern an alluring look over my bare shoulder. He doesn't need any more encouragement than that.

"Your brother's clothes are two sizes too small for me everywhere except the waist," Stern chuckles as he struggles to unbutton the jeans. "I must have really wanted to wine and dine you to squeeze myself into his stuff."

That martini I had at Morton's has given me a real buzz, but it's being with this man that makes me feel light and dizzy at the same time. In the pool, we kiss. Wrapping my legs around him, we float around the pool together, making out like a couple of teenagers—which I actually was when we first met, now that I come to think about it.

The pool has revived me and I am no longer sleepy. Paddling over to the shallow steps, Stern keeps me on his lap and inserts his hard cock into me. It is the most sublime sensation to be floating together, joined in such an intimate way.

I can't help myself. I start tilting my hips and rubbing against him. "I was wet before the water, just so you know," I tell him this in between our kisses.

"I would have been rock hard for you all evening, Carrie, if those tight pants had allowed it."

"You would have scared everyone away from the restaurant, Stern."

This is us, making love and laughing together about how strange our lives have turned out, and in such a short space of time as well.

Floating to the edge, Stern leans back and lets me ride him. I use his cock like a big dildo, rising up and down so I can feel all his length and then grinding myself down on him so that my clit can rub on the base. Of course, I come in big, shuddering gasps, falling back so that my head hits the water with a splash.

Stern leads me to the bedroom, holding my hand, smiling at me, and completely comfortable with the magnificent way he looks. Pushing me down onto his perfectly made bed, he mounts me like a ravenous mercenary looking for the weak spot in my defenses.

My arousal is so fierce that I come again with no problems, even though my clit is still exquisitely sensitive after my first orgasm. When I slowly open my eyes and see his face, I wish, I wish with all my heart that my lies had not pushed this wonderful man away at the start.

We are both really tired afterward. Stern spoons me as I curl into a sleepy ball and begin to doze off.

"You can move in with me here if you want," Stern murmurs gruffly. "At least I have ceilings in the bedrooms."

For one magic moment, I imagine living with Simon Sterns, a security genius billionaire. How safe it would make me feel to have him close by. But reality strikes and I shut it down.

"Not possible. Miles would tell my parents I moved out and they have a right to know where I decided to live."

His voice growls. "We will talk about this in the morning."

And the way he says it tells me that Stern is not the kind of man who gets to hear the word no very often.

***

Leaving Stern to sleep, I head out for the pool at daybreak. The faint trace of martini is still sloshing around in my system, but a few minutes swimming in the pool with the tether harness around my waist gets my blood pumping. There is nothing quite like swimming naked in the early hours of the morning.

When I lift my face out of the water, I see Stern watching me. He looks stunning in a pair of swimming trunks that somehow manage to make his butt and thighs look even better when he turns to put his glass of juice down on the patio table.

I can see where my fingernails raked down his back when I came last night, and get a tiny bit embarrassed. I remember screaming quite loudly, enjoying the privacy of being alone with

Stern in his own apartment with no one listening in to my shrieks of pleasure.

"Could you get used to visiting here over the weekend at least?" He doesn't even say good morning to me, and I know he spent his first few waking moments thinking how to get me back.

"Good morning to you too, Stern," I say, slicking my hair back. I unclip the harness and wade over to where he is standing on the edge of the pool. The clothes we were wearing last night are still scattered over the floor. "And the answer to your question is still no. Miles takes brothering seriously. After what happened last time, do you honestly think my parents would just allow me to waltz back here unchaperoned?"

Stern is no longer paying attention to what I am saying. His eyes are wide as he turns his head to hear something inside. His phone is still where I left it in the entrance hall. Pivoting around with astonishing quickness, he strides inside and slides the doors closed after him. But the doors don't snap shut, so I can hear who is coming in.

"Morning, Stern," my brother grunts and I hear him throw a set of keys down on the side table where I put Stern's phone last night. "I tried calling you, but your phone's on silent. The deal is done. The Delgardos accepted the quote and the arrangement. They sent me back here because they want you to sign off on it ASAP. The daughter's ex is still hanging around online, so I will have to get our cyber guys onto that next."

Silence, then. "What's up? Why are you so quiet? You look like you've seen a ghost, Bru."

Stern gives a big, fake laugh. Jesus. I can tell that he has had no experience with deceiving people! Moving as slowly as I can, I duck down behind the edge of the pool closest to the living room.

Stern gives another strained bark of laughter. His performance is so bad that I think he could win one of those Golden Raspberry awards.

"Ha! A ghost! No way that's possible. Bru."

Miles's voice is tired but curious. "No, there's definitely something off about you. I know what it is. You're happy. How did that happen?"

Another nervous fake laugh from Stern. If the situation wasn't so dire, I swear I would jump out of this pool and strangle him.

He comes straight out and says it. "I have a girl staying over."

Miles lowers his voice to a theatrical whisper. "In the bedroom? Jeez, I'm sorry, Bru. It's been so long, man. I mean, like, never before. You always stay at theirs so you can make a clean getaway straight after the fucking is over."

Stern interrupts. "Shut up. Don't get all forensic over my previous encounters.... They meant nothing to me."

To my horror, I hear the sliding doors hiss open and my brother's voice enters the patio. "She won't hear us out here, Stern. I want you to know, I'm happy for you. Just make sure she's not like Belinda if you are thinking about getting serious."

Stern must have turned around because my brother whistles. "Whoa! She left quite a mark on your back with her nails! She must be a real tiger!"

The two men laugh, and I can tell that Stern is leading Miles over to the furthest corner of the patio away from where I am half-submerged under the water.

"Hey, never mind about me, Milo." Stern is starting to sound more relaxed, thank goodness. "I wanted to ask you, how is it going in the loft with your sister?"

Miles sounds bored like he wants to get back to talking about Stern's booty call in the bedroom. "Carrie? She's a good girl. An angel, really. She's going to help me get the loft into shape. My family knows I need someone to look after me. It's not easy being single again. I'm lousy at housework."

Stern's voice gets lower. "Aren't you worried about Carrie living in the Big Bad Apple? I mean, it's New York.... The bird's gotta fly the coop and have some fun sometime, am I right?"

A thumping sound comes from the wall. I hear my brother groan as pain floods through his hand. He must have punched the wall hard.

"That's what I will do to any son of a bitch who tries to get fresh with my little sister! I will kill any motherfucker who lays a hand on her!"

I feel the shock coming from Stern. "Sure, brother. And I'll help you do it."

"Thanks," Miles says in a shaky voice. "It's just that my parents made me swear on my life that I would protect Carrie when she was here. I think something bad happened to her last time, but I'm not sure."

Stern tries to calm him down. "Isn't your reaction a little extreme? How old is Carrie now?"

"I don't care! She's my little sister and any man who tries to take advantage of her is going to die."

I hear Stern patting Miles's back. "Come on. Let's go inside and have a cup of c—"

I am about to breathe a sigh of relief when I hear the worst thing ever.

"Stern, what are my clothes doing next to your pool?"

Chapter 16: Stern

During my eight years of service in the armed forces, I was exposed to my fair share of sticky situations, but I have to say that this particular one tops them all. It's dangerous. Not in a life or death type way, but dangerous to anyone who values consistent and regular normalcy the way I do.

My brain spirals as the synapses snap into situation-resolution mode. In the real world, the clock records the passing of one or two seconds. But in my mind, time has slowed down.

There is no doubt those are Miles's clothes, and it will only look guilty if I deny that. A man knows his own clothes because of the recognizable wear and tear. Besides the fact that my shoulders and neck are huge compared to my friend's and I have no business wearing them for that reason alone.

Why do I have Miles's shirt and jeans in my apartment? Computations flash in my mind as I search for an explanation. I need a good explanation for my friend's clothing being here, and then I need Miles to leave.

A memory is retrieved and brought to mind as a possible solution. I think hard, back to the message I got from my credit card provider. Do I want to activate the purchase 'accept or reject' feature? Why? Because the card had been used to pay for feminine items at Bloomingdale's and... and for a housekeeping service.

"Good question, Miles. It's a long story, but you're going to laugh at the end of it." Propelling Miles back into the living room, I give a rueful laugh.

"I use a house cleaning service. I asked them if they would pop by your loft and clean there too. As a way of saying thank you to you for sealing the Delgardo deal. The housekeeping service must have accidentally mixed up our laundry. Last night, I just grabbed the first two items of clothing out of my closet and took them with me to the patio.

"My girlfriend and I went out for a swim last night—you know how things are in the dark—and after getting out of the pool I had the clothes on before I noticed something was off. So, I just dropped your clothes right there for the cleaning service to pick up next time they come."

I try to read Miles's expression to see if he swallowed my story. He must have because he changes the subject. "Girlfriend? You have a girlfriend now? When did that happen? I thought she was just a one-night stand."

Balling my fists to stop the tremors of relief from showing in my hands, I shake my head. "Oh no, mate. First of all, you got to thank me for that house cleaning service I got you."

Miles grins, slapping my left bicep by way of a thank you. "Yeah, I let things slide a bit."

Lowering my voice to a loud whisper, I jerk my chin towards the bedroom door. "I will speak to you later about... you know, the girlfriend situation. In the meantime, can you flick the Delgardo paperwork over to me? I'll run through the estimate while you go catch up on your sleep."

I want to slap my face with frustration as I say the words. My sweaty gym clothes are at the loft! The situation is getting so complicated, this time it's me who wants to punch the wall. "Wait! I think it's best if you go straight to HQ. Use the private suite onsite if you need to sleep and I'll catch up with you there later."

Miles yawns and nods. "Yah... sure. All right. See you later. My body clock is out of whack. And good luck with...," he says, pointing to the bedroom door and winking, Miles finally leaves.

That is when I start to shake all over. The adrenaline surging through my body has put me into enormous "flight or fight" mode. I never want to feel like that again when chatting with my buddy, like he's the enemy and I have to defend my actions against him.

The sliding doors open. Shivering, with her arms wrapped around her, Carrie runs through to the bathroom to grab a towel. We are both too shocked to speak for what seems like a long time.

I am galvanized into action. This should not be happening to us; we have nothing to hide. Or maybe it's just me who has nothing to hide?

"Carrie! What did Miles mean when he said something bad happened to you last time you were in New York? Was he talking about me? About us? What the fuck?!"

She is still shivering, possibly even in shock, but I am too pissed to think of anyone but myself. As far as I can tell, it is only me who stands to lose everything if Miles cottons on to our liaison.

"Did you tell your parents I took advantage of you? Well, you obviously didn't tell them who it was, but did you say you weren't a willing participant in what happened? Did you lie?'

Slamming the palm of my hand against the bathroom door, I bellow at full volume. "When are the fucking lies going to stop!? When are you going to tell your family that you wanted me from the first time we laid eyes on each other? As much as I wanted you!"

Carrie is shaking, but this time it is from suppressed rage and not the cold. Shoving me back as she passes by to get to the bedroom, she starts to get dressed. Her long red hair is dark, with water still dripping off the ends. "I was a teenager when it happened, Stern!" Her voice is low but controlled. She doesn't look at me as she steps back into her clothes. "My family was all I had to help me when you weren't there!"

I see red. "You can be a bitch sometimes, Carrie, you know that? If you had just told me the truth from the start, do you think I would have ditched my best friend's wedding to go fuck his little sister?"

She shouts right back. "Don't deflect, you fuck! It didn't matter who I was! It was you who shirked your responsibilities!"

My responsibilities as the best man at the wedding I doubted should have even happened are being thrown in my face now! I have heard of some people blaming men for not checking a female's driver's license before having sex with her to make sure she's of legal age, but for Carrie to hint that I should have done that is ridiculous.

"I'm leaving," I stomp into the walk-in closet to change into a new pair of sweats, "don't forget to get rid of my clothes at the loft before Miles fucking finds them. I am so tired of playing these lying games, Carrie, you have no idea."

I know it is the adrenaline talking, but I can't hold back. The more pressure I put on Carrie, the more she will realize how stupid it is for us to continue going behind her family's back. I'm her boss, sure, but there must be plenty of bosses who date their employees out there.

Belinda wrote the "no sex, dating, or affairs in the workplace" contract clause after she married Miles. I suppose she didn't want to risk her husband doing the same thing all over again with someone else. Damn it.

I am going to have to do something about that if I want to go public with my new relationship. Belinda rules over the HR department like a mini despot. And I know she will sense something is going on if I ask her to change it now.

Pulling the light cotton sweater over my head, I keep talking, even though my voice is momentarily muffled. I pull out the sock drawer and then crouch down to pull them on.

"And another thing—it's killing me that I can't be honest with your brother, Carrie. Frankly, all this cloak-and-dagger bullshit we are doing just makes me happy that I have no family of my own to get in my way. You are eventually going to have to pick a side, sweetheart. Mine or—"

I hear a door close. Grabbing my sneakers, I run out into the bedroom. Carrie is not there, so I run out into the living room. And then the entrance hall.

Looking up above the elevator, I see the light on the numbers is going down.

Carrie has left me once again.

***

I am done running after my best friend's sister. Carrie is in New York City and not likely to fly the coop. If she did, it would be way more suspicious than if she came straight out and told

Miles about us. She doesn't answer any of my messages or pick up my calls.

But this time, I'm not worried because I have her in my sights. This is new territory for me. I have never had to pursue a woman before, nor had one constantly running away from me as if I were some grumpy ogre.

My dating life is, and always has been, nonexistent as far as "going steady" with someone goes. I would attend some gallery opening and pick up an interested woman there, or be called upon to quote on some famous woman's home security, and we would fuck a few times. End of story.

It happened often enough for me to not worry about a dry spell. I had a built-in, steady supply of women ready to bed me at the drop of a hat. I used my information resources to check that none of them were married or in the middle of a messy divorce if they wanted to repeat the event, but mostly one-night stands were all I ever agreed to.

And I always stayed away from anything that had the potential to get messy too. My job has always been the reason I get up in the mornings. Before that, it was the Corps. I don't think that is ever going to change.

One of the reasons I keep women like Samantha Carson at arm's length is because I know how selfish and demanding she can be. We went out for one date about four years ago and that was enough for me to be able to read her motives like a book. Besides, the only person who gets to be selfish and demanding in my life is me.

Fumbling with my phone, I try calling Carrie. Answering service. "Carrie, please pick up. I'm sorry I was a grouch."

I have never had to chase after a woman like this before. Not only is Carrie the youngest woman I have ever fucked, but she is also the most elusive.

I am not so fond of getting my rocks off that I don't look at fucking someone from all sides of the equation before actually doing it. That's one of the reasons why I got rich: I always double- and triple-check before doing something—until

I met Carrie Maitland that is. Or rather, Caron Leslie.

And yes, I can tell when a woman is interested in dating my wallet. That's why all of my sexual liaisons have been with wealthy, powerful women. They know how to play the game and do it well.

Carrie is not one of those women. She's different. I have feelings for her that I never had for those other women. One night was never going to be enough for Carrie and me.

Trying to stop myself from wondering what it was that made her run away from me again, I call her phone one more time. It goes to her answering service.

"Carrie. If you have blocked my number, you should re-read your contract. It specifically forbids you from doing that! I want to see the work you have done on the mural mockups so far. Call me!"

The moment I hang up, I regret my message. So, I call back. "Er... Carrie? Sorry about the other message. Please ignore it. Please call me. Let's sort this out like adults."

***

I'm going crazy. It's been five days since she walked out on me. She's put up a firewall between us, communicating to me about the mural project through Gail and Mannie, which technically she's allowed to do.

She even checks before she goes to Apollo on First to see if I am there. I guess she doesn't want to be stuck in the office with me alone again. Not that I could keep her there if she wanted to leave.

Every employee gets their fingerprints uploaded onto the database when they start work at Sterns & Co., so any employee can leave my office when they want to. Every time the door opens, it gets time and date stamped on the mainframe.

Kicking the leather waste basket across the floor, I try Gail's number again. She picks up and, bless her, she sounds understanding.

"Yes, sir?" That's our code. Gail always calls me "sir" when Carrie is in the room with her. "Hey,

Gail. What are her plans for this weekend? Any chance of Carrie forgiving me yet?"

"Hold on, sir. That information is on my laptop. I'll just go and access it for you."

Walking noises are followed by the sound of a door closing. "Boss, it's only been five days. Please give Carrie time. I'm still trying to find out what you said or did to make her so upset. Do you know?"

I play back the fight Carrie and I had after Miles's terrifying unexpected visit. "Look, I can't ask Miles for his pass card back—he'll get suspicious. Is that what she is angry about?"

Gail's leather desk chair squeaks as she settles into it. "Hey, that's on Miles and you and your arrangement to treat one another like frat bros precedes this. But might I suggest that you think a little bit into the future? You can't have Miles moseying into your apartment whenever he feels like it forever."

I need to explain it. "Before this, I lived in the barracks. Privacy is not a big deal in the Corps."

"You're not in the Corps anymore, Boss. And you might want to have a bit of a think about what you said to Carrie that made her sun go behind the clouds."

Chapter 17: Carrie

Gail makes sure that I never have to lay eyes on Stern again.

"Not unless you want to, sweetie?" Gail asks me, "Do you want to see Mr. Sterns again?"

It's not like me to be constantly warring with someone. I can't even stay mad at my mom when her strict rules make my life miserable.

In retrospect, my teenage years seem more like a prison sentence than the last days of my childhood compared to how free kids are in the States. But most South African middle-class children are overprotected by their parents, because of a combination of fear about the crime rate and their strict Puritan principles.

Even then, I was able to find something to smile about. But I am really struggling to see the upside of being with Stern now.

"I would prefer not to see Stern right now, Gail. We... I left him under strained circumstances."

Of course, I had told my friend about spending the night with Stern. It was such a relief to have someone I could finally confide in. A girl needs to share her secrets. It's the most chicken soup for the soul thing a person can do!

But I haven't told Gail about the horrible things Stern said to me that made me leave. I have enough respect for him still to not want to lower other people's opinions about him.

I try to explain. "The first time we were together, Gail, he made me feel like one of those desert flowers that open up when it rains. And he shared so much of himself with me, so I know all about his hard life."

Gail snorts. "Hard life, my ass! He's a billionaire."

I giggle at the face she pulls and the way she pretends to make the money rain with her hands.

SECRET BABY FOR MY BOSSY BILLIONAIRE   211

"I'm talking about his childhood, Gail. He was an orphan, you know. He joined the Navy as a way of finding somewhere he belonged. His mother didn't want him so he was put into care at a young age."

Her face gets somber as Gail gets sad. "Oh my God. I never knew. I always thought Mr. Sterns was born tough and rich right off the bat."

Shaking my head, I explain, "No one wanted to foster him or adopt him, so he stayed stuck in the system. Stern laughs about it now, saying that it must have been because he looked like trouble, but I think that's his way of coping with the constant rejection. Anyway, he was raised to such a hardscrabble life that I suppose becoming a Navy SEAL looked like a holiday in comparison."

Nodding, Gail agrees with my assessment. "Do you make an allowance for that when he treats you shabbily?"

"No way! I'm not a doormat!" It makes me smile when I remember all the times the hyper-rugged Simon Sterns treated me like a precious porcelain doll. "But he seems to have developed some kind of rejection for family life—or at least he does not understand its dynamic. The only loyalty he feels is towards his brothers in arms."

Gail takes in all this information while swinging side to side in one of the desk chairs.

We are in my little cubicle space in the architectural development space at Sterns & Co. HQ. It's where all the panic rooms and security monitor rooms are designed to fit into the original architectural structure's blueprints.

It's highly top secret. Sometimes, villains can obtain blueprints online or from a municipal planning office, and then they use them to see how they can breach security. With Sterns & Co., no one knows about the built-in security measures except the people in this room and the clients.

Gail told me this really funny story about how one client forgot to tell the realtor selling their house about the panic rooms and concealed monitoring. They came back from vacation to find the realtor and the buyer still trapped in their house.

I wish I could ask Stern if the story is true. I miss him, but frankly, he has missed the mark if he thinks he can talk about my precious family like that and get away with it! He doesn't even know how often I talk to them online and how many hours over the weekend I sit watching videos of them. I miss them so much, but I am determined to make it in New York so I can create the perfect home for myself before they visit.

"Where are we going out for cocktails tonight?" It's no fun going back home to the loft every evening. Sure, I'm downhearted, but I'm only twenty-three years old, for God's sake, and Manhattan is packed with bars and clubs.

We are both dressed in cute, summer dresses and strappy-heel shoes. It's easy enough for us to go straight from work to one of the dozens of cocktail bars lining the streets.

Tapping the edge of the black credit card on her front teeth, Gail looks thoughtful. "Okay. A couple of cocktails never hurt anyone. Maybe we can pick up a couple of guys and go for supper somewhere after?"

I test the suggestion in my mind, but my heart nixes the idea. "Um... maybe next time."

Gail probes deeper. "Too soon? Come on, Carrie. If you want to get over the boss, you have to meet other guys. What do they say? If you fall off, it's best to get straight back onto the horse again."

I smile. "Yes, I think that is what they say, but I haven't fallen off the horse, Gail. I just slipped out of the saddle."

My friend grins. "Girl, if Stern is so big you need a saddle to ride him, I think having a little disagreement is the least of your problems!"

"Ooh, Gail! You have no idea!"

We fall about laughing with tears leaking out of our eyes. And then we go to fix our makeup in the bathroom before heading out.

Like we always do, Gail and I accept the drinks that get sent over to us from a couple of guys at the bar. For a young woman who was never allowed to go out at home—or when staying with Miles too, for that matter—meeting some nice men and chatting is thrilling.

I'm not looking for someone else, but I want to see if I would ever feel about another man when I see him for the first time, the way I did with Simon Sterns. What always happens after one drink, we pair off into couples.

I end up with the younger man called Darryl because Gail is thirty, and in her own words she "doesn't have time for some young fool playing her.'"

The guy I end up talking to works at one of the news networks. He is interested in my accent. "You're Dutch, right? One of those countries that speak English as a second language. Am I close?"

"Not even in the same ballpark. I'm South African. A country that has no less than eleven official languages, all of them spoken with atrocious accents! But my parents are American. They moved there when they were young. Bought a small hotel on the coast. It was nice."

"Was?" I have to give the young man ten out of ten for picking up on that. Or else he must have heard something at the news network where he works.

"South Africa has never been perfect. But the thing that ruined my life the most when I was growing up was the crime. There's lots of crime and zero punishment. So my mom never lets me go anywhere by myself."

"Hey," my new friend from the news network says, leaning forward to pat my knee, "we have loads of crime here in New York too. You got to be careful everywhere nowadays."

"Let's drink to that!" I offer to buy him a drink. I like it when he chooses a Mexican beer with a slice of lime in the neck. We have a good laugh over the half-eaten lime slice looking like a bad hairdo after he sucks on it. Our conversation jumps from our countries' sports to our favorite restaurants to how much we both want to go to London.

Gail is also having a good time. Eventually, all four of us turn our chairs to talk altogether. "Have you told Darryl what you do for a living, Carrie?" she's got a twinkle in her eye when she asks me. It's so sweet because I can tell that Gail is very proud of my talent.

I blush. "I don't like to brag...."

That makes the two men beg me to tell them. Relenting, I do. "I got the commission to create the mural at Apollo on First. I think I've been on a permanent party since I found out!"

Darryl bombards me with questions. "That's Simon Sterns's new architectural project, isn't it? I think he bought one of KidSuper's first artworks. Have you been to his office? What is hanging behind his desk?"

"Hey!" Gail laughs. "Don't fanboy over the man. He's flesh and blood, just like the rest of us."

"And bone too, from what I hear in all the art circles!" Darryl's friends sniggers, and elbows me in the ribs. I think he must be on his fourth cocktail. "I heard they found him in the toilets at the Met during the Picasso exhibition, getting head from the sponsor's ex-wife!"

I can't help it. I feel myself getting red in the face. My skin is tingling with a heated combination of humiliation and jealousy. That's the horrid thing about sex with someone you adore. It makes you think you don't care when, in fact, you do.

"That's a rumor, nothing else!" Gail snaps at the man. "Well, it's time for us to call it a night, guys.

It was a pleasure meeting you. Come and see Carrie's mural when it's finished."

They beg us to stay. "C'mon, ladies. The night is young. Let's go for dinner somewhere."

But Gail is resolute. "We do yoga early on Saturday mornings. Sorry."

Darryl grabs my arm lightly before I can pick up my Montblanc crossbody bag. "Carrie? Please can I have your number? Are you free during the week?"

I shake my head. I wish I had never come out for Friday night cocktails. If nothing else, this has made me realize how far I have let myself grow complex feelings for the man I must now call boss.

"Sorry, Darryl. This was a one-off. But come see the mural anytime. I'm still in the design phase, but I hope to start implementing the design soon. It was lovely meeting you. Goodbye."

A few seconds later, we are out on the sidewalk, teetering to the corner to hail a cab. "You realize that Stern is going to be there when you present the layout to Mannie?"

Not even a few strong cocktails are enough to stop Gail from worrying about me. Taking her hand and threading it through my arm, I reply. "I guess I can't put it off forever. If he hadn't told me about his sad childhood from the get-go, I don't think I would ever be able to forgive Stern for what he said to me at the apartment."

"What did he say exactly?" We turn to face the oncoming traffic, looking out for a cab with its light on.

I think of the best way to recount the details without making Gail hate Stern as much as I used to. "He said he's glad he doesn't have a family because they just complicate things."

Gail whistles with disapproval. "The man reeks of being a manipulator and a user, Carrie. I know men like him—they litter the penthouses and offices of Manhattan like so much crap! Too self-absorbed and career-obsessed to think of marriage until they are in their fifties. Are you sure you want to give Stern the benefit of the doubt?"

"I don't think that's Stern's end goal. After all, he wants us to go public with our relationship. But

I can't have that happen because my parents would go ballistic! Literally ballistic!"

My friend looks at me with one eyebrow raised. "Your folks don't want you dating a billionaire?"

Laughing and shaking my head, I shut down the conversation. "It's complicated. Here comes a cab with its light on! Shall we stop by Saks for a little shopping?"

Gail accepts my change of topic. "Let's see how the traffic is. We might not be able to get there before seven. I guess we wasted a bit of time flirting with those poor guys at the bar!"

Chapter 18: Stern

When I look at my phone screen, it's Gail calling. "Yes?" No time for polite hellos and how are yous?

She sounds hesitant. "Boss, sorry for calling so late, but you asked me to keep you updated.... You know that Carrie has filled me in on some of your relationship details? Are you okay with that?"

I have no experience with what women talk about when they are alone together. I suppose sports and the financial markets are not high on the priority chat list—I'm not completely clueless—but other than that, I have no idea.

I'm thirty-five years old and I have never overheard women talking in private.

"Tell me what she said and then I'll know how to reply, Gail. I can't promise anything until I know how much detail she went into."

"Oh golly gosh! Not that kind of shit! If Carrie tries to tell me what you are like in bed, Mr. S, I just shut that right down! That's not an image I want sticking in my mind, thank you very much!"

We laugh for a long while. I haven't laughed in ages, so long I have forgotten what it feels like. "I'm relieved to hear you say that, Gail. So, go ahead, shoot."

"Carrie told me about... about your childhood, Mr. S. I know it's not common knowledge, about you being an orphan and then joining the armed forces when you were a teenager. It's not like you have a Wiki page or anything like that, but I thought you should know... that I know."

"Know what?"

Gail sighs. "Do I have to spell it out for you? Very well. You can be a bit of a grump sometimes. A jerk. You're kind of intimidating. Not your muscles and height, although it is that too. You're in a really bad mood sometimes. And it makes folks scared of your temper."

I am shocked. "Is that what Carrie told you about me? That I have a temper?" I am devastated that Carrie feels afraid of me. I would not touch a hair on her head.

"No! Not Carrie. She's remarkably understanding and tolerant of you, Mr. S! She says you were probably such a cute little boy who had to form a hard outer layer to stop yourself from being hurt by all the rejection—shit like that. I... I think she really gets you, Boss. And I can see why you want to be with her. I'm just saying."

"Gail, can I call you back just now, please." Disconnecting the line, I walk out onto the apartment patio and breathe deeply. The surge of emotion boiling inside me has me shaken to the core.

I have never analyzed why I feel it is so easy to share all of my life with Carrie. It just happened from the start. Sure, I loved the way she looked in that white lacy lingerie of hers, but once we got to know each other on a more personal level I wanted her to know everything about me.

Walking to the edge of the balcony, I look down at the view below. For so long I used to do that, ignore the skyline and stare down at the street instead. This time, I look at the famous Manhattan skyline all around me. And for the first time, I feel the weight of my loneliness crushing in.

Turning my back on the view, I go back inside and press Gail's number. "Hey, sorry about that. My takeout delivery was at the door. Thanks for sharing that with me, Gail. Any more news?"

"Carrie has been talking about using some of her advance money to buy a house in Simon's Town in South Africa, Mr. S. I think she wants to go back there after the mural is finished."

Now that is the kind of news I don't like hearing. But this time, I am self-aware enough not to let my bad mood show. "Hmm, really? Anything else?"

Gail chats a bit about how Mannie loves the mural concept and would like to put a meeting on the books. "But Carrie wants the meeting to go down with both me and Mannie in the room with you at the same time. That's good news, though. It means Carrie can't trust herself to be in the same room as you, Mr. S, in case she succumbs to the burning passion she bears for you in her heart and allows you to sweep her off to the boudoir."

I can tell she is being sarcastic. "Oh ha ha, Gail. Very funny. Give me a buzz if you come up with any more brilliant ideas for Carrie to forgive me—and go mad with the card if you need anything."

When Gail disconnects, the wave of loneliness comes back. Moving to the study where my laptop is set up, I click on a page I have been visiting more and more lately: Upstate and out-of-state real estate for sale.

***

Another week goes by and I'm getting desperate, enough to text Gail for the third time that day. What about if the two of you go out for dinner? And I'll pretend to be at the same restaurant as a coincidence?

Gail's reply comes back. I don't know, Boss. That sounds a little bit stalker-y to me.

I no longer care if I am coming across like the grumpy boss. Just ask her! I'll book a table under your name and send you the reservation deets. And thank you. S.

Suddenly, a bright idea hits me. Slamming my office door behind me, I stalk around the mezzanine balcony, heading for the elevators. Two minutes later, I am in Miles's office. "Hey, buddy. I heard your divorce is being finalized soon. Want to go out and have something to eat?"

Miles looks up from his desktop as I walk in, a sorrowful expression on his face. "You heard? Yah, it's true. I can't believe she went through with it. But I suppose I should be grateful that the lawyer managed to get a good settlement for me."

Leaning against the door, I fold my arms across my chest. "How come?"

Miles is happy to share. "One of the investigators found out that Belinda has been funneling her bonus checks into an offshore account instead of declaring them as joint assets. So she caved in and stopped her demands the moment my lawyer confronted her about it."

I whistled softly. "Jesus! What a bitch. She wanted to take you to the cleaners and get off scot-free."

Miles tries to joke. "Well, she failed! I feel a lot better knowing that. Serves her right for refusing to give me a blowjob for the last five years!"

Ah. Men jokes. I love them so much. We laugh and high-five. "So? What about it? Want to go out to one of the places around here this evening?"

Miles nods. "Sure. Carrie has been cooking for me at home every night, so she'll be pleased to get the night off."

"Yep, you bet." Throwing him a thumbs-up, I back out of the office. Mission accomplished. When I am out of earshot of Miles, I call my fixer. She's the woman who can get me tables at all the restaurants and tickets to all the shows whenever I want them.

"Hey, Monique. How are you?"

Her voice sounds stressed as it crackles over the line. "I know that tone of voice, Stern. You always use it if you need a big favor."

Laughing, I explain my predicament. "I know this is a tall order, Monique, so please try all the places. I need a table for four, but booked for only two. Got that? And it must be one of the best tables. And then I need a table for two somewhere far away from my table, so it looks coincidental that we are at the same place. The table for two must be booked under the name Gail Patterson."

I hear Monique writing all of this down, her pencil scratching on the paper. "Jeez, Stern! Anything else? Like the fillings out of my back teeth?"

Typical Monique. She makes it sound so hard, but I have earned a lot of goodwill in this city because of my charitable donations and sponsorships. "Oh yeah. I need it to be in one of the most romantic restaurants. Tables a good distance away from one another, comprehensive wine list, the whole shebang. And please let the restaurant know that they can double book the table for two because I am going to ask them to join me at my table. Okay?"

"You old charmer, you," Monique teases me. "Sure thing. I will sort this out for you and then text you the time and place."

My assistant puts all our new clients on a list so I know who to call after their security systems have been installed. I wait for Monique to get back to me by going down the list.

Most of them are way too important to deal with customer service face-to-face, but they always take my calls because, in their eyes, I'm one of them. "Good to hear your voice, Stern." One of my new clients in the political arena gets straight to the point when he picks up my call. "I need to up the security in my fleet too, not just the office and home."

We chat for a while about personal and work vehicles, and how to integrate a system into both fleets. "Do you need us to train your current staff on how to handle a possible emergency, or would you like us to re-staff your domestic transport sector entirely?"

The politician gives a bark of laughter. "That's the problem, Stern. Poor Burt has been with me from the start. I don't know how to break it to him that he should retire. But if I'm to be honest, if a terrorist or kidnapper jumped out in front of our vehicle, I think Burt would have a heart attack."

We make an appointment for me to visit the house in person. That's part of my job; giving staff the chop when they can't cut it anymore. But then again, re-staffing a politico's driving fleet with trained security personnel will add another eight million or so onto an already thirty-million-dollar security detail.

And that's just one client. Sterns & Co. has hundreds of wealthy and powerful people on its books. Keeping safe is a global industry now.

The cell phone rings on the desk. I say goodbye and hang up the landline before answering. It's Monique.

"Hold your horses, Stern, because I got you a good one! Are you sitting down? Great. How does dinner for two at a table for four, and another table for two that will be nixed when they join your table at Per Se sound?"

"You're right, Monique. It sounds great. And thank you for coming through for me like this. How did you manage to pull it off?"

"Oh, a little Monique magic. Per Se had a cancellation. They were just about to put it on the concierge chat, but I got it first."

There is a very secret chat site where all the fine dining and booked-out theater seat cancellations get posted. Only concierges at the five-star hotels know about the chat site. They go on the site whenever a resident or visitor tips them big and asks them to get them a table or a seat for something that is usually impossible to get into.

But Monique isn't finished yet.

"There are conditions attached, though, Stern. You have to get there early, at seven. And tell the table for two, Gail Patterson, to get there even earlier if you are planning on making a move for them to join you. Is that okay?"

I promise Monique that I will abide by those conditions. The second the call is disconnected, I get busy texting Gail. It makes me smile because she has basically become my wingman since Miles is off-limits now.

Per Se. Table for two under the name of Gail Patterson. Columbus Circle. 18:45. Sharp. See you there.

I wait for Gail's reply, trying hard not to hold my breath. She sends me the thumbs-up sign and I can breathe again. This is my chance to show Miles how good Carrie and I are together. Maybe then he will come to like the idea of his best friend and his little sister being together.

And then again, maybe he won't.

Chapter 19: Carrie

Gail catches up with me as I am busy leaving the Apollo on First. My work is really painstaking now. The lobby is a huge space, but fortunately, I only have to do one side. I'm in the process of enlarging my mural concept so that it fits the wall. Doing that is no picnic!

"How did you know it was quitting time for me, Gail?" I am pleased to see her and lean in for a warm hug.

"Call it intuition." My friend gives me a naughty smile. "Oh, very well. I called the lobby guard on duty and asked him to give me a heads-up when you began to pack up. I have a surprise for us."

I raise my eyebrows. "I like surprises."

"Good, because you are going to love this one! I have a connection with restaurant bookings. They had someone cancel for Per Se this evening, so I said we'd take it."

Rubbing my eyes wearily, I am not so sure about this. "I don't know. I'm bushed. I've been up on ladders and scaffolding all day. And to be honest, I'm looking forward to having the loft to myself tonight. Miles is going out partying with Stern."

Gail looks at me in a kind of searching way. "And you're not worried about that? Stern going out with Miles, two men on the lookout for girls?"

Feeling my shoulders slump, I have a confession to make. "You know how it goes after a fight, Gail. You have a big falling out and you leave. You tell the man you don't want to see him for a long time or you ghost him for so long that you forget what it was you fought about in the first place?"

My friend grins. "Oh boy, do I ever! Is that what happened with you and Stern?"

I nod. "Yah. Although I can remember what our disagreement was about. Stern is starting with such a disadvantage to me that my heart keeps telling me to forgive him. And then my head goes crazy thinking about all the things I wish I had said, and all the things I want to say."

Gail pats my arm. "I get the picture. Are you sure Stern isn't pulling the 'poor little orphan boy' schtick with you so that he can play on your heartstrings?"

"No way! He only told me that the first time and never referred to it again. But so much time has passed now that I don't know what to say if he speaks to me."

"Pfft! Girl, please! You won't have to worry about that until the meeting with Mannie. In the meantime, what about an early dinner?"

"Just to be sure, we're going out to eat, right? I don't think I can handle another run-in with someone like Darryl. It makes me feel so guilty when I have to tell them I'm not interested."

"Don't feel guilty!" Gail insists. "They bought us a round of drinks and we got the next round. Fair is fair. We had a nice chat with those guys, and that is that. You don't owe a man anything except respect and friendliness so long as he shows you the same. Now, go home. I'll pick you up at a quarter past six."

I walk to the subway but decide against it. It's so hot and crowded at the end of the work day. There are no cabs. And the sidewalks are too stuffy and polluted to walk all the way to the Village.

For one moment, I want to chuck it all in and go back to Simon's Town. Then I get my second wind and make it to the bus stop. Saying a silent prayer for special bus lanes, I get back to the loft in a good mood and plan what I am going to wear to the restaurant when I get out of the shower.

Turns out, Per Se is quite a big deal. It's meant to be one of the most romantic old-school restaurants in Manhattan and has three stars. Time for me to bring out the big guns. I choose a daring black '70s-inspired wrap dress I got from Lord & Taylor. It's mid-length with bell sleeves, and a V-shape plunging neckline with a split up the middle of the skirt.

After putting the dress on, I bounce up and down a few times to check that it is decent. It passes the jiggle test, definitely more sexy-elegant than straight-up sexy.

Shit! My phone rings. It's Gail, and she's already waiting for me outside! I tell her I'll be down in a jiffy.

Quickly running to the bathroom, I pat moisturizer on my skin and spray some perfume in the air to walk through. I give a silent thanks to my mom for putting sunscreen on me every day of my life so that my skin is soft and dewy.

A quick slick of mascara and I'm done. Grabbing my stilettos in one hand, I run downstairs. Arriving at the cab panting and laughing, I wave the shoes at Gail in the backseat.

We head to Columbus Circle. This is one of my favorite routes, and I keep a lookout for the park and the trees. "Do you think my hair will be dry by the time we get there?" I ask Gail while pressing the windows to open so that the hot Manhattan air will help.

"You can work the damp hair look, Carrie," my friend reassures me. "But keep those windows open. Give me your comb so I can lift the back."

In the end, we decide to knot my hair on top. "Just make some soft curls and tendrils to hang down," Gail is like a scientist in a laboratory the way she's fixing my hair. "You can get away with it because it is a more formal style."

I see Gail paying the driver with her black credit card again, and something jogs my memory. "Please let's pay with cash next time, girl. Stern says that those people who provide us with good customer service prefer that."

Gail just stands on the sidewalk outside Per Se with her mouth open and her eyes showing happy shock. "Carrie! That's the first time you've ever said 'Stern says' to me! It's a sign!"

Laughing and blushing, I tell my friend not to be such a goof as we walk inside. The host notices us immediately and finds Gail's name as soon as she says it. We are ushered into the beautiful, low-lit space and shown to our table—

"Carrie!" my brother's voice calls to me, so I turn around. Miles is seated at a square table with the most handsome man in the room, city, country, and possibly the world, sitting opposite him: Simon Sterns.

"What are you doing here?" Miles addresses the question to me, but I can see his eyes are on Gail when he is talking.

It feels like a dream as Gail tells the host that the two men seated at the table are her bosses. And then Miles stands up to shake Gail's hand and introduces himself, leaving Stern and me to look at one another in solid silence.

The last time I saw Simon, he was yelling at me from inside his bedroom walk-in closet. I wish I could shrug my shoulders and say "Awkward much?" out loud, but I can't risk tipping off my brother to the existing tense situation.

"Would you like to join us?" Miles suggests. "I'm sure they can find two more place settings for you. This is such good luck. I was wondering when my sister was going to introduce me to her new friend."

Stern nods to the host and two more chairs are brought for us to sit on. The servers get busy setting down tableware and napkins as Miles and Gail chat like old friends. "I've seen images of you on the website, Miles," Gail says to my brother, "but your hair is so much redder in real life. It's hard not to see a family resemblance between Carrie and you."

Stern gives me a slight smile and I feel him rub his foot against me under the table before he speaks. "It's actually easier to find a member of the Maitland family without red hair than it is to find one with it. Statistically, that is really unusual. It got pretty confusing at Miles's wedding, I can tell you."

Biting my lower lip, I hope that is the end of Stern referencing the day we first met, but Miles is having none of it. Focusing on Gail, my brother explains. "Stern was a lousy best man. He didn't even give a reception speech. We are out on the town tonight because we have something to celebrate, Gail—I'm not married anymore!"

My friend is charming. "If you're happy about that, Miles, then so am I!" Gail flutters her lashes, managing to look cute and sophisticated at the same time.

They get busy ordering expensive champagne and asking one another about where they were born and where they went to school. I feel kind of panicked because the more Miles and Gail get on, the more it will look like Stern and I have a problem with each other.

Pushing back my chair, I tell Gail I'm going to the ladies' restroom. She just waves her hand and doesn't even look at me because the champagne is arriving. My friend is putting on a really good display of being interested in my brother's boring chat about what he studied at university!

I'm staring at my reflection in the mirror when Stern comes into the restroom. I'm so shocked that I let him take me by the hand and lead me to one of the cubicles. He slides the door lock and then grabs me by the shoulders, pushing me against the door.

"Carrie. Are you in or are you out?"

He towers over me, but I am not afraid of him. I can see the desperation in his gorgeous blue eyes, and that makes me realize that all the cards lie in my hand. And yet, back at the apartment, Stern said he has no time for family, and my family is so important to me that I can't even begin to explain to him what it feels like to love that intensely.

But I love Stern intensely too. It cut me up at the bar when Darryl told me that Stern goes to art exhibitions and fucks high-society beauties. I don't want him to be with anyone else, because it will hurt me to know that.

"I'm... I'm in. Yes."

"God, you look so hot in that dress, sweetheart." Stern's mouth descends on mine and we kiss. Leaning against the cubicle door, I let his hands untie my wrap dress so that it falls open. I am wearing a pair of black lace G-string panties underneath, but one rip and Stern has broken the thin lace elastic and pulled them off.

I am fumbling with the zipper in his pants, rubbing the thick outline of his cock underneath. My intentions are clear. I need his cock inside me now.

There is no time for us to think about where we are and what we are doing. Balancing myself with one hand on the door, I allow Stern to lift my left leg so that I can half-mount him. It helps that I am wearing high heels.

"I want you so bad," I murmur so that only we can hear it. I feel his fingers sliding into my pussy as his thumb stimulates my clit. I am dripping wet, so ready for him that I am almost coming already.

He releases his rampant cock from inside his pants, and I know how much I have missed this. Pushing me against the door, Stern slides his massive tool into my achingly wet pussy. I can feel every inch of him as he gets ready to pound me so hard.

There is only the sound of us fucking in the narrow cubicle. We can no longer hold back. I start to pant and moan as his long, slow strokes start getting faster. Gripping his broad shoulders with my hands, I wrap my leg around him, trying to get him closer.

"Fuck it, I can't hold back. I'm going to come," Stern groans, really pounding me hard as the door behind me shakes from the force of his movements.

"I want you to come inside me so hard," I'm so turned on, I can't focus on anything else but the exquisite tenderness of my clit. "I want you so bad."

Stern comes first. His knob expands so much when he does that it seems to press something inside me. I start coming as well, scratching at his fancy dinner jacket and grinding my pussy against the base of his cock.

Pulling out of me, Stern uses his pocket handkerchief to wipe himself off and then hands it to me. He knows tissue paper sticks to cum like glue. "Thank you. I'll see you outside."

And then he's gone. Feeling so lightheaded, I sway back out to the mirrors. My hair has come down.

I look really fucked.

Chapter 20: Stern

I guess having a short, no-nonsense haircut pays off big time when I return to the table and no one notices how rumpled I look. My body reacts when I remember what just went down in the restroom cubicles and I almost get hard all over again. I sit down before my luck runs out.

What shocks me the most is that Miles has not even noticed how long I was gone from the table at the same time as his sister. And while I kind of get off on living dangerously because of how I spent my life as a young adult, I never want to be carried away by my emotions like that again.

Gail turns to include me in the conversation. "You haven't even touched your champagne, Boss. Are you on a cleanse?" I can see from the twinkle in her eyes that she knows exactly what I did in the restrooms, but she is just too loyal to hint at it.

Right then, I resolve to promote Gail just as soon as I can. She's one in a million. Grinning, I take a sip of champagne and smile. "Please call me Stern, Gail. Just about everyone does."

Gail doesn't reply with the obvious remark, which is "What does your mom call you?" because Carrie has told her about my upbringing and background.

All she does is raise her glass and say, "Stern it is, then."

What I love the most about Per Se is how they pace the service to the table. There is no rush for them to start serving appetizers and I am glad they don't because that might make Miles wonder where Carrie is.

I see her walking back to the table. Her hair is down, falling like a river of fire over her shoulders, her pale, heart-shaped face tinted with a touch of pink in her cheeks. But it's those silver-gray eyes of hers that make me smile.

"Where were you all this time?" Miles wants to know.

Carrie points to her hair. "Having a bit of a crisis with my hair. Up or down? Sometimes that question can keep me in front of the mirror for hours."

I think I better add my own touch of humor here. "Women and their hair. If it isn't that, it's something else. Am I right, Miles?"

This is my best friend's clue to drop in a sarcastic comment about how long Belinda takes to get ready to go out. Only he doesn't.

Putting on a fake understanding expression, Miles acts all outraged. "Bru! You mustn't belittle a woman's presentation process! It is a sacred ritual. And what would you know about how important it is anyway? You've never even lived with a woman in your life."

I am shocked but in a good way. This is the first time in six years that Miles has not brought the conversation back around to Belinda! And he is trying to score points with Gail.

Miles turns back to focus his attention on Gail. "I love your hair, Gail. It suits you so well." And then the two of them ignore Carrie and me as they launch into talking about ethnic hairstyling techniques in South Africa.

After risking a look at Carrie, I can see that she's enjoying how her brother has taken a shine to her friend. Our eyes connect and she gives me a little smile. My stomach flips because she is so beautiful and I want to believe that she is mine.

Our appetizers start to arrive and everyone turns their attention to the food and wine. By the time the sweet courses start to arrive, Gail and Miles have turned their attention back on one another again. Angling her body towards me, Carrie dares to speak to me.

"Did you set this up?" Her voice is soft and does not carry over to where Miles is sitting. He would not be able to overhear anyway; he's in deep conversation with Gail, so I risk being honest. "Yes. Are you glad I did?"

She nods. "It was a good idea. Recently, Miles has been almost as grumpy as you are. So, thank you for pushing him back out into the world of dating."

I pretend to be shocked, but still keep my voice to a low growl. "Me, grumpy? No way. I just call it like it is. How can I be over the moon when you keep insisting on keeping us a secret?"

Carrie hesitates, but then the moment is lost as Miles cuts in. "Shall we go clubbing? Can you get us into one of those fancy nightclubs where you're a member, Stern? I'm in the mood for dancing."

My friend's enthusiasm is great to see. He's been down in the dumps for so long, and I have not been much help because of my own problems weighing me down. This is the chance I have been waiting for. I risk hinting to Miles at how I feel about his sister.

"Sure, buddy. But I have to tell you how amazing it is to see Carrie outside of the work environment. Not only is she a talented artist, but—" I turn to Carrie and address the comment straight to her. "—you look so damn sexy in that dress."

It's almost as if everyone at the table is holding their breath as we wait for Miles's reaction. By the look on his face, I can see a flood of different emotions fighting for supremacy there. But eventually, one emotion wins. Discomfort.

"Jeez, Stern. For fuck's sake. That's my little sister you're talking about. And you are old enough to be her father, besides the fact that you already have a girlfriend." He turns to Carrie. "Sis, maybe wear something less revealing next time."

I did not think Carrie could get whiter, but she goes pale. I can't help it. I feel the righteous anger boiling up inside me and I am about to explode.

Then Gail swoops in to save the day. Smacking Miles playfully across the arm, she bursts into laughter. "Whoa! You nearly had me fooled there, Miles. I thought you were being serious for a moment. There is nothing I hate more than a serious fool, you know what I mean?"

She soothingly massages his wrist. "It's hard when a sister grows up and spreads her wings, isn't it? I have three younger sisters, and I am very strict with them. But wouldn't you know it, they are all happily married with kids now!"

I can see Miles melting under this tender treatment. I give Carrie's knee a squeeze under the table, but she doesn't look at me.

Gail turns to give Carrie the soothing treatment too. "Don't you dare let your brother tease you like that, Carrie! You are a grown woman of twenty-three years old. A beautiful, sophisticated, talented, young woman. Miles, tell your sister that your joke was in poor taste."

Miles is put on the spot. He can't insist he was serious now without looking like a mean son of a bitch. "I'm sorry, Carrie. For what I said. I keep forgetting how old you are now." A rallying look comes into Miles's eyes. "But Mom and Dad told me to—"

Gail butts in before he can finish. "You know what I loved the most about turning twenty-one? The fact that my parents could no longer tell me what to do! Oh, and did I forget to add that I could also drink alcohol? Which reminds me—let's have a round of coffee before we hit the club."

Our server sees me look around and takes the coffee order. It arrives with the most delicious petit fours, giving us the perfect topic to change the conversation.

My heart is still pumping so fast. My plan is in ruins. Miles is still dead set against my attraction to his sister.

I have never felt this level of frustration and despair since I left the Corps. It is the same kind of feeling I got when one of my fellow Marines got injured or killed in the line of duty. That burning desire to set things right at all costs, that need to fight for justice. It's this feeling that made me the world leader in security consultation for the elite, but it brings me no comfort here. I don't like feeling like this about my private life, that's for damn sure.

God help me, but I have to see this evening to its conclusion. The food tastes like ashes in my mouth. I can't be with the woman I want because she happens to be my best friend's sister.

The emotional swing that happened between the restroom and now is dizzying. I try to hold Carrie's hand under the table again and this time she lets me.

I wait for Miles to get wrapped up in his conversation with Gail again before I risk looking at Carrie. Our eyes meet and I can read the surrender in her eyes. She has given up on the idea of us.

It takes every last ounce of discipline I possess to keep acting naturally. I guess I am clutching at straws when I speak.

"Hey, sorry about the inappropriate remark I made earlier, Carrie. I keep forgetting that you kind of work for me and Mannie. Belinda, your brother's lovely ex-wife, frowns on any man complimenting a pretty woman when she deserves it."

That catches Miles and Gail's attention. Gail reacts first. "You were married to Belinda! Oh my God. I remember Carrie telling me something about that. Belinda is the head of the department I am in. I was in inter-staff relations, but now I act as a liaison between HQ and the architectural division at Apollo on First."

It is a masterclass in how to inject information into a conversation without giving too much away. I hope Gail can read the gratefulness in my eyes.

Miles smiles ruefully. "I guess I picked up my ex-wife's narrow mindset from living with her for five years." Turning to Carrie, he continues. "Sis, I'm sorry for the rude way I overreacted. Gail is right. I was out of line."

Carrie gives me a look before replying. "I think you should apologize to Stern, Miles. He is not old. And I think that I would be right in saying he is not old enough to be my father."

That is a step too far for Miles. "Hang on." I see him do some calculations in his head. "There's a twelve-year age gap between the two of you. That's plenty old. When he was dating his first girlfriend, you were being born."

It is my turn to drop a truth bomb. "Nope. When I was twelve years old, I was kept in a boys' orphanage waiting for a place in the foster system. The only female there was the super's wife. And she's doing time in prison now for beating a small boy to death with a tire iron, so she doesn't count as a woman I knew on any level."

Carrie gives a small cry and grabs my hand over the top of the table. Thankfully, Miles doesn't have a problem with her doing this, and it's not because he wants to act like a nice guy in front of Gail either.

"Bru, I was out of line. I am so sorry." Trying to mitigate any damage, Miles asks Gail if he can see her home. "Let's walk if that's okay. I need to digest some of this lovely food and hopefully clear my head of the wine too. I am not really in the mood for clubbing anymore."

"Are you acting all nice because you found out that Belinda was my boss?" Gail is teasing Miles and attempting to lighten the mood.

Miles grins. "Yes! But also, I just want to walk you home. Good night, you two. See you at the loft later, Sis. Thanks for the meal, Stern."

To say that Carrie is sad after her friend and brother leave would be an understatement. "I should go," she tries to smile at me but fails miserably. "I wouldn't put it past my brother to check the door entry schedules to see what time I get home."

"When can I see you again?" I want to know. "I think we are making progress. He seems more receptive to the idea of us."

Carrie shakes her head. "I don't think we should see each other as lovers again, Stern. I can't handle this emotional push and pull."

Chapter 21: Carrie

I can read Stern's face so well by now. I can see he refuses to see it from my point of view.

"What a classic Carrie move," he growls, shaking his head. "You act like I don't have feelings when you come straight out and say things like that. You know that, don't you?"

He's hurting, and that makes me feel bad. I don't know what to do. "My family will always be against you walking casually back into my life, Stern. I want to get out now before it is too late."

His gorgeous blue eyes narrow. "So, you told them about me… about us? And they have a problem with that?"

My eyes get wide. "It's going to come out sooner or later, Stern! I can't keep it a secret forever. And to answer your accusation more fully—no. I have not told them about us."

He settles down. "It's going to come out sooner. Definitely sooner. If I have anything to do with it. Sooner."

I should have realized that being the action man that he is, Stern would want to take control of the situation, bending the results to adapt to his iron-strong will. "And you don't have a problem with that?" I need to know. "I mean, you won't come out of it smelling like roses, Stern. There's been too much water flowing under the bridge for that to happen."

He gives me one of those charming grins. The one that never fails to melt my heart and makes me agree with everything he says. "I don't mind what people think of me, Carrie. Surely you must have noticed that about me by now?"

Like the rest of the service at Per Se, the bill is presented and paid for with seamless efficiency and grace. I thank Stern for the lovely meal as he takes my hand and places it in the crook of his elbow. But I am burning to know something before I succumb entirely to his will.

"If I am to act as if you do have feelings, Stern, it might help if I knew what they were."

His town car has pulled up to the curb and the driver is standing with the door open, waiting for us to get in. Stern holds my hand and watches me settle into the softly cushioned black leather seat before he steps back onto the sidewalk.

When the driver is back behind the wheel and the engine rumbles as it starts, Stern lowers the car's window and closes the door. Leaning in with his elbows on the edge, he smiles at me. "I'm not coming back with you. I've had enough of Miles's paranoia this evening already." He steps back again, bending over so that he can still see my face as the car begins to pull away from the curb.

"You want to know my feelings?" He waves goodbye. "I love you."

As the car joins the traffic, I turn my head back so I can watch Stern get smaller in the distance. His hand drops to his side, but then he raises it and pats his heart. Then he turns and starts walking away.

I have a lot to think about. So much in fact that I don't even notice it when my brother does not come home that night. I wish Miles would move to another apartment, another city! He is getting in the way in so many ways, I can't even list them.

This is my problem. When I search deep inside my heart I can sense there is a very dark part of me that still hates Simon Sterns. Loathes him would be a better word.

No matter how amazing the sex is, no matter how much he spoils me, I don't know if I can forgive him for what he did to me when I was a young, innocent eighteen-year-old girl. That isn't me being vindictive and mean-hearted—that is me being honest with myself.

That gives me a lot to think about. When I leave for work the next morning, I wonder whether I should be diplomatic and discreet with Gail when I next see her. This might be the Big Bad Apple, Manhattan, the city where dreams can come true or fizzle out, but I am only twenty-three years old at the end of the day. I have no idea whether it's appropriate to talk about sex at work.

One thing I do know is this: Belinda makes sure everyone follows the rules when it comes to relationships at work. Everyone except herself, that is.

"Good morning, Rick," I greet the security guard sitting at the desk in the lobby entrance when he buzzes me in. The building is still technically under construction, but I don't have to wear a work helmet because this section is finished. "Did the scaffolding technician check the second level?"

"No such luck, Carrie." Rick is a cool guy and has forgiven me for giving him such a shock when the elevator doors opened on me giving Stern head. "Please stick to the one level until the clamps have been tightened. I swear the top platform was swaying like a tall tree in the wind last time you were up there."

"You know what?" I step back and have a look at the outline of my mural design that is halfway complete on the wall. "I think I'm going to head back to HQ and print out the next section. So that it is ready for when the scaffolding is secure."

I am starting to feel a little bit hunted, because I know that sooner or later, Stern is going to come looking for a reply from me. How can I explain my complex attitude regarding how he treated me in the past?

It's typical Manhattan madness, rush-hour traffic, so I have time to think as I walk to HQ with my head down, looking at the cracks in the pavement for inspiration. Heading up to the design floor, I greet each member of the staff as I pass their cubicles before sitting down at my desk.

"Hey, girl!" Gail bounces into the cubicle with a beaming smile on her face. "How did it go with the boss last night?" Then she notices my solemn face and frowns. "Please, please don't tell me that it went to shit after we left. I don't think I can take much more of the drama, Carrie."

I reassure her. "No! Not at all. It was lovely, and thank you for arranging it. Stern and I got the chance to—"

Noticing Gail's expectant face, I break into laughter. "—Ha! You are naughty, Gail, you know that? I am so not going to tell you what happened in the restroom. Stern and I got the chance to iron out some issues. That's all I can say for now. What about Miles and you?"

Gail gives me a wink. "I don't kiss and tell, Carrie. But I had a lovely evening too." Looking down at the open computer screen and staring at my design, she searches for the right words. "Umm... do you have any idea why Miles is so dead set against you two getting together? It seems a bit old-fashioned for your family to allow Miles such a huge amount of freedom while they treat you like a nun in a cloister."

Pointing down at my lap, I sigh. "I'm a woman. The youngest child with two older brothers. Need I say more?"

Gail huffs, but pats my shoulder kindly. "Good luck, girl."

I'm all alone in my booth, doodling on my sketchpad and then uploading the pattern onto my computer. When the phone rings, I know who it is already. The man is like an Olympic sprinter waiting to race to the finish line!

"Hey, Stern. Thank you for a wonderful eve—"

"Do you love me too, Carrie?"

Oh, shit. I don't know what to say. I spent half the night worrying about what to say during this moment. "Love is such a big word, Stern—" It is a crap start to a very difficult conversation, and he knows this.

"It's three little words, Carrie. It's no big deal."

Trying to lighten the mood, I crack a joke. "Four words, if I say your name too."

Silence at the other end of the line. I try to fill the gap with word salad. "Fine, I will be honest, Stern. I think we owe each other that much. I love having sex with you. I love spending time with you. I love talking to you."

He makes a sound that tells me he's not satisfied. "That sounds damn well like love to me, Carrie. So, say the words."

"But—" There, I got the most important word out. "But I have a small, tiny fraction of hate for you too. We can't be together without acknowledging that, but I think it is always going to be there. I don't see any way it's ever going away unless something miraculous happens. No fine-dining experience, no fancy shopping spree, and no job commission is ever going to diminish it."

This time, the silence at the end of the line is deafening. Then, I hear him breathing, angry puffs, like the way a bull snorts when it wants to kick the rodeo cowboy off its back. "What have I ever fucking done to make you hate me, Carrie Maitland!?"

The line goes dead. I knew this was going to happen. Stern is an "all-or-nothing" kind of guy. He wants all of my love, and I can't give it to him because I love my little family more.

Trying to concentrate on my design, I send the latest section of the mural over to the print station to be enlarged. I will use it as a guideline when I trace it onto the lobby wall. Pushing my chair back, I decide to go pick up the print myself, but a shadow blocks the cubical exit.

It's Gail. "What have you done? Stern just called me and he sounded pissed."

Shaking my head, I don't even have the strength to explain. "The man was born to be miserable, Gail. What can I say?"

My friend's eyes are wide with shock. "He's picked up the contract extension option, and Mannie just okayed it. But then again, Mannie does everything Stern asks him to do."

Screwing up my eyes, I try to remember my contract wording. Giving up, I ask Gail to explain.

"That means you will have to paint murals on all the lobby walls, Carrie, not just the one."

I almost faint. The lobby space is huge. It will take me years to finish. "B-but that's impossible for one person. It will be time to knock Apollo on First down and build a new one by the time I finish."

Gail rolls her eyes. "Why do you and Stern keep sabotaging one another, Carrie? Please go and talk to him. I think he's on the mezzanine level. I know he will see you."

Closing my lips together into a thin line, I shake my head. "Fuck him! He is incapable of having a rational conversation! I'm going back to Apollo on First. He just wants a reaction, and I'll be damned if I give him one."

Slumping her shoulders, Gail stands aside to let me pass. "Go, I won't stop you. I will tell the boss you agree to his latest outrageous demand, and maybe that will give him the satisfaction he is so obviously craving."

Laughing and giving a careless wave of my hand to my friend, I leave. Remembering to stop off at the print station to pick up the new design outline, I splurge and catch a cab across to First Avenue instead of walking.

I keep cash on me now after what Stern told me. My face softens as I think about how much he cares for the people who provide a service for him. Why can't he be that understanding when it comes to me?

"Hey, Rick. I'm back again," I announce. Inclining my head over to the mural sketched on the wall, I ask with a wry smile, "Did they fix the scaffolding yet?"

Rick gives me the thumbs-up, but can't speak because he's on the phone. Placing my long, aluminum drafting tube against the first platform, I use the ladder to climb up to the second platform. There, I begin to measure the section where the new outline is meant to go.

This is why I don't wear dresses to work now. Only leggings or pants will allow me to get up and down ladders without giving all of the lobby visitors an eyeful from down below.

Today, I am wearing tight black leggings with a giant T-shirt hanging off one shoulder and a white vest underneath. My hair is in a casual ponytail, and I have tekkies on my feet.

I have fallen into the habit of calling my running shoes "tekkies," which is what they call sneakers in South Africa.

And it just so happens that one of those lobby visitors is down below me right now. I nearly fall off the scaffolding when I hear his deep voice behind me.

"Hey, Carrie! I thought I would drop by and say hello. I love what you have done so far."

Looking down, I see someone I recognize. It's Darryl from the wine bar.

Chapter 22: Stern

I'm coming up outside the building, striding quickly because I'm in a bad mood and I'm trying to walk it off when I see Carrie leaning against the scaffolding ladder and talking to some preppy bastard in a navy-blue Brooks Brothers suit.

Barging into the lobby the moment Rick unlocks the entrance door, I stalk over to the happy couple. "I'm sorry. Am I interrupting? I didn't realize your workload was so light, Carrie, that you could spend the day yakking to some random civvie who walks in off the street."

Shooting me a dark look, Carrie ignores my satirical remark. "Stern, please can I introduce

Darryl Vonn to you? Darryl, this is my boss, Simon Sterns."

I don't look down at the hand Darryl is holding out towards me, so he drops it. "Pleased to meet you, Mr. Stern. I love what you have done to the building's interior. I'm a bit of an art collector myself."

The guy can't be more than twenty-five years old and he makes me feel like I'm old-school. Inhaling slowly, I fight my aggression down. "Darryl. Vonn. Got it. I know your family." Gritting my teeth, I shake his hand. "Sterns & Co. installed the security at Spencer Vonn's private and business addresses."

"He's my uncle on my dad's side of the family. Good old Uncle Spenny. He's got quite the art collection himself."

Keeping my expression neutral, I reply, "Yes. I know. I saw it when your uncle invited me over."

This tight little trio is quiet for a beat as everyone thinks about what to say next. Carrie gives it a shot. "I invited Darryl to come and see the progress we are making on the mural, Stern. I was just telling him how it looks like I will have to extend the project for another ten years because you want me to do the entire lobby."

If Carrie is expecting me to take back the extension by forcing me to admit how large-scale the project has become in front of preppy Darryl Vonn, she's in for a surprise.

"How did you two meet? I'm obviously not working you hard enough if you have the time to go hang out in cocktail bars." I take a flying guess that's where Carrie met this character. I remember the notification coming through on my bank app, alerting me to drinks being purchased at The Wayland last week.

"Yeah," Darryl says, grinning, "we met at a cocktail bar not too far from here, but the night ended abruptly because Carrie and Gail had an early morning yoga class."

As my frown melts away, I look at Carrie and see a naughty spark in her eye. She's enjoying this! She's teasing me with this poor young guy, hoping to make me frantic with worry. I guess I deserve it after the stunt I pulled with the lobby.

I shake Darryl's hand to say goodbye and then growl at Carrie. "Come upstairs when you have said goodbye to your visitor, Carrie."

I see Rick giving me a worried look when he sees me get into the elevator. I bet he doesn't want to see Carrie giving me oral again. But this time, I have my sexual appetite under control. I want an answer from Carrie, one way or another.

Gail picks up the special line I had installed in her office. "Who's Darryl?" I keep my interrogation short and sweet.

Gail is not impressed. Whispering so that no one else in the office can overhear, she lets me have it. "Y'all giving me whiplash with these mood swings, Stern! Leave the poor girl alone."

"I can't," I confess. "I love her. I need to know if she feels the same way about me."

That keeps the line silent for a beat while Gail takes in this new bit of information. "Fine. But please remember that you started your relationship with secrets and lies, Stern. So, please don't get upset if more secrets and lies are going forward. And you should admire Carrie for not throwing the words 'I love you' around like candy at Halloween—saying it obviously holds a deep significance for her."

And then she hangs up. Dropping my phone on the desk, I go to the floor-to-ceiling windows and look out. I stay there until I hear the elevator doors open.

Carrie sounds relieved. "The buttons in the elevator work for me now. Is that some fancy security feature?" She comes in, clutching her aluminum drafting tube like a bouquet.

"Sit down." Turning from the window, I move back to the desk and sit down. "Please, Carrie."

She sits down opposite me, crossing her shapely legs so I can see her practical footwear. She has customized the sneakers herself by writing "left" on the right shoe and "right" on the left one.

I can't stop myself from smiling when I see it. It's such a Carrie thing to do.

"I know it's scheduled for you to make the design presentation in situ at the end of the month, Carrie. You only have to do one mural for now. But I would like to pick up my option to extend the contract."

"In situ?" she raises her eyebrows.

I explain. "It's Latin. It means 'at the place' where the mural is going to be. Basically, it's my complicated way of saying that Mannie and I will want to see the sketched outline laid out to full scale. We'll probably want to see some kind of progress when it comes to painting too. Not a lot, just some of the colors need to be laid down."

She doesn't move. "Aren't you going to emotionally pressure me about something, Stern? Make some taxing demand on my feelings? Ask for me to pick a side?"

Shaking my head, I stare out the window. "What's the point? I have to be content with you loving the sex for now. Maybe I'm trying to rush things because I'm not getting any younger. While you, Carrie, you have all the time in the world."

"Can I travel to South Africa please, Stern?"

That definitely makes me turn and look at her. "This is unexpected. Is everything okay at home?"

She nods, clearly pleased to see that I am taking the news well. "Yes, all is well. I call home every morning before I come to work. I need to go because a part of the mural includes these amazing vibrant Ndebele tribal patterns, and I can't find the ones I want to copy online. But I know where I can photograph them in South Africa…."

My heart sinks as I think of Carrie going back home. I want to protect her, so I don't like the thought of her going anywhere without me. But I have to take a leap of faith and trust her on this one. "Sure, sweetheart. Go if it's important to you. Take the jet. It'll be more comfortable."

Finally, I have said and done the right thing. Bouncing up from the chair, Carrie comes to hug me—which of course turns into a kiss. The next thing I know, she's sitting on my lap with her legs straddling me.

"Stern, why are you so good to me? I love it when you are sweet-natured. God knows I don't deserve it."

Burying her face against my chest, we sit peacefully together for a long while as I stroke the long red hair falling down her back. "I've never told anyone that I loved them before, Carrie, so you must forgive my impatience to know if you feel the same way. I'm sorry."

I feel her hands slip around my neck and her soft lips as she kisses my jaw. "Stern, it's not you, it's me. But I promise you that I am not sleeping with anyone else. I've only ever had sex with you, so you can relax." She gives a small laugh as she runs her hand downwards. "You satisfy me completely, so why would I need anyone else?"

Of course, when she fumbles with my zipper, she finds me hard. "Ooh," Carrie coos in my ear, "it looks like someone is happy to see me."

The next thing I know, she is on her knees in front of me, hauling my rampant cock out of my pants and licking it with her eyes closed. Suddenly, her eyes open and she sees me watching her. A naughty expression flickers on her face.

"I want you to fuck my mouth, Stern. And then I want you to fuck me hard. Bend me over your desk and give it to me."

I almost come in her mouth right then when I see Carrie slide her hand down the front of her tight leggings. She begins to finger her clit with lush, leisurely strokes. "Mmm," she sucks my knob and then licks the shaft, "you taste so good."

The way she is fingering her pussy is totally turning me on. Biting my lower lip, I manage to get out the words. "Any chance you can step out of those pants of yours, sweetheart? I would love to get in on that action in your panties."

The leggings are made of Lycra. She peels them off her legs and steps out of them, leaving them in a puddle on the floor. She looks more like a wicked high-school girl now than she ever did five years ago. Next, she pulls off the big T-shirt and throws it onto the floor too. With only the string strap vest and her socks and sneakers on, Carrie resembles a cheerleader.

When she bends over to untie her shoes, I tell her to leave them on. I can see her pussy slit glistening wet as she bends down. Pushing her against the desk and bending her over, I feed all ten inches of my cock into her, not stopping until I hear her moan with satisfaction as my balls touch her labia.

She's shaved down there. I can feel how soft and smooth she is when I reach around and start to finger her. "So sensitive," Carrie tells me, "but sooo good."

I know she loves it when I slide my cock in and out of her tight slit. It looks unbelievably hot when I see how her juices are making my shaft soaking wet. I have to finger her clit again, loving the way it makes her ass tilt up as she grinds back against me.

For one delicious moment, I withdraw and bang her beautiful rounded ass with my cock. That makes Carrie turn around and sit on the edge of the desk, spreading her legs wide for me. Her eyes flutter as she says the magic words.

"Want to fuck this?" Her fingers are busy, rubbing her clit and then circling her wet snatch.

"Or do you want to watch me come without your cock pounding inside me? Because I am close."

She wraps her legs around me and pulls me closer, guiding my cock with her hands to rub against her clit before sliding back inside her. I bang her hard, and she loves it. Lifting Carrie off the desk, I carry her over to the leather couch. "I don't want my pretty princess to bruise that gorgeous ass of hers on the wood," I growl.

Giving a wild laugh, Carrie lies down and lets me fuck her to my heart's content. I hear her come, but I can't stop to ask her if it was good. I am too fixated on my own orgasm. It seems to mount and mount some more as I get close. This has to be the longest orgasm I have ever had. Stars seem to burst in front of my eyes when I eventually reach my peak and come off.

Collapsing against her neck, I can't find the words to thank Carrie for the most monumental fuck of my life. Then, I am dimly aware of her using me to have another orgasm herself. I love the little grunts she makes as she rotates her hips up and down my cock.

I think I might have even drifted off to sleep… but then we both come alive when we hear the elevator spring into life!

Chapter 23: Carrie

"When are you going to learn to lock that darn elevator door, Stern!" I'm half laughing, half panicked as the elevator pulleys and cables hiss upwards.

"Do you think I do this often?" Stern is laughing too as he fastens the buttons of his shirt. "But you're right. I'll get an emergency elevator stop button installed under my desk, like one of those old James Bond movies."

That makes me giggle, which ends up sounding more like a snort. For some reason, I have the good sense to give a quick spray of perfume into the air before the elevator doors slide open... and my brother, Miles, steps out.

His head is down, and he has some papers he's concentrating on, but then the smell of scent makes him look up, a confused expression on his face. "Jesus, Carrie! Lighten up on whatever you like wearing. It smells like a drag queen's makeup case in here."

I try to look as if butter wouldn't melt in my mouth as I clasp the drafting tube on my lap. "Isn't that so funny, Miles, because Stern was just saying that he likes it? How can you not adore L'Interdit by Givenchy?"

He shoots me a confused look. "What by who? Sounds like mumbo jumbo to me, Carrie. Smells like mumbo jumbo too, if you ask me." Ignoring me, Miles begins to talk to Stern about the laser sensors for a museum in Europe.

I get up to leave while my brother is distracted, but Stern is not having any of it. "Carrie, aren't you going to tell Miles about your trip?"

Whipping his head around as if he is suspicious of me, Miles gives me a narrow stare. "Trip? What trip? You've only just started working on the mural, Sis. You can't take a break now."

I return his stare with an intense one of my own. "Actually, I can. And you're not my boss anyway, because Mannie is. Stern says I can travel to South Africa—I really need to find a design concept for the other walls."

Miles begins to grumble. "You're lucky I'm not married to Belinda anymore, Carrie. If I was, you can bet the farm I would tell her about your little jaunt on company time."

Muttering under my breath, I threaten him with what I know. "And then I might have something to say about you spending the night away from the loft...."

Stern seems to be enjoying our brother and sister bickering, but he interrupts her. "You both seem to have forgotten that I'm the client. Carrie is free to go wherever she likes for inspiration."

Grumbling louder, Miles shakes his head. "Then you have to hire an assistant, a driver, and send two—no, three security personnel for my sister. My parents would flip out if they knew she was traveling around the country without a chaperone."

Feeling malicious, I make a suggestion. "I can take Gail. She's the official Milano-Sterns go-between. And Stern can arrange for us to hook up with a driver and security on the other side."

My brother starts to backtrack immediately. "Whoa! Let's not be hasty now. Gail hasn't even been consulted." I hide my laughter because I know Miles wants to bring Gail around to the loft during my absence.

Stern steps in. "I tell you what. I'll arrange for someone to go with Carrie. You will never find a safer escort than I can. I'm still linked into all my old SEAL special ops teams."

My brother still looks unsure, so Stern plows on. "There's an armored vehicle expo at the Dubai Convention Center next week that I'm attending. So I'll be a few hours' flight away if there is an emergency, Miles, but I'm hardly likely to be more helpful than your own family on their home turf. How does that sound?"

The thought of inviting Gail around to the loft without me being there to cramp his style is too tempting for my brother to resist. "Okay. Sure. Please be careful that they don't leave Carrie alone in public or outdoors. I'm serious, Stern. You do not want to know how dangerous South Africa is."

Stern looks unfazed. "I do know. We have clients there, remember? Carrie," he says, shooting me a wicked look out of those gorgeous blue eyes of his, "wheels up at seven this evening. Okay?'

I give him the thumbs-up and then make my exit. I have a lot of packing to do.

***

My phone vibrates and I know it's Stern. I'm going to be your escort to Cape Town, Carrie. Don't worry about Miles. He thinks I'm going to Dubai.

I text back. Wheels up at seven indeed ;)

The black credit card Gail is so fond of using is on file at Bloomingdale's now. So, I spend the rest of the day shopping for presents for my family after grabbing a quick shower at the loft. I have to admit to going a bit nuts on gifts and souvenirs. I miss them so much and can't wait to see them all again.

I am so grateful for the opportunity my parents gave me. They paid for all of my tuition and school fees and medical bills, and that came to quite a healthy sum of money over the last five years. This mural is going to be my calling card, my way of saying to the world that I have talent and nothing is going to stand in my way.

I was thinking about buying a small house in South Africa, something I can use as an investment while I sort out my new life in the States. I'm holding back on that for now, because I need to know if Stern and I can make it work.

When the commissions for my art begin rolling in, I can set up my own place and bring my little family over here to live a comfortable life of ease. I really need to make it on my own, without a handout from Stern.

Asking the cab to wait for me downstairs because all the gift bags are in the trunk, I rush up to the loft and pack. Cheekily, I write a lipstick message inside the bathroom cabinet that reads "Hi Gail." I know my friend will like that even if my prim and proper brother might not.

It feels like a million bucks when I direct the cab driver to Teterboro Airport and tell him to head for the private entrance. The drive, made in bumper-to-bumper Manhattan traffic, allows me to unwind and catch up on some texts.

Hi Mom—guess what? I got permission to come back home for a bit to do some research. I'm no good at working out when the plane will be landing, but I should be there tomorrow. You can light the fire for a braai because your daughter is coming for dinner! (Please don't tell anyone else until I have verified these details. Thank you, Mom. Love, Carrie.

A "braai" is the South African version of a barbecue. My parents are Texans through and through, so it's a family joke that the kids use the word braai because my mom and dad say that it will always be a barbecue for them.

I have one headphone in and I'm listening to my favorite music as I chat with the cab driver. It turns out that he visited Durban in South Africa once because he has relatives there.

"It's a small world," I try to sound upbeat, "but I wouldn't advise you to visit there now!"

"Yes," the driver agrees, "my relatives want to move away from there now. Too much chaos. Beautiful country, but the corruption and crime are so bad."

My heart skips a beat when I see Stern waiting for me. I can never quite believe that such a handsome man could fall in love with me. I'm not falsely modest. I have a certain appeal because of my rarity value. Men go cray-cray for natural redheads and heart-shaped faces with silvery colored eyes, especially when they are a nubile twenty-three years old.

But Stern is next level on every scale. His body is built for the gods. His dirty yellow-blond hair color—especially the way it falls over his forehead when he's busy and then he moves it with a careless flick of his head—his aquiline features, and his big, beautiful cock. He has all of these things, plus wealth, so why isn't he dating a supermodel?

The flight attendant is a man. He shows me to my seat and tells me about the flight while

Stern chats with the pilot. The attendant is busy showing me where the one thousand trees and ten hectares of jungle are going to be planted or preserved after this flight.

Stern takes his seat opposite me. I can tell he's pleased our little plan went so well. "I have been wanting to get you alone for a heart-to-heart conversation for a real long time, Carrie Maitland."

My mouth pulls into a joking grimace. "That sounds ominous, Stern. And here was little ol' me hoping that you were going to induct me into the Mile High Club."

The jet begins to coast forward and I do my best not to grab the armrest. The seats are made of soft leather and colored a light beige color. There are eight seats, spaced in facing pairs. I try to imagine what it must be like to live in such luxury, but it's like a dream.

Making a beckoning gesture with my hand, I lean back and relax. I am fighting the urge to stress about flying. Ever since I heard that control freaks are the worst flyers because they find it hard to trust the pilot!

"Okay. Go. Give me this heart-to-heart you have been promising us, Stern."

He is watching me fight to relax with the trace of a lopsided smile on his face. "I wanted to see more of you from the first day we met, Carrie, but your brother put the kibosh on that. I mean, look at how he reacted at Per Se. It was a fuckup. It was best for me to let you go. The company was still gaining ground and I had my hands full. Don't you agree that was the best move?"

My stomach knots as travel sickness and sorrow fight for dominance inside my head. "Um… I was too young to know the consequences of what we were doing, Stern. I was barely eighteen." The plane surges forward and up. I have to hiccup down my travel-sick tummy. "I know you love to analyze the crap out of everything, looking for all the imperfections, but I promise you one thing—"

I close my eyes as nausea floods me. I hear a soft pop and the sound of something fizzing. "Oh God, Stern, please no champagne right now."

Hearing Stern laugh, I open my eyes. He's leaning forward and holding out a glass of Alka-Seltzer towards me. The pop was the sound of him taking off the lid. "You promise me one thing?" There is kindness in his face, and I can imagine him putting a field dressing on one of his injured team and waiting for the CASEVAC to arrive.

Taking the glass with a nod of gratitude, I drink the fizzing water down. Embarrassed to have such a human moment in front of my lover, I place my jacket over my face to hide my shame. I hear Stern tell the flight attendant to show me to the restrooms, and I follow the kind man there.

It's as luxurious as the rest of the interior inside the restrooms. The pale skin on my face has a slight green tinge, making my silvery eyes look large and luminous. How can I tell Stern how badly I needed him to choose me over Miles? Then, and now.

Until he does, that kernel of hate in my heart will never go away.

The jet lurches. Gripping the door handle, I stagger out. Bless my amazing traveling companion, because he has gone to chat with the pilot to give me my space. When he comes out again, my warm feelings for him have returned.

"You were saying?" Stern places a cool hand against my forehead. Then I feel his fingertips pressing my wrist to feel my pulse.

"I was saying—I promise you one thing, Simon Sterns—that we will never know what the best move was, will we?"

Chapter 24: Carrie

Now & Then

What happened to me on the day of my brother's wedding four and a half years ago haunts my nightmares and dreams. I got nightmares whenever I thought about the pain my lies caused everyone. I had hot and heavy dreams about lying in Simon's arms again almost every lonely night.

I was still a kid then, now that I come to think about it. Made to play adult games out of curiosity and lust.

The fake persona I put on for Simon Sterns' benefit was the teenage equivalent of playing with Barbie and Ken and then bumping their plastic bits together in the dollhouse.

I can remember what happened so clearly after my mom dragged me away from the reception. We went back to the loft in one of the limousines, my mom scolding me all the way. I said nothing. I was so shell-shocked from losing my V-card and then having the man who took it ask me to move in with him.

Was there a connection between Simon and me? Wasn't there a connection? Whatever chemistry is, whatever instant attraction causes two people to fall in love at first sight, I know that stuff happens, because it happened to Simon and me.

When Simon asked me where I stayed so that he could send someone there to collect my stuff, I knew in my heart that I made him happy. Being with each other made us both happy.

So I don't need to emphasize how deeply unhappy I was when my mom scolded me and kept a beady, watchful eye on me until we got on the plane back home. My dad stayed behind to go visit his folks in the care home in Marfa.

Brody and his wife Alma looked after the bed and breakfast in our absence. I can remember how my brother hugged me and then pushed me away from him, staring into my eyes. "You okay, Sissy? You seem a little bit… I don't know… deflated."

I tried to act normal. "Deflated like an old balloon, Boetie? That's not much of a compliment!" Boetie is a South African slang word for "brother." My siblings and I liked to use slang terms because they always made our mom angry.

My fake upbeat attitude seemed to fool my brother. After giving me a pat on the back, he stepped back and began discussing business details with my mom.

Alma was pregnant and blooming. Her dream was to buy a small holding close to the Cape Peninsula Wild Game Reserve and set up an animal hospital. She's Afrikaans but speaks English too. Which is a good thing because the Maitland family is not big on being bilingual!

My parents can speak Spanish and understand a few words of Afrikaans, but leave the Afrikaans side of the business for Alma to run.

This is a good thing because most of the English-speaking South Africans have left to return to the countries their parents or grandparents originally came from.

"Howzit, Carrie?" Alma hugged me. "Good to have you back home. Hey... can I talk to you for a minute, please?" She looked over at my mom to check if she had noticed our conversation, but Mom and Brody had their heads together, looking down at the laptop screen.

"Sh-sure, Alma." I followed her all the way down to the bottom of the garden where the herb boxes are kept. It's our usual cover if we want to talk privately. If someone asks us what we are talking about, we tell them it's about herbs.

"Carrie," Alma says, rubbing her tummy bulge and looking down at it with a loving expression. "You know you can always talk to me, right? I'll never tell a soul. I'm invested in your happiness, but I can also see you have grown up into a beautiful young adult. I would never try to squash that out of you."

I waited for Alma to make her point. It was hot out here in the garden. The grueling South African sun beat down on my head.

"Did you become intimate with a man at Miles's wedding?"

"What?!" That got a reaction out of me. "Why are you asking me this?" Alma did not say anything back. She just crossed her arms and waited. Eventually, I had to confess. I was blooming with love and pride from having slept with the hottest guy at the wedding.

"Yes. I did. Please don't tell Mom or anyone else. I said I wasn't feeling well so that I could stay at the hotel with him."

Alma shook her head. "Hotel weddings. Such a bad idea—all those bedrooms. Did you use protection?"

"No... but it's okay because no one gets pregnant the first time they have sex, Alma. Everyone at school says so."

My sister-in-law's eyes got big. "What about disease? How could you know if he is clean?"

Swept away by my teenage crush, I giggled. "Believe me, he's clean. He's cut, you know, down there. Oh my God, Alma, it was so lovely. I want to see him again, but I guess I'll have to settle for texting for now."

"He gave you his number?"

I explained to my sister-in-law the problem. About the lies and being dragged away by Mom before I could say goodbye. I got all teary. "I left him sleeping so peacefully.... Oh, Alma, we were making plans for me to move in with him and—"

"No, Carrie. You're wrong. That man had plans with this 'Caron Leslie' person. The moment that poor man finds out how old you are, he's more likely to call his lawyer to start planning his defense! You're not eighteen yet! What were you thinking?"

Plucking random flowers of lavender and thyme off the bushes, I whispered something about love at first sight.

That made Alma laugh. "Love? Bullshit! What was his name, Carrie? And for your sake, I hope he wasn't also lying about it."

Shaking my head, I denied her accusation. "No way. He told me everything about himself. And I found out from Mom who he really is because he was Miles's best man—Simon Sterns."

Alma clutched her belly with shock. "Carrie! No! That's your brother's boss. Your brother's best friend!"

Pouting, I kicked out at the grass. "I don't care. We're in love, Alma. I have to get back to him."

Grabbing my shoulders, my sister-in-law gave me a shake. "Now just you listen here, Missy! You are going to pretend it never happened. You got that? Leave the poor man with a little dignity if you say you love him. The last thing Simon Sterns needs in his life is a scandal involving the underage sister of his Logistics and Applications Chief!"

Pushing me towards the patio sliding doors, Alma continued to scold me in an under-voice all the way back to the steps. "And go put some cover stick on those love bruises on your arms and neck, Carrie. You're lucky that Mom didn't notice—because she's under the illusion that you are still her good little girl!"

But I could not forget him. I lost weight. I couldn't sleep. I cried into my pillow at night, desperate to feel his strong hands pulling me into a fierce embrace, his deep voice murmuring in my ear as we planned our futures together and talked about our past.

Sometimes, I would just lie in bed, staring at the ceiling, whispering his name over and over again as I tried to make some sense out of the passion he caused to grow inside me. "Simon Sterns. Simon Sterns. Mr. and Mrs. Simon Sterns."

It went on for months like that. I wrote my exams and finished school. And then one day, I decided to stop dreaming and start doing. I called Belinda. I would be able to con her better than I could Miles.

"Hi, Belinda. Sister. Can you hear me okay? It's Carrie Maitland here. I'm calling to say thank you for the wonderful bridesmaid gift you and Miles gave me."

Every bridesmaid got a memento locket shaped like a heart. They had been specially engraved and arrived by courier a few weeks after the wedding. Mine said "to the best little sister in the world" on the back.

Belinda suspected nothing. "Thanks, Carrie. I hardly got to see you. Miles and I got your thank-you note, but it's nice to hear from you. I was sorry to hear you were sick after the ceremony."

Giggling nervously, I spun yet another lie. "Yes, apparently some bug was going around. It must have been all that air kissing and stuff. This guy helped me get home, Belinda. I would love to thank him too, but I don't have his contact deets. I was wondering if you could help me connect with him."

Belinda sounded distracted. "Sure, what did he look like? Or do you have a name?"

"H-he was your best man, Belinda—"

My new sister-in-law clucked her tongue with irritation. "Don't talk to me about that prick! He left us one speech short! Yeah, I know a bug was going around, but he should have put on an adult diaper, or something, and sucked it up!"

Trying to stifle my laughter, I managed to reply. "I dunno, Belinda... those pants the guys were wearing were pretty tight."

"His name's Simon Sterns. He's the boss, fuck him. He doesn't deserve your thanks."

It bursts out of me. "Please let me thank him, Belinda. He was so kind to me—" There's a break in my voice and I was on the verge of crying. "You see, he made an effort because I was alone. And I can't find him on any social media or anything—"

Belinda sounded bored. "Fine. Send the thank-you card to the company, care of myself, and I will make sure to give it to Simon personally. But I promise, the no-good prick doesn't deserve it."

Only staying on the line long enough to give me her address, Belinda hung up.

Simon never replied to my letter. Or any of the other ones I sent afterward. I blamed myself up to a point, but then I stopped caring. Being ghosted by a man who took your V-card tends to do that to a woman. It was like I was some kind of a love lobster—an animal that develops a hard outer casing to protect it from hurt.

Stern hurt the teenage me really bad. That's where the hard kernel of hate inside me comes from. My love lobster outer layer bottled that up nice and tight for me.

But the moment I saw him again, I knew the love was bottled up inside me too. And for now, the love is winning.

When I wake up on the jet, we are close to landing. "Has my beautiful girlfriend been burning the candle at both ends by any chance?" Stern wants to know as the jet taxis to the hangar slowly.

Stretching and covering my yawns with my hand, my eyes twinkle at him. "Thank you for dropping me off at Cape Town, Stern. I'll catch up with you in Pretoria, okay? Text me the name of the hotel."

I can see he is surprised. "Pretoria? Aren't we sticking together like we planned?"

It's time for me to put the kibosh on that. "Stern, I love you. I love my brother too. And I am grateful for your constant vigilance in protecting me. But this is my town. I know my way around it like the back of my hand. I don't need you to escort me here. I need to see my family alone, Stern. Surely you understand that?"

Slumping back into the soft beige leather seat, Stern regards me keenly, his blue eyes like lasers, raking me up and down. "Isn't it time for me to meet the parents?"

Throwing back my head, I laugh. "Not unless you want to lose your Head of Logistics and Applications. Don't forget you told Miles you were going to Dubai."

As the jet starts the descent to land, I wait for Stern to agree to what I am laying down. He has that stubborn look around his mouth and his jaw is set in a way that shows he's ready to disagree.

Chapter 25: Stern

Now & Then

I can see that Carrie is anxious and I don't want her to be. "Sure, sweetheart. I'll tell the crew to escort you through Customs. See you in Pretoria. A heads-up would have been nice, that's all."

She gives me that dazzling smile of hers and then kisses me. It's not a sensual kiss. I love it when Carrie is all enthusiastic and spontaneous, like a cute kitten playing with a ribbon. "Thank you, Stern! You are my knight in shining armor!"

I watch as she clambers down the steps, moving to the golf cart as the steward carries her case.

She's wearing those sexy high heels she knows I love, so I called ahead for the golf cart.

Carrie is all grown up. From the expensive products she uses to keep her hair so glossy to the sophisticated cut of her cream-colored rib knit Peter Do dress, she is a woman now. I met her on the cusp of womanhood and helped push her over the edge.

If only she had not lied to me. If only I had been able to track her down before things got so complicated. I would have swept her off her feet and married her the moment she turned eighteen.

I decide here and now that I will no longer allow my bromance with Miles to get in the way of my romance with his sister. He can just shut up and learn to live with it or move on down the line.

Sure, Miles and I have been there for one another and he's going through a bit of a rough patch right now. But he has no right to dictate the terms of who I can love.

The steward climbs on board. "Miss Maitland has gone through Customs, sir. The pilot called ahead for a town car to be waiting for her on the other side of the Arrivals gate."

Thanking him with a nod, I don't say anything about flying onto Pretoria. I'm all fired up and ready to go in, guns blazing.

"Keep the jet in the hangar. I'm going through Customs here too." Not batting an eyelid, the steward goes to tell the pilot. Leaving my luggage on board, I sprint for Customs. Fortunately for me, I manage to fall in with another private flier who eases me through Customs with them.

I don't want to catch up to Carrie—I want to follow her.

She keeps insisting her family hates me, but I bet if I got the courage to visit they would end up seeing how right I am for their daughter. And I want to drop a word in the Maitlands' ears about lightening up their constant fearmongering and overprotectiveness too!

How bad can it be here anyway? Yes, the squatter camps, called 'informal settlements' in South Africa, are bad. The camps begin almost as soon as the taxi leaves the airport and continue until the Cape Town suburbs.

It's so strange seeing the juxtaposition of poverty and suburbia together. But the middle-class areas are showing signs of wear and tear.

Peeling paint on walls. Roof tiles faded by years of bright sun and no upkeep. Cracked fencing and potholes dot the roads. Thinking back to when Miles and I came out here a few years ago, I can see a distinct difference.

It's sad. The country has so much potential and the most beautiful wildlife in the world, but it looks like a wreck.

I know Miles's old address. He might have chosen to make the States his permanent home, and who can blame him, but he remembers his childhood here fondly. I guess it was different for him because he was male.

"Hey, Boet," my driver doesn't take his eyes off the road as he talks, "what are you visiting Simon's Town for? Holiday?"

"I'm here to visit family." It sounds nice being able to say that. Everyone in South Africa is either a "sister" or a "boet" or "boetie," meaning brother. I guess it's their way of saying that they are all in this together.

"What do you do?" I can see the driver glancing in the mirror at my lack of luggage and pristine Italian designer suit.

"I'm in security. I make sure the bad guys stay away."

The man sniggers. "Easier said than done. We have tried everything in South Africa, but my auntie's house was burgled last week. They took the microwave, TV, alles." He moves his head on the word alles—meaning they took it all.

"I don't do that kind of security. More upscale. Believe it or not, but the more money someone has, the more likely they are to be made a target."

"Your family must be proud of you, Boet," the driver says as the highway flashes past.

Family. I remember growing up at the orphanage. The endless competition to be first in line to get food. The rules and strict discipline. The harsh punishments.

No one can tell from my accent now, but I grew up in the South. A place that feels like a nightmare to me. How I had to hide my head under the sheet to escape the mosquitoes until it got too hot underneath them. Then I would pull the sheet back for the biting to start all over again.

I was always a large boy, but gangly from lack of food, so no one considered me a threat.

"Y'all get to the back of the line, Si." The eldest boy would push me out of line, giving me a little kick to show me he meant business.

We were a motley crew of rejects. Every single one of us with a crack-addicted mother and nonexistent father. I put up with the bullying from the age of three until I turned nine. When the latest eleven-year-old bully tried to pull the same shit on me, I fought back.

"C'mon, Si. Why you got to be so uppity? Get to the back!" A hard shove pushed me out of line. But that time I straightened up and pushed right back. I was skinny, but it was all sinew, strong as whipcord.

"Reckon I'll stay at the head of the line if it's all the same to you." And when he pushed me again, I popped him in the nose. Apparently, my fist felt like the knob from a walking stick when it broke the bridge.

From then on, I made sure all the preschoolers got their meals first before the older boys ate.

It made sense for me to go on protecting by signing up for the Marines. My Southern accent faded, becoming nondescript as I learned to blend in with the rest of the recruits. My physique and height had gone gangbusters in high school as I fought my way up to the top of the totem pole.

I played sports well enough, always on defense, and in the Marines, I got to do it for real. Defend.

By the time I began training to join the Military Police, I was generally described as a stone-cold killer. I wasn't all the time—only when I needed to be.

And now I am cursing the fact that the taxi can't drop me off at the Maitland's guesthouse like a normal person. I ask the driver to leave me at the corner. This makes him whistle.

"Sir, please. It's too hot. And it's uphill. Yus-sis, man, you'll cook!"

He's concerned for me because I paid him double in dollars and told him to keep the change. I have often heard Miles say "Yus-sis." It's the Afrikaans pronunciation of "Jesus."

"I'll be fine. Thanks for the lift. Go well."

I wait for him to do a U-turn and drive away before I set about doing reconnaissance. It is my mission to get Carrie's family to welcome me with open arms, but I'll take anything at this point.

Walking up the narrow dirt road, I reach the end of the Maitland's property boundary. There's a footpath trail cutting through the bush in front of me, so I use it to climb the slope.

Finding a spot under the shade of a line of blue gum trees, I decide it's the best place for me to wait to spring my surprise on Carrie. Leaning against a boulder with my arms folded, I watch for her to come out onto the patio.

This is one of the most interesting aspects of small South African towns. You are only ever a few blocks away from hardcore outback bush. The grasslands are called the "bushveld," and the more forested, rocky areas are called the "bundu," meaning the wilderness.

Because the Maitland home is on the outskirts of the suburb, the house is only a stone's throw away from the complete wilderness: long grasses, scrubby trees, and the special fauna and flora kingdom called "fynbos."

Observing the Maitland's building, I can see it's got massive security. Electric fencing, CCTV around the perimeter, intercom at the gates. I have never felt more like an outsider than I do right now. I could wish for nothing more than an invite to go inside.

There is no guard, and I get the feeling that the CCTV is just there to monitor movement and light because the camera is not set to scope out all the angles.

There's a rustle in the bushes, and a bird emerges on a branch, looking at me sideways to see if I'm good for some food. Digging in my pockets, I unwrap a crumbled cracker from the jet and throw it. In the distance, I can hear the rumble of a waterfall. Far away, but somehow not far enough, I can hear the bark of a baboon scout.

This is such a beautiful, fragrant spot, I can understand why the Maitlands are proud to call it home. Tourists must fight tooth and nail to come and bide a while here.

The house is built into the hillside, so that the guesthouse is on one level with the Maitland house and garden below it, overlooking the waterfall's valley full of fynbos and wildlife.

The sound of voices tells me the patio door is opening. Carrie comes into the garden with a cool drink in her hands. A small boy follows her, and then another two after him. It's crazy, but they all have red hair and they are all holding presents.

The boys look so cute as they roughhouse in the garden, bickering over whose present is best and occasionally coming over to Carrie to have a sip of a cool drink or have her rub sunscreen on their skin.

Am I feeling sad that I never got to experience growing up like this as a kid? You bet! I feel cheated and furious at those responsible, but that is all water under the bridge now.

I think about how it sculpted me, molded me into the man I am today, and I relax. Picking up my phone, I call Carrie.

I watch her tell the kids to be good as she gets up and goes inside to fetch her phone. I like that she didn't take her phone outside with her so that she could give all of her attention to the kids.

"Hi, Stern? Are you in Pretoria already? That was quick."

"No. I decided to stick around in Cape Town. Any chance of a date?"

I watch as she holds one finger up to the three boys and begins to edge over to stand next to boxes of herbs in planters. "Stern! You can't! I can't. I mean, you must know that you can never show your face around here."

I'm shocked by her outrage. "Jesus, Carrie! Why would they hate me? I'm your boss."

A little boy with bright red curls runs over to where she is standing. I hear Carrie saying to him. "I'm coming, Marcus. Just wait, okay?" Then she comes back on the line. "You can't come here, Stern. I haven't told my family about us yet."

It's time for me to come clean. "I think you're making a mountain out of a molehill, sweetheart. Turn and look left."

I see her whipping her body around and looking to the right, holding the phone to her ear. "Left, left. Towards the waterfall." I am using a lightly teasing tone because I need her to know that my being here is not the end of the world.

We are both wearing sunglasses: me, Ray Bans. Carrie, Chanel. But it doesn't matter because our eyes lock on one another just the same. I'm sitting on the incline, above the wall's line of sight, in precisely the same position a sniper would choose if he wanted an easy shot.

I might be almost half a Klick away from her, but Carrie recognizes my black suit and blue shirt. Raising my hand, I wave at her.

I hear the little red-haired kid's voice and see him come over to her. "Who are you talking to? Who are you waving to?"

The kid is at that age when he's got a lot of questions about the world. Carrie sounds stressed. I can hear it in her voice when she hisses into the phone.

"Stern! You can't come here. Listen, my family knows it was you who took my V-card at my brother's wedding!"

Chapter 26: Carrie

I am panicking so badly that I can feel my heart galloping like a runaway pony. I should have known this was going to be Stern's play all along. He wants to take our relationship to the next level, and this time he wants to do it with my parents' blessing... but that is something my parents will never give.

"So?" Fortunately, he sounds as if he is in a reasonable mood. "You were a few months short of your eighteenth birthday. That's not exactly the end of the world."

But all I can think about are those three little boys playing with their new toys in the garden. "It's not that—" I try to explain. "It's how you treated me afterward. They will never forgive you for that."

Even from almost five hundred yards away up the hill I can see Stern get all riled up. He sits straight, clamping the phone to his ear with aggro body language clearly on show.

"Will you at least give me the chance to explain to them in person, Carrie? I'm not a coward. I didn't even know you were Miles's little sister or what your real name was until a month or so ago."

"Come and play with us! You be the bad guy!" the little boys gamboling around behind the trees call out to me.

"Please can we not do this now, Stern?"

A wave of relief washes over me as I see him standing up. "Sure. My bad. Can you please call me a cab? I'll be out of your hair as soon as I can go."

This is what I wanted, but the way it is happening is not what I want. "Stern... I'm sorry. But you had a very small window of opportunity to do the right thing four and a half years ago and you missed it. I'll see you back at the hotel tomorrow, okay?"

I'm talking to dead air. Feeling like a balloon with all the air let out of it, I use my search engine to call a cab company to the Maitland Guesthouse. I try not to cry as the tall, well-built, dark-suited figure under the blue gum trees begins to walk back down the road not looking at me.

***

When I see Stern at the hotel the next day, he is somber. It makes my heart bleed to see how hurt he is from my rejection. Dropping my case, I run over to him with my arms outstretched.

"Honey! Do you forgive me? I just could not face the drama of introducing you to everyone on this trip."

He hugs me close and I can feel him inhaling my perfume. His body relaxes as we embrace.

"There's nothing to forgive, Carrie. It was my bad for overstepping the line."

I want to kick myself for being so mean to him when he was only trying to make up for what happened so long ago.

"Come on. The car is waiting to take us back to the airport." He picks up my case and waits for me to walk out before him. He's sad, and it's all my fault. If only I had told him the truth from the start… but then he never would have fucked me and my life would be completely different.

The drive back to Cape Town International is quiet. I try to fill in the gap with nervous chatter. "People come from all over the world to see the traditional huts painted with Ndebele patterns. Did you know that, Stern?"

Shooting me a small smile, Stern raises one eyebrow to show me he's interested in hearing more, so I continue.

"The tribe of the Ndebele came from all over Southern Africa at one stage. Their fondness for decorating houses, pottery, clothing, and walls stretches back to the eighteenth century. The patterns were originally used to communicate the homeowner's status and standing within the community—tell a story about the occupants."

"A bit like those brownstones that stick a marble lion outside the mailbox?" Stern asks me with one of his gorgeous smiles."

"Bingo," I said, returning his smile. "And what I love about the art form is that it was originated and applied by the women of the tribe. The higher the status of the occupant, the more intricate the pattern would become to show that the man could afford to have many wives working on the painting!"

That makes him laugh. "Ha! Carrie, that's amazing. But all of the patterns you are using look intricate."

I nod. "Yah. The Amasumpa motif means courage and strength, and it has elements of spearheads represented in the design. The iSekhetho motif means unity, good luck, and harmony."

"I knew I made the right decision in handing this project over to you, sweetheart." Leaning over, Stern takes hold of my hand and suddenly everything seems right in my world again.

Squeezing his hand, I shift on the seat to be closer to him. "I can't wait to show you the traditional Ndebele patterns for real, Stern... and thank you for being with me on this trip. It means a lot to me."

We have healed our rift by the time we reach the airport. What have I done to deserve such a wonderful man in my life? He might have done the wrong thing all those years ago when he never bothered stepping up or following up on our one-night stand, but his behavior now is really helping me forgive him.

It is a short flight from Cape Town to the massive Johannesburg-Pretoria metropolitan area. It is like a different planet compared to the Mother City of Cape Town. It is in a different province for starters, but because it is in the middle of the Southern Africa plateau with the warm Indian Ocean currents creating dry winters and rainy summers, it has a completely whacky climate and geography as well.

"God, it's so yellow." Stern is looking out of the window at the miles and miles of grassland and rolling hills beneath us.

"The Pretoria rural area is like one large game park," I tell him. "All that yellow grass on the hills—it feeds the cattle."

"I've seen something like this before," he tells me. "It is similar to the Great Plains—only with cattle instead of buffalo."

"It's not temperate." I like being able to share my local knowledge with Stern. "But it has a very hot, dry climate because it is on an elevated plateau. And the area is way more populated compared to the Great Plains. The dominant tribe here is the Xhosa."

"So do we have to travel further inland to reach the Ndebeles?" Stern is starting to sound genuinely intrigued.

"Yah. I am going to try and hook us up with a local tour guide when we are at the hotel. You booked one at a hotel close to East Pretoria, right? That will give us the best access to the village of Mapoch."

Mapoch is about ten miles outside of the city of Pretoria. It is a Ndebele village dedicated to tourism and cultural education. Stern shoots me a questioning look. "Yeah. But do you mind me asking why that is? What's wrong with us staying in Pretoria city central?"

This is no time for me to sugarcoat it. "The inner cities can be bad. You don't want to stay there. All the nice hotels have moved outside of town and the suburbs."

He looks surprised, but not shocked. I see that look on so many visitors' faces when they begin to learn the harsh reality of African life.

"The divide between the rich and poor gets wider every year, Stern. As a country, we are where India was seventy years ago. With a free population divided into different tribes and cultures, but one that has zero education because of the new ruling government siphoning away all the funds. And unlike the forgiving Indian mindset, the mindset in South Africa holds a lot of anger and resentment."

"At least India invested in its future by ensuring most of the kids went to university," Stern comments dryly.

"That is not the African way," I try to explain. "For hundreds of years, the local people relied on tribal units with a big chief in charge of everything. And then the settlers came and ripped that working system away from them. When the settlers finally loosened the stranglehold the old government had on everyone, it was natural for the local people to go back to trusting a tribal chief. No one was prepared for how corrupt someone in charge can become when their friends and neighbors hand them power and money on a plate."

"This I know," Stern agrees. "But that's a global problem, believe me."

The sun hits like a hammer as we walk down the airstairs. I blink and put on my Chanel sunglasses. The humidity is indescribable.

I can feel the sweat begin to drip before we settle into the car and the drive to Pretoria begins. This is my country, and I already have the South African search engines installed on my phone, so it is me who calls the tourist guide company.

They arrange for a guide to meet up with us at the hotel in the morning. If I'm honest with myself, I am looking forward to spending the night with Stern in a five-star hotel room overlooking the endless vistas of African bushveld.

But it is not to be. Stepping out of the bathroom, I let the towel drop before climbing into bed with him.

"This is a luxury," I whisper in his ear, taking great pleasure from stroking the beautiful muscles on his chest and stomach. "Just you and me alone with no one to interrupt us or judge us...."

Stern continues to read the stats off his tablet for a beat before laying it down on his torso to look at me. "But I'm judging us."

Pulling away from him, I ask Stern what he means by that. Picking up his tablet again, he dismisses me entirely. "I don't have a family, Carrie. Family means so much to me that you wouldn't even believe it. And until you choose to let me into the family side of your life, I don't think we should continue our physical relationship."

I can't let it go. I have to show him how much I love him even though our timing has been so off. Rubbing my naked breasts against his body, I duck under the sheets and start sucking his cock. He gets rampant so fast, so I know he still wants me.

His cock rears up like a thick serpent as I lick his knob and suck his balls. I know that if I peek above the covers, the tablet will be gone.

Moving my hand between my thighs, I start to caress my clit. The thrill of it makes me so turned on that I know I am only a few featherlight strokes away from coming.

I feel Stern lift my ass to lie on top of him and his warm mouth begins to lick me out as I gobble his tasty cock with relish. I want to tell him how amazing it feels to have him suck my pussy while I eat his throbbing shaft.

I love how the veins bulge as I wrap my hand around it and jerk him off. I can tell from the way he is thrusting inside my mouth that he is close to coming, so I use his mouth and tongue for stimulation as I come hard.

The sticky come squirts into my mouth. The spasms last for a long time, which is fine by me because I am still coming as well.

But when we are finished, Stern picks up his tablet again as if I am not even there.

***

I am ready early the next morning. I didn't have anything else to do last night except sleep next to Stern with his back turned to me. Somehow, I have to make this right, but I don't know how.

Looking in the mirror, I check that my outfit is comfortable and practical. A loose khaki shirt with the sleeves rolled down. Long cargo pants with a utility belt that holds a water bottle. Brown socks tucked into old hiking boots.

I've worn this outfit for the last ten years every time I went out into the bush. A battered old hat with a pull-down net completes the ensemble. This is not the time for a fashion statement.

Stern doesn't have much to say to me as we go down to the lobby. He's dressed in a similar outfit to me, but he makes it look so hyper-masculine and rangy that it's almost as if he owns the outdoors look.

All he said by way of chatter in the bedroom was good morning. So much for our romantic holiday.

It's a long, jolting trip to the closest Ndebele settlement in Mapoch. We have our own hire car. A black SUV Land Rover.

We follow the tour guide with Stern silently driving. The guide is very helpful showing us around once we get to the village, but we keep a respectful distance so that it doesn't look like we want to stick our noses into the people's day-to-day normal life.

The villagers are so kind and welcoming when they see me taking photographs. I watch Stern follow some of the children to the small gift shop. I don't know what he buys in there, but the children come out squealing with joy.

We are invited to have a late lunch at the small restaurant that serves visitors. It's proper traditional food: meat cooked over a woodfire, griddle bread, and a thick tomato, green pepper, and onion sauce the South Africans call "monkeygland sauce" for some strange reason.

"The most significant design elements of Ndebele geometrical patterns are lines—which represent purity and pride, triangles—which represent houses, and zigzags—representing the famous Mpumalanga lightning and thunderstorms we get around here. And, of course, the black, yellow, red, and green colors."

The guide moves around the village perimeter that has been demarcated by a grass fence called a boma before continuing.

"Black symbolizes the spirit world because there is still serious ancestor worship in the culture. The color white symbolizes cleanliness. Red stands for power and passion, and yellow is for fertility, hope, and happiness. Green is for farming. Before paint, the Ndebele used clay, mud, and manure to create their colors."

Stern has mentally and emotionally checked out again, so it is up to me to thank the guide. "Thank you. I think I will stick around and take a few more pictures if that is okay." I shake the guide's hand. "Please accept this as a small token of our appreciation."

I give the guide a tip in dollars because the South African Rand currency is very volatile. She thanks me and goes back to her car, but she hesitates.

"I was not joking about the famous Mpumalanga thunderstorms, Madam. And it looks like one is on the way. Please, won't you follow me back out again? The roads are kak."

Kak is a famous South African word for shit. "We'll be fine, thank you." I wave her goodbye. "Don't worry about us. I might not sound it, but I'm actually South African. Cape Town."

The guide guns the engine and gives me one last warning. "Cape Town is a paradise compared to this region, Madam. Be safe."

Chapter 27: Stern

A roll of thunder follows the stark streak of lightning that flickers across the evening sky. In the last few days, I have come to understand my best friend's mindset a bit better. I can see why Miles wants to have kids.

I can remember saying to Miles a while back. "You're getting a divorce over a dispute about having kids? Isn't your love for one another enough without bringing kids into the equation?"

Miles had given a definitive shake of his head. "I can't go through the rest of my life with only a partner as my family, Bru. Belinda is just someone I happened to meet and fall in love with.

She's not my blood. And just because I love her doesn't take away from the fact that I don't like her anymore. I can't. Not after she changed her mind over such an important issue."

I mentioned the fact that not every woman was able to have children, which seemed a bit hard-hearted of Miles in my opinion, but he didn't budge.

"Then we should be able to adopt together. Someone to carry on the family legacy is important to me, Stern. But to take the option off the table completely is a deal breaker for me."

Finally, I can understand what Miles was going on about. I want a family. I want Carrie too, don't get me wrong, but when I saw her at the house with those three little boys running around the garden with her, my heart longed to join them.

I've been grumpy for so long because maybe that's my brain telling me it's time to settle down and start working on that family I've been wishing for all my life. But I can't do that so long as Carrie keeps shutting me out.

"We better get going before the storm overtakes us," I say to Carrie as she takes another photograph.

"I'm nearly fin—"

Another clap of thunder drowns out her reply. I see mothers coming out of the brightly colored huts, calling for their children to come in out of the approaching storm. By the time the last child scuttles inside, the first few large drops of rain have started to fall.

Finally, Carrie puts away her phone and we head back to the car together. Glancing down at my phone, I see it's nearly six in the evening. Time flies by when you're blocking out all the things you want to say….

Closing Carrie's door, I run around to the driver's side, clutching my ranger hat so that the strong wind can't blow it off. My shirt is drenched by the time I close the door on my side.

"I'm starting to understand why the local people have so many lightning patterns as their symbols," I said, cracking a little joke as I press the starter. "Let's hope this SUV can handle rain on the road."

"This isn't rain," Carrie replies gloomily. "This is a deluge."

She was right. No matter how fast the wipers flicked the rain off the windscreen, a sheet of fresh drops took its place. It was hopeless trying to make progress back to the main road.

There was no cell reception, so we were having to use road signs for guidance, and like the rest of the country's infrastructure, that was missing too.

"They steal the road signs for money. The metal gets recycled for scrap," Carrie said in a gloomy voice. "I don't like this at all, Stern. We have zero visibility and don't have a clue where we are or where to go."

"Think we should pull over?"

Carrie shakes her head. "No way. I don't want to be stuck out here in the middle of the night. That's even worse."

We sit and chat about our options for a while as the engine idles softly. "I think we should drive forward along this road slowly," Carrie reasons aloud, "and then the worst thing that can happen is we encounter another vehicle. I'd rather do that than wait in the dark on the side of the road."

My training kicks in. "Sheltering in place is recommended, Carrie. I can drive into the bush if you are worried about someone criminal finding us parked on the roadside."

"But I'm hungry... and most of the water in my bottle is finished. I just want to get home."

I let her convince me because I can see that Carrie is not handling this situation so well. Telling her to keep trying to get a signal on her phone while it charges, we drive on.

After half an hour, it's clear that we are headed in the wrong direction. We must have missed the road back to Pretoria in the dark or else the road sign was stolen. I can't get a bead on our surroundings because every feature is obscured by rain and darkness. Carrie can read the worry on my face.

"We're screwed, aren't we?" I can hear the fear in her voice. If this was the backwaters of some two-bit town in the States, we would have a fighting chance, but out here, it's different. But I don't tell Carrie that.

"Best we pull over, sweetheart. Before this cloud break washes the road out from underneath us."

Our pace is so slow now, we could walk faster. I can't risk running into a stray antelope or some other poor nocturnal animal. Checking the gas gauge gives me no concern. There is still just over half a tank.

"Sure, okay. Let's do that," Carrie said, giving a defeated sigh. "I have no idea where we are or what direction we should be heading in."

I speed up, looking for a side road or driveway we can park in, but all we see on either side in the fleeting headlights is mile after mile of bush.

I must have been going about forty miles an hour when it happened. Carrie screamed, her eyes straining to look ahead as I scoped from side to side, looking for a turnoff.

"Watch out!"

A line of small boulders block the road lane ahead of us. They have been positioned at that perfect point in a dip in the road so that the line of sight is obscured for the driver.

I can see in the headlights that they are big rocks, some bigger than a gridiron helmet. Someone had to have been busier than a beaver carrying all of them to block the road. And they did so for a specific purpose—to disable every normal car except a hardcore off-road vehicle.

The Land Rover crashes over them. The chassis seems to give a loud groan as the rocks scrape the underside. Some serious damage is being done there.

Gripping my wrist, Carrie screams at me. "Keep on driving, Stern! For the love of God, keep on driving!"

I am slowing down because I want to check the chassis. "Carrie, what happens if those rocks damaged the brake line?"

Her silver eyes are wide with fright as her nails dig into my wrist. "Drive, Stern! If you stop, they will get us."

I don't need any more explanation or encouragement than that! Gunning the engine, I shoot the SUV forward. Not daring to take my eyes off the road, I ask for more information.

Carrie is panting with fear. "They place rocks across the road to break the car.... When the car stops, they catch you. They have guns, spears, knives.... They use anything to intimidate you into surrendering... and then they kill you."

"What the fuck do they want?!" I can tell from the way the car is shaking and hiccupping that the engine has been damaged. Maybe the fuel line or the brake fluid.

"They want the car. That's a no-brainer. But then they keep you alive and torture you to get your bank codes and fingerprints. Once they have those things, they kill you so that you can't report the crime."

"Who the fuck are 'they'?" I am seriously concerned now. This has turned into an extremely dangerous situation.

"Tsotsis, Stern. Even you must have heard of those gangs in the States."

I am urging the car to continue, but the engine is sputtering and I can tell a piece of the engine is dragging on the road. "Yes, Carrie. I have heard about tsotsis. They are the most dangerous local gangs in the world. Ruthless killers without remorse, killing indiscriminately, but with a special hatred for anyone with money."

"Yah," Carrie says miserably. "How many kilometers ahead of them do you think we are now?"

I don't have the heart to tell her that we are a pathetic five kilometers away from the stones at best. "We better ditch the car before it starts going slower than a running pace, what do you think?"

Carrie gives me a hopeless look and then nods. "Are they running after us? Maybe they have called off the hunt because of the rain."

My face is grim as I reply. "Carrie, if a gang of murderers have gone to the trouble of hauling several tons of rocks to block the road, then I think I would be right in saying that they are not going to be put off by a thunderstorm."

I want to hug her, to reassure her that everything is going to be all right, but I've never been one to preempt the odds. I need to scope out the land first before I can make a judgment call.

My mind is made up. Swinging the wheel to the left, I drive off the muddy road and into the bush. The car seems to complain about the sudden change of terrain. The engine coughs and splutters some more and then cuts out completely.

I'm out of the door in a flash. "Come on, Carrie. Bring your water bottle and unplug the charger." Popping the trunk, I take as much kit as I can with me wrapped up in one of those tarps they lay down to stop the dirt from getting trekked in: tire iron, jumper cables, gas can, jack.

Taking my hand, she follows me back to the road and over to the other side. "I thought you said we should shelter in place." Carrie has to shout above the drumming sound of the rain. I am guiding her deep into the bushes on the opposite of the road to where the car is.

"If they want the car, they can have it. If they want us, we are going to make that impossible for them."

Because I am so tall, I can see the flashlights bobbing over the road as our pursuers race after us on foot. I don't tell Carrie this of course. "Come, sweetheart. Follow in my footsteps and don't worry. Everything is going to be all right."

By now the flashlights have reached the SUV and are roving over the landscape, looking for us. The hunt has begun....

Chapter 28: Stern

We speak to one another in low voices to keep our spirits up. "Soften the way you pronounce any sibilant words, Carrie," I tell her, "because the s sound carries the furthest at night."

Carrie is fighting to keep calm. That can't be easy as we tramp through the tall grass. Some of it is so high it reaches to my waist. I understand how nerve-racking it must be for her, because she can't see where her feet are landing. It is completely dark all around us as the stars and moonlight have been blocked by rain clouds.

"You want me to lisp?" Carrie wants to know, but she is already softening her sibilant sounds by saying "lithp'" instead of "lisp."

"Yeah. Sibilant words travel the furthest at night. It depends on which way the wind is blowing, so we better do it to be on the safe side." I'm softening my s sounds too now.

I go first, beating a way through the grass, hoping the noise my boots are making is covered by the drumming rain. I manage to get my bearings every time there is a flash of lightning. My training proves to be very helpful now, because my nerves are relatively steady. I have the will to survive so I can bring Carrie safely home to her family.

We might be in alien territory, but the rain will have sent even the most dangerous animals to seek shelter. And that is something we should be doing soon too. The last thing I want to have to handle is a snakebite or lion attack.

"I see a rise on the horizon," I tell Carrie. "We should head for that hill and set up watch on the incline. We have a better chance at getting a signal there."

Carrie doesn't reply. She must have a lot on her mind right now, probably wishing that we had stayed in the safe environment of New York. I'd take a concrete jungle over a real one any day. But I am worried about her family. They will be expecting a phone call from her tomorrow morning so we need a signal for that.

No one will miss me if I am gone. Sure, Miles would be bummed out and possibly a few of my clients. But the only person special in my life is with me right now, and that is why we have to fight to survive this.

The wet shirt sticks to my body, and I begin to worry about us keeping warm. So long as we are walking as fast as we are right now we can stay warm, but we can't walk forever. I hear Carrie stumble and curse behind me, so I halt.

"We good?" What's the point of trying to stay dry now? The flicker of lightning shows me how pale and bedraggled Carrie's face is. Soaking wet strands of hair stick to her cheeks and forehead. Droplets of moisture run down her nose.

"I'm good, Stern. Don't worry about me. Let's just get to the hill."

I shake my head. "We can't do that while the storm is raging. The chances of us being struck by lightning increase if we climb the hill. I'm trying to avoid all the tallest trees as it is."

Carrie nods and makes a small circle with her finger to show me that she is ready to continue walking. Using my belt, I strap the small plastic gas canister to my back so that the funnel can catch water. I make sure Carrie's water bottle is uncapped too before we carry on walking.

The landscape is eerily quiet once the rain begins to taper off. After about an hour, the sky clears and the moon comes out. The steady drip-drip of water running off tree branches surrounds us. In the long time that we have been walking, the foliage has changed.

The grass has gotten shorter and denser. Lots of clumps and tufts of grass for us to fall over as we get closer to the hill.

"Oh my God! I am so tired." I hear Carrie trip and stagger. I go back to help her, but she waves me away. "I'm fine, Stern. Please tell me that we are close to the koppie now. I think I must need glasses or something, because I can't see a thing."

"Koppie?" My voice is a question.

"It's what we call a hill here." Straining my eyes, I search for the outline on the horizon. We are much closer now because the outline is large. Slipping my wet arm over her shoulder, I give Carrie a comforting pat. "We can't be more than five klicks away now, sweetheart. You are so brave for coming this far. Only a few more miles now."

After one long shuddering sigh, Carrie wipes her face and trudges after me. "Did I tell you about the time a gang of tsotsis did this to a tourist bus? When the bus stopped, the gang climbed on board the bus and held up over fifty American tourists at gunpoint. They came to this country to enjoy a pleasant safari trip and ended up losing everything."

I want to keep her focused and upbeat. "Don't you worry about those tourists. Insurance would have them covered."

"That's not the point," Carrie insists. "I am struggling to see an upside in trying to fight this.

Maybe we should just leave our phones and wallets in the grass for them to find and they will leave us alone. They have the rental car. We have nothing left to give them."

"We will talk about this later." That is all I have to say. "We can recalibrate the mission parameters once we have found shelter."

Carrie gives a little snort of laughter. "You sound so serious. Not talking without lisping. Finding higher ground. Mission parameters.... I mean, what are mission parameters even?"

As pleased as I am to hear her laughing, I keep focused on the job at hand. "They are to stay alive and find a way to rescue ourselves, Carrie. I have no doubt that the only reason why that busload of tourists was not eliminated is because the gang did not want to waste ammo."

She stays quiet after that. I hate to be a grump about it, but I need Carrie to understand how bad our situation is right now. One misstep and we are toast.

A trill of birdsong breaks the silence. "I can't believe that we have spent the whole night trekking away from the scene of the crash." I can tell from the way that Carrie is speaking that she is flagging badly and close to exhaustion.

"It's a good thing," I say in an encouraging voice, "because I will finally be able to tell which way is east."

But when the rosy dawn begins to break on the horizon, it brings bad news with it. The hill is an escarpment. The only way we can climb higher than the grass and bushes is to scale the rock face. One look at Carrie and I can tell she's reached the end of her reserves of strength.

"I can't," she pants as we crawl as high as we can up the loose scree. "You go up, Stern. I'll wait here for you to come back down."

We aren't talking much anymore. Me, because I understand how bad our situation is, and Carrie, because she doesn't have the strength.

"Hunker down on the rocks here and I'll climb up alone." I hate leaving her behind, but we really need to find a cell tower signal and get a lay of the land. "Stay out of the sun and drink your rainwater sparingly. Every drop counts."

"Every drop counts," Carrie repeats after me, a faint smile lingering on her lips. She gives me a little wave as I begin to scale the rock face.

It's not as easy as it looks. What advantage I have from being tall and strong I lose because of my weight.

"Are you okay?" I hear Carrie's voice hiss up at me as I accidentally kick loose a small rock.

"Yes," I have to grunt, I am panting so hard. "Keep your voice down and stay hidden."

The sun is high over the horizon by the time I reach the edge of the escarpment. Pulling myself over the last rock, I roll onto the surface, groaning and breathing in fast gasps. Up here, I am getting a taste of how hot it is going to get later on.

That's how it is out here in the African savannah: blazing heat during the day and cold at night. And when the weather isn't doing that, there are always the thunderstorms.

After catching my breath and wiping the perspiration off my face, I crawl to the edge and look over the landscape. I am not going to stand up and make myself a target for the gangs to see.

All there is to see for miles around is grass and bush. Interspersed into the scenery is the occasional koppie or cluster of boulders, but other than that, there is nothing. No sign of civilization. I see movement, but it is only a herd of antelope grazing peacefully in the distance.

I am starting to get a better understanding of where we are, though. We should be heading southwest, with our faces against the sun. Northwest, from what I can remember from looking at the Ndebele village on the GPS system, heads into even thicker bushland and rough terrain.

We must have hiked over twenty klicks in the rain last night. I am so proud of Carrie for doing that. The rain helped. All we had to do whenever we got thirsty was open our mouths. Walking in the heat might be different.

I have only a third of the battery power left on my phone and no reception. Carrie has less than ten percent of battery left, but she has two bars of reception. It must be because her phone was bought in South Africa.

Using some of the precious battery power, I search for the emergency police number, shielding the screen with my body so that I can read the details. "One-oh-triple-one. Easy enough to remember."

I dial the number. It just rings. I check the battery. Only five percent left. I don't know if I should hang up and redial or hang in there. There is no information voice to tell me where I am in the queue.

Finally, someone answers. "Emergency Hotline. How can I direct your call?"

"I'm not sure of my location, but our last stop was the Ndebele Village of Mapoch. Mpumalanga. We need help. Our car broke down after it was sabotaged by a youth gang. Our last known stop was somewhere along the R568, heading for Kameelpoort. Put me through to the police please."

Silence as the controller searches for information. "Putting you through now."

The phone rings again for a very long time. For Christ's sake! It's got to be almost eight o'clock on a Wednesday morning. How busy can they be?

I start to sweat again from sheer desperation. "Kwaggafontein Police. This is Constable—"

"Hey, please listen. Our car was sabotaged during the storm last night. Youth gang. My partner and I had to run into the bush to hide. Can you send a helicopter to scout for us, please. We are on the escarpment—"

This time it's me who is cut off. "No, no, no. No helicopter, Boss."

Biting back my words of frustration, I maintain my calm. "Can you send a rescue vehicle, please? We left the road during the night, so I am unsure of our position, but you can call the car hire and get the last known GPS. It's based in Pretoria—"

"No, we got no police cars here. No petrol."

"B-but you're a police station. How can—"

"Come to the station, Boss. You can make a statement here and get your case number. Easy. Quick."

It feels like I have dropped through a rabbit hole to a different world. "We can't. We are stranded on the escarpment in the bush. We are being hunted by a tsotsi gang—"

"Tsk, how! That's dangerous, dangerous. You must come to the station and make a statement. We got no cars here. Only the police chief and he is busy."

I am losing my faith rapidly. "We must have walked into one of the Nature Reserves because there is no sign of a cell tower—"

The phone cuts out. The battery is dead. Carrie and I are alone without any help coming from the outside.

Chapter 29: Carrie

I wake up when Stern drops onto the ground in front of me like some kind of cool superhero after climbing back down the rock face.

"All you need is a cape and a pair of tights and you are sure to get your own franchise, honey." I stretch and yawn and then smile up at him as he stands up straight.

Stern is smiling too, but I know that he is forcing himself to. "How are you feeling after that grueling hike last night, sweetheart? Good?"

He offers me his hand and I can't help letting out a small moan when I stand. "Ugh. My muscles are killing me. Dozing off while leaning against a pile of rocks is not recommended."

Trying to peek at his face to see his expression, I have to ask him outright, because Stern is unreadable. "Did you manage to get a signal?"

"I turned my device off to save the battery, but I know they can use it to trace us so I guess we will have to leave it on. Your phone died." He gives me a brief rundown of the useless conversation he had at the top of the escarpment.

I try to be Zen about it even though I am desperate to speak to my family and let them know I am all right. "Typical rural police stations. They have no money because the police chiefs always take all the funding. It's the African way."

Stern replies with biting sarcasm, "I am fucking sick and tired of the African way, Carrie. How many tourists have been targeted and murdered by fucking gangs in the last twenty years?"

"They usually pick local people to rob and murder actually, so it doesn't make international news. But a lot of the farmers have been murdered, which is sad. It looks like they haven't followed us. That's got to be good." I can't help being a little bit upbeat this morning. The sun is mild and my clothes are dry. Not everything is hopeless.

"If those fucking little bastards think that they can mess with an ex-Marine Navy SEAL combat specialist and walk away from it, they better think again!" Stern growls, glowering at the horizon with his eyes narrowed.

He steps next to me, searching my face for some sign of what emotions I am feeling right now. "Carrie, I swear on my life that I will protect you. Even if we have to hike out of here on foot, even if we run into trouble, you have nothing to worry about. Got that?"

I nod because Stern is very believable. "Did you see any landmarks while you were up there? Get a bead on where we should be heading?'

"Yes." Rubbing his hands up and down my upper arms, Stern gives my face one last check before hunkering down on the sand to draw a kind of map for me in the dust. The rain from the thunderstorm last night has already sunk straight into the ground with only a few puddles left in the rock hollows.

"I managed to make out a radio tower. It is close to being accurate as a marker to the west. Back towards Pretoria. I think we should start walking towards it. Once these hills are behind us, my phone might get a signal."

"H-how far are we talking, Stern...?" I don't want to sound like a Debbie downer, but I'm feeling wretched from the long walk in the thunderstorm. Every muscle on my body aches.

Stern looks grim. "We'll get there, Carrie. Even if I have to carry you on my back."

Looking across the endless vista of baked red soil and waving yellow grass, I don't like our odds. But it's the only call we can make under the circumstances. "Are you sure we shouldn't just backtrack to the road, Stern? I mean, maybe the gang took the car and ran."

"That's heading back towards danger, Carrie. And there is every chance they are stalking us right now. Like you said, the poverty in these areas makes a thousand-dollar smartphone very tempting. They must know we have our devices with us. They know we have no cell phone reception. Rich pickings for some hooligan with a grudge against us."

I am so used to thinking of Stern as the invincible boss man from New York that it's hard to see him exhausted from lack of sleep. I wish I could be more helpful to him, but I know nothing about these kinds of situations.

"Head west?" I suggest.

"Yep. Let's get as many miles under our belts before noon. We can take shelter during the heat of the day, maybe take a nap."

After taking a brief stock of our kit, Stern ties the tarp full of tools over his shoulders and we set out. He sets a fast pace. I have to jog sometimes to keep up with his long, rangy stride.

"Only wet your lips with the water, Carrie," Stern is cutting through the grass ahead of me, leaving me to follow in his wake. "We have to conserve our resources."

Sometimes he uses the tire iron like a machete, swiping the grass with it before sticking the tool back into his belt. The man is relentless. His steps seem to eat up the miles and I do my best to keep up. He offers to carry me, but I give him a small smile and tell him I am all right.

Looking up at the bright blue sky to see where the sun is positioned, I request a stop after a while. "We must have been hiking for hours, Stern," I gasp, collapsing into the shade provided by a small boulder. "Please can I have a sip of water now?"

Joining me next to the boulder, Stern puts his arm around me. "You are the most amazing woman; you know that, don't you? I had you down as a complete diva because of all those complaining emails and texts you would send Miles, but I was so wrong."

The water feels like liquid gold as it flows down my dry throat. "I don't write diva-ish messages to my brother!"

"Oh yes, you do. You blamed the toxic work environment at Sterns for the breakdown of his marriage because you said the company is not pro-child or pro-family."

I stick to my guns. "Well, it isn't. You said so yourself. There is no time in your life or the company for such insignificant additions."

Stern gathers up his outrage to disagree with me, but then suddenly he gives up. "I'm so tired, I can't remember what I said in the past, sweetheart. What can I say? I was a big grump. If I close my eyes for a quick fifteen-minute nap, will you stand guard?" He turns his phone off and looks at me for confirmation.

Even though I am exhausted, I promise Stern I will stand guard while he catches some sleep. Using my back, he leans against me and closes his eyes. It gives me the perfect opportunity to stroke his hair and stare at his ruggedly handsome face.

"I do love you, Stern." I am talking half to myself and half to him. "But our history is so complicated. I hope we can jump over the hurdles that are facing us."

I could not stop thinking about how distant he was from me after the last time we had sex. Sure, he basically allowed me to fuck his face to get my rocks off while I sucked his delicious cock, but it's not only his cock I want in my life. I want his heart too. And I don't know if Stern would be totally invested in that because of that darn complicated history of ours.

Pulling the net of my hat down over my face to stop the flies crawling over my skin, I settle back to watch over Stern while he sleeps....

***

We both wake up and find out it is late afternoon!

"Carrie!" It is Stern shaking me awake. "We need to put in some serious hiking before nightfall. Come on!"

Scrambling to my feet, I start to apologize, but Stern cuts me off. "It doesn't matter, Carrie. You were tired, I understand. Let's get going."

As I take one more small sip of water from my bottle, Stern holds his hand up in a fist shape. Even I know that means I must be quiet. And then I hear it too.

A harsh male voice calling to another. "Basondele! Basondele!"

Is the sound traveling so far because of the silent bushveld surrounding us? Or are they really close? I am trembling, beyond terror. The tsotsis have managed to hunt us down.

I see Stern quietly turn on his phone and wait for it to boot up. Then he uses the translation app to type in a word. Basondele. It sounds like ba-son-deh-leh. The Xhosa word gets translated on the app. They are close.

The tsotsis are talking about us. They know we must be hiding somewhere close by. But we weren't hiding! We just took a nap and overslept! If only I had stayed awake and we carried on walking. And now it is too late.

Turning off his phone again, Stern whispers in my ear. "I am going to reconnoiter where they are. Stay here. I promise not to let anything bad happen to you, Carrie. I love you."

I want to scream for him not to leave me, but he is gone. Ducking under the tall grass to stay hidden from view. I can hardly breathe, I am shaking so badly.

I am only twenty-three years old. God help me. What about my darling little family? How will they go on without me?

Praying is not an option because I have already lost hope. All I can do is clutch the dead phone in my hand and hope that they will go away if I throw it to them.

"Umfazi ulapha!" A loud shout comes from above me. One of the tsotsis has climbed up onto the boulder and looked down to see me cowering there. I know that the Xhosa word for woman is umfazi, so I know they are talking about me.

Shrieking with terror, I throw my phone at him. Four skinny youths pop out of the tall grass in front of me. They are grinning with happiness to find their prey.

"Umfazi onemali." The chief youth approaches me, picking up the phone off the ground and wiping the sand off it. He isn't talking to me. He is talking to the rest of the gang.

"Where is the other one?" the chief youth wants to know. They must have noticed that two seats in the car had been sat in. He speaks English poorly, but I can understand him. He must be the eldest, no more than nineteen or twenty years old. Close to my age but with a world of difference in our lives. They are all dressed in faded shorts and shirts.

They have flip-flops on their feet, eroded from the harsh ground. Probably wearing the old school uniforms they kept after dropping out of the useless education system. Probably the only clothes they have.

They will make enough out of their crimes to keep their families alive, but the main share of the money they make from stealing and robbing will go to the local chief.

Shaking my head, I manage to stammer a reply. "Gone. Different direction." I point back the way we came. "Looking for help. We can pay. Whatever you want. Just don't hurt me please."

Harsh laughter comes from the skinny youths. They are enjoying my fear, talking among themselves about me in a jeering tone. "Where are the keys? To the car? We want the keys."

The keys! Of course, that is what they want. But I have to be sure. "Is-is that why you are chasing us? For the keys?"

The chief gang member shakes his head. Then he withdraws a long kitchen knife out of the back of his ragged pants. "No, we chase you. We kill you. But we want the keys first."

Chapter 30: Stern

It's best these hooligans think that I am further away than I really am. Carrie is handling her first encounter with murderers amazingly well. I think she knows deep inside her heart that I would never let anything happen to her.

The five youths bicker amongst themselves for what seems like a long time. Their method of communication seems only to consist of shouting at the top of their voice, always talking over each other. It sounds aggressive, but I see it for what it really is: an attempt at dominance.

I have seen this before in the orphanage where I grew up. All the kids who came from abusive homes could only speak at full volume. It was their way of being heard above all the chaos.

The biggest youth is trying to turn on Carrie's phone. They don't know the battery is dead until she tells them.

"I'll give you my password. But you will have to take me back to the SUV first to charge the battery." She is talking calmly, low-key, and very neutral.

"The other one. Is she going back there?" the leader wants to know.

"Yah," Carrie nods her head with convincing trustworthiness. Pulling the charger out of her pocket, she holds it up. "See? If we go back to the road, my friend will be there with the keys. We can charge the phone and I will open it for you."

"We know how to open phones without a passcode." The leader sneers at Carrie and I see her shaking with fear.

They have no idea that I am only a few yards away, lying down in the tall grass and constantly observing them. I have to pick the right moment because I can see that three of them have kitchen knives hanging from the canvas woven belts that are keeping their pants up. The last thing I need is a hostage situation.

"The vehicle will be worth a lot more if it comes with the keys. You can have it over the border and into Zimbabwe in a few hours. You won't be able to do that if you have to get a mechanic to override the starter system first." Carrie's voice is steady as she reasons with them.

"That one, the one you drive with, is she back at the car?" One of the youths comes and stands over Carrie, fingering his knife in a threatening way.

"Yes!" Carrie is quick to show her courage and prove that she is not afraid of them. "But you will get nothing if you hurt me. My friend is not stupid. She will not stay by the car if she sees I am hurt."

"We catch you. We will catch her." The leader and three of the youths chat among themselves as Carrie fights to stop her hands from trembling.

They decide to go back to the car. It is their main payoff after all. The leader jerks his head to Carrie, indicating that she must walk back with them.

I figure they want to be out of the thick veld grasslands before nightfall. The sun is already beginning to set in the west. I will take them out as soon as it is dark enough for a surprise attack.

This is a very dangerous time for me. I have to follow close behind the gang without them noticing. Keeping my eye on the thorn tree branches around me, I move every time the wind blows. It disguises the sound of my footsteps.

I have to run crouched over. Yes, I am running. These guys are going fast. I can hear the noise Carrie is making as she pants. Those bastards have taken her water bottle and are forcing her to jog to keep up with them.

When she flags and stops, bending over to catch her breath as she clutches her side, there is always one of the gang to come back and wave a knife at her.

"You! Keep up! You lazy woman! You are all lazy."

He snatches the hat and net off Carrie's head. She cries out, trying to grab it back. "Please! I have to wear a hat. The sun will burn my skin."

But all they do is laugh. This is their land and their turf. They can run for long distances without water or a hat. They think they are indestructible, but I am going to change all of that tonight.

After one hour of hard jogging, the gang breaks for a rest. Carrie hasn't asked for a toilet break, which worries me. It means she is dehydrated. She looks wrecked. Her head hung down with her hair over her face. At least the sun has gone down now.

The sky is lit up with the most beautiful red and orange sunset, but no one is looking at it. One of the youths clutches his stomach and says something.

The other four wave him away from them. I understand the word they are saying. Voetsak. It means "fuck off" in the Afrikaans language. That much Miles did teach me. Literally, it means "use your feet to leave."

Grumbling and swearing in his language, the youth walks deep into the grass to use the toilet. Only, he never gets the chance. Throwing his knife onto the ground, he unbuckles his pants to squat.

My arm snakes around his neck as I pounce on him from behind. "Wrong time for you to lose your knife, buddy," I hiss the words in his ear as I choke him out. He goes limp like a rag doll and I ease him down to the ground so that the sound of his falling body doesn't alert the rest of the gang, not because I am worried about him getting hurt.

Picking up the knife, I use it to cut strips off the tarp. The goon is out for the count but I'm not going to risk him coming back after us. I tie the jumper cables tightly around his wrists and ankles and then use the tarp to stuff his mouth and tie the gag around the back of his head.

Am I worried that he might suffocate while he is unconscious? Not even a little bit. This gang signed their death warrants when they came after the woman I love.

Carrying the rest of my kit in my hands after picking up the knife, I circle back to the encampment. They are all chatting, completely unaware that the hunters have become the hunted. One of the shit heels picks up a small rock and throws it at Carrie.

She cries out when it hits her arm. Laughing like hyenas, they begin to look for more rocks to throw at her.

Quickly scoping out the landscape before the last of the sun's rays leave the sky, I make up my mind. I start moving to the outcrop of boulders next to the encampment. I have to reach the top boulder before they start to wonder when their friend is coming back from his toilet break.

It's the smallish boulder at the top I am interested in. Slotting the car jack into the crevice at the bottom of the boulder rock, I start to winch up the jack. Chewing my lower lip, I pray they can't get a bead on my location from the noise.

The leader says something that sounds like impatience and then points to the section of grass where their buddy went to the toilet. I pump the jack up faster, using all of my strength to lever the boulder up. I keep thinking that the jack will break, but it comes as part of the Land Rover kit so I know it can lift a couple of tons.

I feel the rock shift! The grit underneath it crackles as the boulder begins to tip and finally, to roll. It happens so quickly there is no time to react. I have already vaulted down off the rocky outcrop as the boulder gathers momentum, crashing down the slope towards the gang's temporary camp.

Shouts and screams as the stone missile smashes to a stop. This is all the distraction I need to strike.

Blasting out of the grass, I tackle the closest youth to the ground. As he struggles to escape my mighty grip, I snap his neck with one twist. This time, I let the body fall. There is no more point in trying to hide.

Three left. "Carrie, come and stand behind me." I don't have to tell her twice. Edging around the back, she puts me between her and the remaining gang.

This is what I wanted. No hostage situation.

The leader is concerned, but not nearly concerned enough in my opinion. He must think he still has a fighting chance. He could not be more wrong.

"Give us the keys. Or we will kill the woman." He brandishes the knife in Carrie's direction.

Time for me to bring the fight to them. With the tire iron in one hand and the knife in the other, I step up.

"I'm giving you one chance to throw down your weapons and surrender." They don't take the chance I give them to live. One of the youths takes out his phone and presses a number. I don't want them calling for backup, so I close with them fast.

The guy with the phone goes down first. One swing of the tire iron and he's toast, even though he tries to duck. The other two seem to think this is the best time to take me down. They both try to jump me at the same time.

They both have knives. One more violent swipe of the tire iron and only one of them is holding a knife now. I lash out at the guy without a knife, breaking his arm with the tire iron and slashing with the knife in my left hand.

He cries out, clutching his belly with his unbroken arm. And then he goes down when he sees the slice I have made in his gut.

The leader is left. I'm still not worried, but I am tired. This means so much to me, I know my strength won't let me down now.

"Look at your friends," I snarl. "You have the choice to surrender or join them."

"Fuck you, you rich fuck."

So much for negotiations. I let him lunge first. He's holding his knife like that scene from the movie Psycho, stabbing downwards with it, trying to catch my arm or neck.

His technique sucks, because all I do is block the blow with my arm. As he comes in closer for another stab, I twist my knife around in my hand so that it points upward.

This is the best way to hold a knife during hand-to-hand combat, because when the combatant comes closer all I have to do is slide the blade under his guard. Which is what I do. The knife blade slides in deep under the rib cage. I step back, leaving the knife in there.

The adrenaline is so high that he doesn't even notice that he has been stabbed. I have heard that when the knife goes in, it feels like a punch. A hard blow, not a burning slice.

The sudden drop in his blood pressure is the only clue he gets that his clock is running out. He looks down and the shock is real because he never felt the knife going in.

His chest cavity must be filling up with blood already because he is struggling to breathe. Carrie runs up and throws herself into my arms.

"We must call for an ambulance, Stern! We have to do something to help them!"

"They had the chance to leave and live, Carrie. They made their choice."

But still, she goes to pick up one of the tsotsis' phones to try and dial for an ambulance. I have a feeling that the local chief has taken all the money for ambulances too, but I don't say that. I'm too busy going from one gang member to the other, making sure that they are permanently out of commission.

The leader is expiring first, and he dies with hate-filled eyes staring up at Carrie and me. What a waste of a life. Put someone like him in the Army and train him up, and he would have made a good soldier. But he chose the wrong pathway in life. Or maybe it was chosen for him.

"Sweetheart," I go to hug Carrie who is weeping quietly, "let's hike back to the car. Now that we don't have these sharks stalking us."

"Don't touch me! You're a killer, just like them!"

Chapter 31: Carrie

I can't believe Stern is so casual about taking people out! He reminds me of some kind of Terminator machine, ruthless and completely unemotional. Maybe it's hysteria, but now he kind of scares me.

"Couldn't you have just knocked them over the head and left them unconscious, Stern?" I'm backing away from him, but he just keeps coming closer, his hands stretched out to touch me. "They are dead. Dead!"

He talks to me like he would a frightened child. "Hush, Carrie. Don't give in to survivor's guilt. They deserved to die. I gave them the chance to run away. They chose to roll the dice with an unknown entity."

It feels as if Stern is an unknown entity to me now too! "B-but it is so final." Staring around the trampled grass, I can taste the blood in the air. "I-I want to go h-home," I say, weeping and shaking, in complete shock at what has gone down.

Wrapping his arms around me, he strokes my hair. "Shhh, sweetheart. I'll get you home if it's the last thing I do. Let's head back to the escarpment. You can wait there while I drive back for help."

The thought of being left alone in the vast swathe of veld makes me cry and shake even more! There is a small part of me that thinks maybe this was Stern's play all along. To keep the car keys in his pocket so that the tsotsis would come after us.

But then I remember that it was me who fumbled the ball by letting us oversleep in the shade of the rocks. If we had kept walking, we would have been at the radio tower by now while the youths hunting us were still miles away.

Inhaling slowly, I shut my eyes and try to forget what I just saw. What I need to focus on right now is getting back to the car with Stern and not slowing him down.

It's as if he can read my mind. "I need to get you back safely to your family, Carrie. Those sweet little boys in Simon's Town would never forgive me if I let something happen to their favorite playmate. How would they play cops and robbers without you being the bad guy?"

This is the first time Stern has referred to my family like that. His small joke kind of warms my heart. It is the first time I see a future for us together. It is the first time he sees me as part of a unit.

"Please don't leave me at the escarpment. I promise to keep up. But I'm scared of snakes and wild animals. It's not raining anymore."

I let him hug me close and stroke my hair. My arms hang down and don't hug him back. I guess I'm just not quite ready for that yet.

"I'm going to do a quick tour to see if the one who went for a toilet break is out for the count.

I don't like the idea of one of them coming after us."

I watch Stern disappear into the tall grass and the sound of his boots tramping through the bushes. It's completely dark now, but the starlight and moonlight make dark shadows on the ground. I get totally creeped out from being left alone with a pile of dead bodies.

"Okay," Stern is back. "I checked his wrist ties. He can wiggle out of them if he pulls the cords hard enough. Let's hope he goes back to his gang leader and tells the bastard to stop targeting innocent tourists."

The horror of what we have been through hardens me. "Good luck with that. There will always be dozens more starving, neglected youths to take their place. Like I said, Africa is a hopeless case."

Heaving myself back up onto my feet, I follow in Stern's footsteps. He goes in front with his long, rangy stride, kicking and tramping the grass to scare away any wild animals. It is a lot easier to walk now that the heat of the sun is gone.

Occasionally, I see Stern looking up at the sky. "What is it?" I want to know. "Do you think they will send a helicopter to come looking for us?"

He grins and shakes his head. "I'm trying to work out which way is east from looking at these upside-down stars of yours. The only one I really know is the Southern Cross."

Of course, he would know how to navigate which way to go from looking at the bloody stars! "Well, when you are through being such a fucking Boy Scout, Stern, can you please explain to me why you let us get so lost in the first place if you can do that?"

He doesn't even look at me when he answers. "Because it was raining, Carrie. All the stars were hidden by the clouds."

That makes me feel stupid, so I keep my mouth shut from then on. When I stumble and fall, Stern stops to lift me. He carries me about one or two miles on his back. I think he knows I have reached my limit.

I feel terrible. It's what Stern said. I feel guilty for surviving, guilty for bringing us all the way out here just so that I can take stupid photos of tribal patterns. My heart is heavy whenever I think of those wasted lives. It's difficult for me to remember how hell-bent they were on killing me once they got the car keys.

When I look around, I can see the grass has been trampled on either side of me. As much as I love Stern carrying me—I can hear the steady beating of his heart when I rest my ear against his back—it's time for me to walk on my own.

"Have you found a track?" I ask him as he gently lowers my feet to the ground. He shrugs and sighs. "It was so easy for them to follow us. All they had to do was follow the trampled grass. I think they lost our tracks when we reached the rocky ground by the hill, but they followed the edge of the grass until they could pick up the trampled grass tracks again."

"We made it so easy for them," I say, feeling awful.

Stern is philosophical about it. "What choice did we have? Sit in the car like quacking ducks?"

That makes me laugh. The further away we get from that spot where Stern went ballistic on those young men, the more relieved and grateful I feel.

And then the grass thins and I see the familiar dirt road in front of us, glinting silver in the moonlight. I go into some kind of shock because I simply stand there on the verge, trembling and staring. After this horrific adventure, Stern has brought us to safety, just as he promised.

I see him move to the middle of the road and take his bearings of the landscape. "Stay here, Carrie," he tells me, "the Rover is a few hundred yards down the road."

I am about to open my mouth and tell him not to leave me here alone, but he is already jogging down the road. My legs give out. They feel like jelly. All I can do is squat on the verge and wait.

It isn't long before I hear the sound of a vehicle coming towards me. The engine is making a racket, but it keeps turning over like clockwork except for the occasional hiccup.

I am too traumatized to believe my ordeal is over, so I scramble back into the grass to wait and see what car it is.

The Rover grinds to a halt opposite me. Stern must have superpowers to be able to see where I left the road. "Carrie, we got lucky. The engine started without a hitch after I added the spare canister of oil, but we better take it slow. The chassis sounds fucked. The brake line is hanging loose." He gets out of the door and goes around to open the passenger side for me—ever the gentleman. "Come on, sweetheart. Get in."

We drive back to Pretoria slowly in silence because I am in a daze. I can't wear the seat belt because it makes me feel trapped, so Stern clips it to the seat underneath me. He is gentle, almost tender the way he treats my strange mood.

It shocks me to think that we were one knife stroke away from becoming just another crime statistic in South Africa. Probably not even important enough to make the news cycle.

"It is so much easier to see the road now that it isn't raining," he says to me by way of conversation. But all I can muster up is a series of monosyllabic ums by way of a reply. He leaves me to recover in my own time.

Only when we reach our hotel does it hit me that we are finally safe. Ringing the bell at the reception desk brings the night shift clerk. His eyes get big when we tell him our name.

"Ag, sorry, Meneer, Mevrou. We didn't think you were coming back. We packed your bags and put them in storage." Every Afrikaans person says "ag" when they want to express an emotion. They say it the same as we would say "ach." "Meneer" is the way they formally address a man, like Mister. "Mevrou" literally means "wife," but I am too exhausted to contradict him.

It seems as though our ordeal has finally gotten to Stern as well. His reply is acidic. "With the fucking crime rate in this fucking place, when a couple of tourists don't come back from their daily activities, don't you think that the first thing you should fucking do is contact the police instead of packing up our fucking cases?"

The clerk takes in our dirty, disheveled appearances. "Did you get carjacked? But I thought you came back here in your rental? I saw you guys drive in on the CCTV."

Stern doesn't say anything. He just holds out his hand for a new key card. The clerk seems to read the room and gets busy programming us a new card. "I will bring your cases up immediately, Meneer, Mevrou. Ek is baie jammer."

"I am very sorry too," Stern sighs, rubbing his eyes as he puts his arm around my shoulder in a protective gesture. "It was my own experience that it's no use calling the police either."

The clerk hands us a room card with a rueful smile. "Yah. Jammer, Meneer. Lekker slaap." He apologizes again before wishing us sweet dreams.

Frankly, I am far more likely to have nightmares. The first thing we do is head for the bar fridge and uncap bottle after bottle of water and finally, soda and fruit juice. I feel my stomach twist with shock as the moisture hits it.

Stern pushes the bottle away from my mouth. "Take it slow unless you want to spend the rest of the night in the bathroom."

That makes me smile. "Oh well, that would be the perfect ending to a lovely last few days."

Flicking the end of my nose gently, he returns my smile. "That's my brave girl. I knew it would not be long before you found the sunshine in your life again."

He leads me to the shower and turns on the faucet. The warm water hits me like the most gorgeous waterfall. Piece by piece, I am starting to come alive.

Holding out my hand to him, I show him that I want him to come inside the shower and join me.

"I am not so tired that I won't get turned on by you, Carrie," Stern warns me. How can I tell him that this is what I want? I need to show him how much I adore him and making love is the best way to do it.

"Well, here is the problem, Stern," I say, managing to smile, "my hands are too tired to lather the soap over my body, so I think you are going to have to step up one last time."

He is happy to do so. Pulling his shirt out of his pants, he gives me a glimpse of his tats before sitting down on the edge of the bath to remove his boots, socks, and pants. He's got a few nasty scrapes and bruises, but that must be from climbing up the escarpment.

The next thing I know, Stern is standing behind me, turning the soap in his hands under the jet of water to make lots of bubbles. It feels heavenly when he begins to wash me. God, but I love the way his strong hands massage my breasts, sliding down my aching back to the crack of my ass before applying the soap in there too.

He has expert knowledge about female anatomy because he knows to keep the soap bubbles away from my pussy and clit. When he wants to caress me there, he uses the warm water as a lube, kneading my clit so gently, but with a steady, arousing rhythm….

I feel his cock engorge and press against my butt. He grinds it into me, sliding the huge member between my thighs and then up my butt crack.

"Stern." I am gasping, I am so turned on by his rampant need to fuck me. "Maybe we should wait, you know. We have been through so much."

Pushing the palms of my hands against the shower glass, I arch my back, pressing my ass against him, opening my legs, and bracing myself. My words are saying one thing, but my body is saying something different. He knows this. He can feel how badly I want his cock inside me.

"I fight hard, Carrie, but I fuck even harder."

And with those words, he slides his thick cock into my tight, wet pussy.

Chapter 32: Stern

The moment I am inside her, I know I can't last for long. I just don't have the willpower. Carrie is so hot the way she presents her pussy for me to fuck, just like the sweetest, tightest gift-wrapped heavenly slit.

I only managed four or five pumps before I cum hard. The view is so amazing, with her legs spread open and her ass arched up for me to access. As I cum, she lets me finger her clit.

After I finish squirting my jizz deep inside her, I drop to my knees with the shower faucet water cascading down on us. Burying my face in between her thighs, I get to work with my tongue on her clit.

Carrie grabs my hair, pulling on it as I lick her out. I give long, rough licks, driving my tongue deep into her pussy before sliding it over and around her clit. She is loving it, loving what I am doing to her.

I can tell she is close, but I am not finished yet. Using three of my fingers, I finger bang her pussy as I lick her clit, darting my tongue lightly over the hard little nub hiding between those plump pussy lips of hers.

She starts to cum over my face, rubbing her pussy slit over my mouth and moaning softly. It lasts a long time, but I let her ride it out, happy to bring her to fulfillment in my mouth and on my tongue.

Carrie collapses on the shower floor afterward, half laughing but still moaning. "Oh, Stern. That is the best way I can think for us to celebrate our lives... thank you."

She is so beautiful; how could I ever let her down? I would have gone mad if any harm had come to her. "Whenever I fuck you, Carrie, it feels as though my body is stuck in the middle of one of those thunderstorms. I swear I saw flashes of lightning when I came!"

We laugh together and kiss. It is now that I make up my mind to ask Carrie to marry me. I know that my life will never feel complete unless she is with me.

***

I want to ask Carrie if I can contact her parents. I need to ask her father's permission first before I put a ring on it. I never had parents to guide me or tell me they were proud of me, but I have to respect Carrie's wishes when it comes to contacting her family. It's a pickle, and I have no way yet of getting around it.

We try ordering breakfast in bed from the hotel kitchen, but they tell us we're too late to order from the breakfast menu. "Sir, you can choose any item off the à la carte or brunch menu, but the breakfast buffet has unfortunately been removed already to make way for luncheon guests."

So we order sandwiches and milkshakes. We skip coffee so that our body clocks can return to normal. I need to carbo load some massive amounts now that my body is finally rehydrated. I finished two sandwiches and fries easily.

Our phones charged overnight, with us sharing the use of Carrie's charger. She is reading the replies to the text messages she sent last night.

"Did you tell them?" I ask her, shifting to lie on my side as I pick at the last pieces of sandwich on the plate. "I mean, I just need to know what to say if Miles chats to me about it."

She shakes her head sadly. "No. I said we got a flat tire. My family... I don't want them to worry about me."

Makes sense. Leaving Carrie to finish her breakfast, I go down to reception and ask to speak to security. An Afrikaans man introduces himself to me and respectfully says good morning, but I can see that he is curious.

"I'm going to need a statement and report from the hotel. Our rental vehicle got wrecked during the storm two nights ago. We were ambushed—rocks placed across the road in the dark—the chassis got badly damaged."

The security man is on the level immediately. "I hope you managed to keep driving, Meneer. If you had stopped, those blerry tsotsi gangs would have bliksemmed jou dood." I get the picture without having to understand the Afrikaans words: bliksem is a lightning strike. Would have struck you dead, that's what he said. Strike us dead. Carrie would be dead if I hadn't taken control of the situation and my training hadn't kicked in.

"We got back on the road… eventually, but the car is fucked."

He looks at me and reads what happened in my stone-cold killer eyes. He looks down at my hands and sees the scrapes and bruises. I don't bother hiding my injuries, but nor am I proud of what I did.

Protection is in my blood and don't get me started on how I feel about those I love being under threat. I might have been the world's biggest grumpy billionaire for the last five years, but love has made me lethal too.

We discuss my options. No, I am not prepared to drive back to Mapoch to make a report to the local police station. Nor am I willing to hang around and wait for someone from the nearest police station to hitch a ride to the hotel, because again, there are no police cars available.

"It's bad, Meneer," the hotel security head tells me, "the police are corrupt. They accept bribes from the gang leaders and pretend no crime happened. Most of them can't even understand English. Tourists have a tough time out here if they are unlucky enough to be targeted."

"That might be a good thing to add to your tourism brochures, don't you agree? Although I don't blame anyone for not being able to speak English—it must be hard out here with three languages to learn at school."

The manager laughs. "Three? I wish! No, Meneer, South Africa has eleven official languages the children have to learn at school. It's crazy, but all the different cultures and languages must be respected and represented. It makes our justice system and education system very complicated. It ends up with no one being able to master any one language properly for the most part."

We decide to return the vehicle to the rental company and for me to take the hit for the damage on my credit card.

"Life is too short at the end of the day for you to waste time filling in forms, don't you agree, Meneer?" the head of security suggests.

"Buddy, you have no idea how short it nearly was." I give him a tip in dollars and go back to the room to wait for our new rental car to arrive.

When I get to the room, Carrie has fallen back to sleep. It gives me the chance to look at her to my heart's content. In my eyes, she is flawless.

Her long, thick, red hair spread across the pillow is like a curling comet's tail blazing through the night sky. Her pale eyelids flicker as she dreams. One hand sticks out from under the covers, sunburnt and pink after her ordeal in the bushveld.

If only I had looked harder for her after Miles and Belinda's wedding. If only I had not given one good goddamn about Miles's tantrum about me fucking someone connected to his family. Now I am stuck between a rock and a hard place, trying to find some way to make it up to the woman I love.

I should have known she was the one. I was just not the same after that night we spent together. I took Carrie's V-card, and where I come from that really means something to a man. It was for better or for worse for me from that moment onwards.

Moving to the patio so that my voice doesn't disturb her, I get on the phone to beef up my alibi. And while I do it, I promise myself that this will be the last time I lie to Miles about me and his sister.

I have killed for this woman lying in the bed behind me, so now it is time for us to make a long-term commitment to each other.

It's midafternoon when Carrie wakes up. I hear her yawning and stretching before she gets up and goes to the bathroom. Miles has sent through quite a few emails and messages for me. It makes me pause to think what my security business might be like without him, but that's going to have to play out depending on the way it goes.

My phone pings to let me know that the new car is downstairs. "The rental replacement is here, sweetheart," I shout loud enough for her to hear me through the door. "Be back in a sec." I like having someone to tell things to. I don't even have a dog to talk to back home.

I go downstairs and sign all the paperwork, taking responsibility for the damage to the car. The extra insurance I took out will pay for most of it, thank God, but the excess is still high enough to make a normal man's eyes water.

But I am not an ordinary man. I am a billionaire and want to pay to make this all go away. My priority is Carrie.

A brochure catches my eye in the lobby. Feeling spontaneous, I flick a text over to Carrie. Taking a quick drive into Johannesburg. Won't be long. Choose a place where we can have dinner. S.

Pretoria and Johannesburg are both capital cities, joined together by a long urban area called the Midrand. Pretoria is head of government administration and Johannesburg is head of government business. But all this means is a chance to enlarge the government and create more teats for corruption to suckle on.

I don't care anymore. I don't want Carrie ever coming back here. I want us to buy a big house in the country together—upstate New York or Connecticut, somewhere like that—and for her family to visit us for as long as they like.

The GPS tells me that I have arrived at the place I saw in the brochure. They are expecting me. The cameras scan me and I am asked to produce my ID before I have even stepped off the parking lot sidewalk. As a security expert, I approve.

An elegant woman steps over the thickly carpeted floor towards me with her hand held out. "Mr. Sterns. Lovely to meet you. How can we help?"

"Thank you. I want to see some diamonds, please."

They don't know my budget, but this saleswoman already has a fair idea about what I am prepared to spend. They saw the top of the range rental car I used to come here, and they can see the hand stitching on my shirt and my made-to-measure suit.

And if I am not mistaken, she also notices the jacket lining is made with a custom woven silk. If her careful observation takes in the cuts on my hands and fingers, she doesn't say anything. She has already made up her mind about what to show me.

"Of course, Mr. Sterns. Ordinarily, I am sure Mr. Clifton would love to consult you about the latest security measures we might use on our premises, but a diamond is always so nice to own, isn't it?" So, she knows who I am, therefore she knows how much Sterns & Co. is worth. I am kind of relieved because now we can get down to business.

We move to sit in a private booth. It is luxurious. Not too cramped, but not too spacious to make it feel social either. "Can I ask you a few questions first, please? Is the diamond for a lady?"

The image of Carrie asleep in the hotel bed flashes across my mind. "Yes."

"Gift or engagement?"

My mind is made up. "Definitely engagement."

The elegant saleswoman smiles. "Lucky lady. What is her coloring like, do you mind me asking?"

"Long, red hair, pale skin with golden freckles sprinkled across her nose and cheekbones. Heart-shaped face. Silver gray eyes. Wide smile. Slim."

Getting out my phone, I show her an image of Carrie. In it, she is laughing, throwing her hair back behind her shoulders, wearing one of her cute summer dresses. "She is like liquid sunshine, her personality, that is. A sunny, sparkling, sunbeam full of love and optimism with a wide streak of hidden strength."

I know that I am sounding goofy crazy in love, but I don't care.

"Thank you, Mr. Sterns. I won't be a moment. What would you like to drink?"

I request a bottle of room-temperature still water. I take a few sips as I wait.

The saleswoman returns with a small tray of stones. My eyes are dazzled when she opens it.

"These stones range from four to eight carats. An acceptable size for a diamond ring that is to be worn every day, but is also an investment. But we don't recommend it be worn to bed at night. We can craft an eternity band out of matching diamonds if you like, for the lady to wear in bed. For the lady's coloring, we suggest a platinum setting. Or white gold if you prefer."

The stones range in color from pure blue-white diamonds to yellow, amber, orange, brown, and red.

"We have pink diamonds in-house as well, but they can be a challenging color for a redhead to pull off."

I remember the subtle shimmering pink color on Carrie's cheeks after her shopping day with Gail. I know that is one of the most special colors for her. "Show me some pink diamonds, please. The woman I am going to marry can definitely pull off a challenging color."

A new tray comes in, full of pink diamonds.

"The pink color is determined by several factors," the saleswoman tells me. "Hue, whether the color is on the red side of the color spectrum or the blue side of it."

Thinking back to the blush on Carrie's cheeks, I know what she would like. "The hue must be on the blue side of the pink color spectrum."

"Of course," she pushes a line of stones closer. "The next is saturation. How dense and intense the pink color is in the stone—is it a pale pink or a darker pink? Lastly, is tone, how much light is allowed through the cut stone because that is what makes it sparkle."

I am drawn to a pink cushion cut diamond. It is so deeply saturated with blue-pink tones that it is almost a soft mauve or lilac when I hold it at certain angles. The saleswoman holds out the loupe for me to use so that I can check the stone for inclusions. It is perfect, flawless, just like Carrie.

The certificate tells me it was mined in Australia and cut by a master craftsman in Amsterdam. A unique provenance. The saleslady offers to show me a video of the seam from which the stone was mined and the technique the diamond cutter used to create the shape.

"That's the one," I push back my chair. "I'll send one of my men to pick it up. I want it set in platinum. Flick some recommended settings over to my email for me to choose from."

"What about an eternity ring and wedding band to match, Mr. Sterns."

"Yes, that too."

"Your future wife is going to be a very happy woman when she sees her new ring."

I smile and put my card down to pay. The saleswoman lifts it delicately. "You are a man who knows what he likes the moment he sees it, I can tell."

"You have no idea." I grin. "that's actually how I first met my future wife! And now all she has to do is say yes!"

Chapter 33: Carrie

"I feel such a sense of relief to be home safely, Stern." I shoot him a grateful smile. "I can't thank you enough."

We are almost ready to land at Cape Town International Airport, but I have to say goodbye to my family before I go back overseas. I miss them so much when I am in Manhattan. And after what happened to me in Mapoch, I can't wait to bring my family to live with me in New York.

Stern is in a good mood. He shrugged off what happened to us in the bushveld as easily as if it were an old pair of shoes he didn't want to wear anymore. Taking my cue from him, I do the same. I will not allow such evil to rule my memories.

We feel safer the moment we step out to the Drop and Go temporary parking lot. "How come it's so different in Cape Town?" Stern wants to know. He is looking around at the clean sidewalks, litter bins, and brand-new signage.

"The province where Cape Town is situated is ruled by a different government," I tell him. "Think of the differences between California and Florida and you will get a small idea about how different Cape Town is from the rest of the country. The only thing they don't have total control over is the water and power supplies, but the city is planning on going completely off-grid in a few years, so it doesn't really matter."

"Are all the provinces like that?" Our driver is going to drop Stern off at the hotel and then take me on to Simon's Town, which is about half an hour's drive out of the city.

Shaking my head sadly, I tell him no. "Only Cape Town is different. It is the oldest city in South Africa. It was founded four hundred years ago by Dutch explorers who wanted to establish a garden here so they could restock fresh vegetables when they docked in the harbor. The merchants settled here to start vineyards for winemaking. Of course, there was the usual enslavement of the indigenous populations, but the intermarriages ended up creating the most wonderful independent culture of mixed-race people who are now the dominant force in Cape politics. To this day, they are still fiercely independent of all the other shit that goes on in Africa."

"Hey," Stern disagrees with me, "when I look out of the window, I still see shanty towns. It's not rainbows and unicorns here, not by any means."

"Yah, sure, but most of the people living in those shanty towns are not local to the Cape. They came here to work and are happy to live in a shanty town so that they can send most of what they earn back to their families living outside the Cape. I mean, look at the statistics, Stern. Ninety-eight percent of all new jobs in South Africa are in the Cape Province."

That shuts him up. I can see him checking out the smooth tarmac on the highway and the clean streets. It is like night and day compared to what we experienced in the province we just came from.

"When were you going to tell your family that you are not ever coming back to live in South Africa? Manhattan is for keeps, isn't it...? With me."

Stern's question takes me by surprise. Just when I think I have him all figured out, he always manages to shock me. "Umm... I need to get out of Miles's loft first. Things have been so crazy with plotting the mural that I haven't had the time—or the inclination—to go apartment hunting."

He frowns. I knew it wouldn't be too long before Grumpy Stern made an appearance. "Can I tell Gail to set you up in a nice place? She can sort out the deposit and the first six months' rent with your advance payout."

I don't want to have to tell him that I need to choose my own apartment because I plan on moving my family in there as soon as I can. That means it must have safety rails and access to playgrounds and so much more.

"I'll get around to it soon. I promise." I let him take my hand. He raises it to his mouth and kisses it. Sometimes, Stern can be so hella romantic it makes my heart skip a beat!

"Why don't you move in with me? To hell with what Miles thinks. He can't jump ship over such a silly thing."

I think of what happened in the past. And when I remember his apartment, all I can see is the uncovered pool on the patio. The inadequate railings. The fact that Stern's penthouse suite only has four bedrooms, one of which he uses as an office and another he uses as a reading room.

"I think we should live apart until we have made up our minds over how to introduce the idea of us to my parents, Stern."

He kisses my hand again. "Can you do that now, today? Please."

I tell him I will try. This is a touchy subject at Chez Maitland. I can just see my mother's face turning purple with rage right now!

The driver drops Stern off at the hotel and then takes me on to Simon's Town. The traffic is light, and we arrive there in record time. My mom opens the door with a beaming smile on her face.

"Carrie! Thank goodness you got back from the north safely! I swear I couldn't sleep worrying about you on those dangerous roads they have up there." Ushering me down into the family's living area which is separate from the guests, my mom asks more questions. "How long did it take for roadside assistance to reach you? I'm amazed you even managed to find a cell phone signal."

My dad comes into the room. "You mentioned something about going up there with someone, Carrie." He bends over and gives me a peck on the cheek hello. "Who went with you?"

Alma comes into the sitting area. We glance over at one another. Alma's eyes are full of caution. I told her I was here with Simon Sterns. Just like I told her what happened between Simon and me at Miles and Belinda's hotel reception. She knows that my brother's best friend fucked me several times over on the day, and night, of my brother's wedding.

"I'm dating someone in New York, Mom. That's who I went with. He's staying out of the picture for now, because I am not ready to introduce him yet."

My parents shoot looks at each other. They do not approve. I can see that.

"So long as you are not shacking up with him, Carrie," my mom insists, "because you owe it to your family to tread the straight and narrow. You messed up once. Please don't make a habit of doing so. Think of all the money we invested in your education. You can't throw that away."

I confess. "He's staying out of the picture, Mom, because he changed his mind about meeting my family when I asked him to pump the brakes. We didn't plan on falling in love in the beginning—we made that perfectly clear to each other from the start. It just happened, and I am not sorry that it did."

My dad is chewing his mouth like an angry bull. "Oh, so he is an inconsistent man, is he? Well, that does not bode well for your future together as a couple, Carrie! Your family must come first... always come first! I will not have you gallivanting off with this man anywhere you like without thinking about the long-term consequences!"

I hang my head. Alma takes this as a sign to step in. "Let's not be too harsh on one another after the fact, everyone." She puts her arm around me and leads me to the herb garden, saying, "Carrie has a wise head on young shoulders, I promise."

The tears in my eyes sting. "Oh Alma, I'm so tired of the lies. I truly believe that Stern regrets his actions in the past. He wants me and all the baggage I come with."

Alma shakes her head as we go to sit down on the bench under the shade tree. "You looked wrecked, Carrie. Is he taking care of you? I think you have lost weight."

This time, the tears start flowing. Swallowing the lump in my throat, I try explaining. "Alma, he is so brave and so good to me. After the last five years, I can't tell you how lovely it is for me to just be able to sit back and let Stern take the wheel."

Alma is not impressed. "That's the least the man can do after all the shit he orchestrated in your life! And as for him taking the wheel—I'm not sure he even has a valid driver's license for that! I don't understand how you can even bear him touching you after the way he treated you after the wedding."

That makes me smile because no one can understand how Simon Sterns makes me feel. I manage to wipe away my tears and blow my nose with a tissue. "You don't know him, Alma, so I'll forgive you for your mistrust. And...," I lower my voice, "the sex is incredible. In-cred-dib-bill."

Since my brother Brody married Alma, we have enjoyed our girl talk whenever we can. While Alma doesn't get too graphic about what happens in her own marital bed, we sometimes like to compare notes and indulge in a little dirty talk.

"Ooh, tell me more!" Alma is caught hook, line, and sinker. "His online bio pics are gorge! What's his body like underneath all of those tailor-made suits?"

I try and stop myself from going into raptures. "Oh my God, Alma, Stern's body is rock hard in all the right places. He has that perfect V-shaped torso, you know. Broad shoulders, trim waist, and lean hips. Not an inch to pinch anywhere on his body, he is super fit. Like one of those models from Men's Health mag."

Alma is hanging on every word. I think she is starting to understand why I was helpless to resist falling right back into Simon's arms. I continue my raptures.

"Well, I might be lying about one thing. He definitely has a few extra inches to pinch... down there! He is hung like a randy stallion, and he knows how to use it too."

We giggle together, darting naughty looks behind us to make sure no one is coming down the path. "Carrie, I totally forgive you for sleeping with him again. There is nothing better than making love to a man with a good body and a big cock."

More giggles before I continue praising my lover. "He's got one of those effortlessly perfect bodies, you know. He has no idea who his parents were, but they must have been physically impressive once. Such a shame his mom dumped him in the foster home at such a young age."

Alma gets serious again. "Whenever I think of someone doing that to my darling boys, I want to die from sorrow. It's amazing that Simon turned out so well."

"Rigid discipline," I tell her. "He makes time for the gym every day. And when he can't make the time, he swims in his pool at night. So he has an athletic build, but with those recognizable brick shithouse muscles, he got from training as a Navy SEAL. He's still a Marine at heart, I think. I know he fights with ruthless intensity."

Whispering, Alma wants to know something. "How does he make you come? Is he good with his tongue?"

Her question makes me shiver with ecstasy at the memory of what happened in the shower.

"Maybe it's because he was my only lover, Alma, but when Simon Sterns fucks me, it is hands down the most erotic encounter of my life! He does the most pornographic things to me but in the nicest way. He strokes my breasts, but then gives my nipples a little pinch to titillate me. He plays with my nipples with his tongue, and sucks them with just the right amount of pressure."

"Ooh." Alma giggles some more, covering her mouth with her hand.

"He seems to know when I'm in the mood for some rough play too," I continue, my half-closed eyes thinking about what Stern does to me in bed that drives me wild. "If he thinks I'm coming too quickly, he sometimes takes his cock out of my pussy and rubs his gleaming knob on my clit. He tugs my hair if he wants me to suck his cock harder. It is so amazing because it keeps me satisfied without inhibiting my rhythm. I even love it when he slides his cock up and down my ass crack because the thought of what he is doing makes me totally orgasmic! If I forget to play with my clit when we do it doggy style, he always does it for me. And his cock is so yummy."

"Gee whiz, Carrie!" Alma chuckles. "Poor Brody is going to get his brains fucked out by me tonight, I can promise you that! Come on. Let's join the real world. Drive with me to pick up the boys from preschool. I need to cool down a bit."

Chapter 34: Stern

Carrie has a little secret smile on her face when she joins me in the Private Lounge at Cape Town International the following morning.

I stand up to greet her and kiss her cheek. She smells gorgeous, her hair and skin. The subtle scent of her perfume rises from her cleavage, intoxicating and rare.

She has another one of her cute sundresses on and a three-quarter-length coat hanging over one arm in case the fall weather is cold in New York. Her toenails are painted pastel pink, something I noticed because of the pink leather thong sandals separating her toes.

Pushing her away from me, I keep her at arm's length so I can read the expression on her face. "No trauma? We good, Carrie?"

She gives me that dazzling smile of hers. "That bit of R and R with my family was just what I needed, Stern. Thank you."

"Look at you...," I say, hugging her before indicating to the steward that we are ready to embark on the jet. "Using the same terminology as the Marines. R and R indeed."

I want to ask her if she got the time to chat with her parents about me, but I leave it to Carrie to bring up that particular topic of conversation. Half an hour later, we are leaving our horrible South African bushveld adventure behind us as the jet climbs to a comfortable air cruising altitude.

I spent last night trying to limit damage control while sorting out that big mess I left amidst the savannah grasslands of Mpumalanga. Carrie was right about that much. I couldn't leave those bodies to rot under the sun. I used a couple of Miles's old business contacts in security to make inquiries for me.

Turned out I didn't need to worry about completely annihilating the gang. The one youth I tied up and gagged managed to free himself. He ran back to the gang leader, a local politician, and told him the gang had been almost wiped out by a motorist.

When the politician began asking questions and found out it was a heist and carjacking gone wrong, he put the kibosh on ordering a vengeance hit.

For an area that still relies on tourism for a large portion of the money it makes, bringing up the death of a tsotsi gang might give the local folks the idea to fight back. I am starting to understand why some of the luxury vehicles in South Africa have flamethrowers welded to the doors.

Carrie loosens her seat belt and comes to sit next to me. She is so slim, we both fit on the wide seat easily. Lowering the back of my chair, I cradle her head on my chest. She travels using an antinauseant now, which has made flying so much easier.

"Stern...," she can sound like a little girl sometimes. I love that about her. "Yes, Carrie?"

"Why did you leave me all alone after that first night we spent together? I tried so hard to rationalize your thinking, but it makes no sense with the man I know you are today."

Oh shit. I wish I had insisted Miles give me the details of the cute red-haired bridesmaid I spent the night with. I should have shut him down right then and stood up for what I wanted.

"I was a coward, Carrie. An emotional coward. Maybe I was still stuck in that mentality I had in the Corps, you know? The unit comes first. And Miles has always been part of my unit. If I had known your real name, I would have come looking for you, I promise."

She shifts in my arms. "But I told you my real name. Remember? I shared everything with you, and you just blanked me."

Am I losing my mind? There is no way Carrie told me that the night we spent together. I think I know what this is. Over the last five years, Carrie has managed to convince herself that she was the one to make all the effort to try and stay in contact.

Fine, I am going to let her have this. "Like I said, sweetheart, I regret it so much. Let me make it up to you in the future. Okay?"

She doesn't reply. I hold my breath, waiting to see if she has another accusation to make about me. But as always, Carrie surprises me. She begins to pull down the zipper of my pants....

I am so taken aback by the casual way she slides her hand inside the open fly and hauls out my cock that I only have a semi when she starts to massage the shaft. Putting her fingertips to her mouth, she lubes them with spit and then goes back to massaging me.

It feels so good when she kneads my knob, pulling the cut foreskin up and down the shaft. It doesn't take long for me to get fully erect. The veins bulge out and my knob starts to throb as it turns mauve with blood.

"Christ, Carrie, that feels so good when you do it," I say, biting my lower lip, I shut my eyes as her stroking gets faster.

"You like that, don't you, big boy?" God, her voice is so sexy when she talks dirty to me like that. "You want to fuck my pussy so bad, but you can't... yet. Because this time, I am the one in control."

"Yes, don't stop, I'm close."

I feel her hand unbuttoning my shirt as I get ready to shoot my spunk hard. I hold my breath as I cum, my cock spasming and jerking in her hand. This is such a fantasy. I have never cum so hard from jerking off before. Everything feels better when Carrie does it.

Leaving me to use my pocket-handkerchief to clean myself up, Carrie goes to sit back in her chair. "That was hot."

All I can do is agree. I didn't think it was possible, but I am more in love with her now than before.

***

Carrie calls Miles on her speakerphone when we land. "Hey, Bro. I am back. I took some great pics. Do you want me to pick up some groceries?"

Miles sounds cagey. "Hey, Sis. Listen, we should talk."

Carrie holds her finger to her lips to let me know not to say anything. "About what?"

"I'm going steady with Gail. We are a couple. Officially. So... I don't want you staying at the loft anymore."

I can see that Carrie is tickled pink with the news. She doesn't seem to care about not being able to call the loft home anymore. I don't blame her—the bedroom walls don't even touch the ceiling!

"Congratulations, Miles. You guys make a lovely couple. Gail is the best. Don't worry about me. I have somewhere else I can stay."

Miles isn't done yet, not by a long shot. "Just make sure that you are not shacking up with some random dude, Sis. I might have to kick his ass then."

Carrie tries to stifle her laughter as she imagines her brother attempting to kick my butt.

"Good luck with that, Bro. But I can stay at an apartment hotel until I sort something out. Please don't tell Mom and Dad."

I am making angry signs and mouthing the words. "That's not fair! He's shacking up with Gail!"

Carrie shakes her head, mouthing back at me. "He's a man! He can't fall pregnant out of wedlock! That's what my family is so paranoid about!"

"Hello? Are you still there?" Miles is still sticking his nose in our business.

"Yah, I'm still here, Miles. I'll let you know the hotel's name once I settle in. And once again, I am so proud of you for moving on."

After she hangs up, I have quite a lot to say about the unfairness of it all. Carrie frowns me down. "You, of all people, Stern, should understand why my folks are not cool with me living with someone. Doubly so if that person is you. I have to go. Can Gerry drop me off at a decent accommodation facility, please? I would prefer it to be closer to the Apollo on First than Sterns & Co. HQ."

Why is it twisting me up inside to see her walk away from me now? She gives me a naughty wink and a smile before stepping daintily down the stairs. My heart somersaults as I watch her crossing the tarmac.

There are a few things I need to find out before I go back to my penthouse, so I use my phone to call Gail. It is so nice to have good cell phone coverage again.

"Gail. I'm back. I need your help."

"Hello, Stern. How are you? I am fine. And now that we have all the polite chitchat out of the damn way, how can I help?"

"Listen, I know you have gotten tight with Miles while we were away. I'm happy for you. But I need you to please try and find out why doesn't he like the idea of me being with his sister?"

I can hear Gail typing on the keyboard as she talks to me. "Miles doesn't like the idea of any man with his sister, Boss. It's not just you."

A frustrated sigh escapes my mouth. "Okay. Fine. But why? Carrie is twenty-three. She is no longer a minor. It makes no sense."

The sound of typing stops. "I think you should be asking Carrie these questions yourself, Stern. Don't you?"

I swear and then apologize for my bad language. "I am getting mixed messages like you wouldn't believe, Gail. Now she is telling me that she did tell me her real name at the wedding and that I ignored her. It's like she doesn't want to understand how awkward it was for me trying to get the information out of Miles after I stood him and Belinda up during their reception."

Gail seems to take pity on the sound of desperation in my voice. "There is nothing stronger than a family unit, Stern. Miles was telling me that his folks still haven't forgiven him for not making it work with Belinda. These things take time. I'll tell you what. I'll give Brody a call. He seems to be on the level."

"Do you have his number? Won't he think it's strange to get a call from his sister's assistant?"

"Hey, soon I will be part of the Maitland family! Miles is already starting to talk about how many kids we want and where our new brownstone will be. Brody will be fine with me calling him. I will ask him straight out why they are so overprotective of Carrie."

"Gail, you are a woman in a million. Miles is lucky to have met you."

Gail chuckles. "Luck has nothing to do with it. Take two lonely people, tired of the shit show that is the Manhattan dating scene. Add a pinch of sexual attraction and a teaspoon of broodiness. Throw in a strong nesting instinct, the one that makes you happy to spend your entire Saturday mornings at Bed, Bath & Beyond, or Home Depot, and give it a good shake. And voilà! You have one happy marriage. Ain't nothing to it."

"You make it sound so easy, Gail." I give a long sigh. "But that was denied to me from the start because of Carrie's age. I suggested she move in with me, and I didn't even know her real age. I could have ended up looking like a real creep. Or at least like one of those older wealthy men who swan around all the social events with a young girl on the arm, oblivious to how scaly it looks."

"You were only thirty, Stern. It would have looked fine. You make a beautiful couple, Carrie and you."

"Gail, please be a doll and do that right now. Call Brody."

Chapter 35: Carrie

Gail has been put in charge of helping me hire assistants. Every mural painter has assistants. They hand the artist paint when they are up on the scaffolding, mix the right colors, and run errands. The only thing an assistant can't do is take a coffee break for the artist! But they are there to hold the ladder for when the artist needs to climb up and down it.

"I think we should reach out to local art colleges. Ask the dean if there is some way the student can gain credits for putting in some time on the Apollo on First project."

Gail disagrees. "Students are not reliable. Let's stick to a straight hire. People need jobs. Let's put on the application that first-time job seekers can apply. That's more helpful."

My friend seems a little bit distracted today. "Is everything going right between Miles and you, Gail? You're acting differently."

She looks at me, and for one moment, I think the truth is going to come out. But then Gail seems to change her mind about confiding in me. "No, girl. I'm good. Miles is a doll. We fell in love so quickly, I just never realized how much baggage comes with it...."

I give her arm a comforting squeeze. "Is Belinda being a pill?"

"She doesn't know yet. Stern has offered me a full-time position with Mannie Milano so we can get around the 'no dating at work' contract clause, but I love it here at Sterns & Co. It's a stupid rule anyway."

That makes me frown. "Gail, I think you should be on guard. I can remember Miles telling me how much power Belinda wields as head of recruitment. She has access to a lot of private information. So long as the communication happens at work, Belinda has the right to monitor it."

My friend shakes her head. "I have so much going on right now, Carrie, I can't think straight. Do you want me to send the candidates over to you? Or would you like me to handle the hiring?"

For one minute, I am tempted to handle the hires myself. I don't want to add to Gail's burdens. She is looking really frazzled. But I know I will be no good at selecting the right person.

"Please can you do it for me, Gail? I'm sorry to be such a drag, but you are better than me at asking the right questions."

Did I say something wrong? Gail looks really stressed after my request. But she shrugs it off and manages to smile. "Sure, girl. Don't worry. I'll get the best assistant for you. Let's get this mural going ASAP!"

I giggle. "Stern would be so chuffed to hear you use a military term like ASAP, Gail. He was teaching me some of them during the trip. FUBAR. That's Fucked Up Beyond All Recognition. BOHICA. That stands for Bend Over, Here It Comes Again. SNAFU. This one is my favorite because it stands for Situation Normal: All Fucked Up."

She tries to muster a smile. "That's funny, Carrie. Thanks. Talk later, 'kay?"

Yes. Something is off about Gail's mood. That is why we are such good friends. We both see the sunny, funny side of life together. That's how it has always been. My brother better not be giving Gail heartache!

I am tempted to pop in and visit Stern, but I don't know what to say to him if I go there. I'm staying in one of those accommodation hotels, the type of place where Manhattan businessmen end up living after their wives kick them out. My room is functional, elegantly utilitarian even. But it reeks of being a temporary arrangement at best.

Stern wants me to move in with him, but I want to wait. I have to be sure. Once bitten, twice shy.

Every time I step out into the lobby there is always some poor dude loitering there next to the mailboxes, looking to see if his lawyer has written him a letter. So depressing.

I am halfway back to the Apollo when I remember something I wanted to tell Gail. Now that I know my way around the streets, I have no trouble turning around and retracing my steps back to HQ.

But when I see two heads sticking over the top of Gail's cubicle partition, I pull back, ducking into the photocopier section. One blonde head looks like she is leaning against Gail's desk with her hands resting on the edge. The other beautifully coiffed hairdo is turned to show her profile. It's Belinda.

"Just tell me the truth, Gail. What is it that Stern has you doing for him?" Belinda has her arms folded. She looks pissed.

I can't see Gail, but my heart goes out to my friend being trapped by the two women on either side of her chair. "You will have to ask the boss what that was about, Belinda. I am not at liberty to discuss it."

Belinda flicks her hair back and glares. "You work for my department, Gail. And quite frankly, I am sick and tired of you sticking your nose into family concerns."

"When last I checked, Belinda," Gail says, her voice steady, "your divorce papers were signed, sealed, and delivered. I am free to phone the Maitland household in South Africa if I want without asking for your permission first—because they are no longer your family."

Shaking some sheets of paper in front of Gail, Belinda lets rip. "Except you used a company phone to do it! First, Stern calls you for a nice little old chat, and then you call Miles. What the fuck, Gail? You used the company's phones to do it, which makes it my problem! I can only gather you got Miles's family's phone number from him because the next number you call belongs to the Maitlands! Now, I want to know what this is about. Why did Stern call you? And what did you say to the Maitlands?"

The blonde butts in. "And what are you even doing calling Miles's private phone, Gail? Are the two of you dating?"

I might be wrong, but I think the blonde is Samantha Carson, Belinda's sister. They are giving my friend a third-degree interrogation.

Gail is silent. This seems to irritate the sisters. "It says here in black and white that you were connected to the Maitland's line for over an hour, Gail! Tell me what you were talking about! I am your boss. You will regret not telling me, I swear."

My tummy swoops up and down. Gail called my old home. What on earth was she talking to my family about for so long? If it wasn't Belinda asking the question, I might want to ask it myself!

I hear Gail sigh. "I am sorry for using the company phone for the call, Belinda. Please deduct the full amount from my paycheck."

This is clearly not the reply the Carson sisters want. "What did Stern say to you?" Samantha taps the desk with one sharp, manicured nail. "We have made the connection that he is fucking Miles's dopey little sister, but where are you involved in all this?"

I know what they are trying to do. They are trying to wear Gail down into giving a snippy reply so that Belinda can fire her. They might still do that because of the international phone call charges. I wish I could go to Gail's defense, but I want to listen if they have more to say.

Belinda lowers her voice so that no one else in the room can hear her. The cubicle walls are segmented into booths, so there is no way of knowing who is using the computers in their booth without looking over the partitions.

"Gail, I can see from your search engine history that you are up to something. You found accommodation for Carrie so that you are free to come and go at Miles's place, isn't that right? You know that you are not allowed to date within the Sterns & Co. staff without reporting it to me first?"

No reply. I see the sisters shoot one another glances over Gail's head. "But what we really want to know is this: why did you call the Maitlands?" Samantha leans forward as she asks the question. "We looked at the CCTV footage during the call, Gail. You were crying. What the fuck was that about?"

Gail glances at her phone and then puts it in her purse and stands up. "Well, would you look at the time? I believe I am entitled to take a coffee break at ten thirty every work day, Belinda. Now if you would excuse me...."

Gail squeezes past Belinda and heads for the break room, leaving the two Carson sisters alone in her booth. I am hunkered down next to the photocopier, ready to dive behind the machine if the Carsons walk past. Only they don't.

"Quick, Belinda! Do it now!" I hear Samantha read a sequence of numbers and letters out to her sister.

"I'm in," Belinda tells her.

When I risk a look, I can't see their heads anymore. They must be sitting on Gail's chair. "What do her emails say?"

Belinda sounds excited. "Take photos of this one, Sam. It sounds important. And this one. Keep an eye out for the fat cow coming back from her coffee break. Although I am allowed to look through employees' in-house communications whenever I want to, they might have a problem with me checking her private account."

"Who are they going to report it to, Bel?" Samantha sniggers. "The buck stops with you!"

Lots of sounds of camera phones clicking and shocked gasps as they read my friend's emails.

"Oh. My. God, Bel. I can't fucking believe it. This is crazy. How could she have kept this a secret?"

"Shut up and keep watching for Gail coming back, Sam! This stuff is a goldmine. We just have to find a way to use it to our advantage now. We can pretend Gail told us or something."

Samantha sounds grim when she replies. "Oh, you bet your sweet ass that we are going to use this, Belinda. This is clearly what all that secret communication was about. Fuck the Maitlands. Fuck Miles. And fuck Stern too if he thinks he can take me out on one date and then ghost me."

Belinda sounds troubled. "I don't know, Sam. I mean, it's not like he fucked you or anything. He even told me he thinks you are an interesting person, and that he wishes you all the best in your search for a partner."

"Fuck him!" Samantha hisses. "Stern is a stuck-up jarhead with a rod rammed up his preppy ass. He is going to rue the day he turned me down."

"Shut up," Belinda snaps. "We have to strategize over this before doing or saying anything. Come on. Let's go."

I crawl behind the photocopier machine and curl up into a ball in the corner. My mind is in a whirl! What is going on?

I hear the Carsons' high-heeled shoes clack past me, but I don't move out of my corner.

Thinking about what they said about the CCTV, I crawl out of the booth on my hands and knees until I reach the exit. Pushing the door open, I go through it. Only then do I stand up.

I want to know more than anything else in the world why Gail was calling my family in Simon's Town! Using my phone to check my face looks normal and my hair is lying straight, I go back into the HR office.

I can't help it. The first thing I do after entering is look around for the CCTV camera. There is one in every corner, all pivoting on a steel arm to get a good view of all the staff. Fuck. Trying to act natural, I walk to the break room.

Gail looks up when I walk in. She is sitting at a table on her own and her face is tearful. This is the first time I have ever seen my friend less than one hundred percent happy and sassy. The floor seems to lurch underneath my feet.

Does she have some bad news from home that she doesn't want to tell me? But no. I was talking to Gail this morning and everything was fine....

Now that I think about it, Gail was not firing on all cylinders this morning. She looked bleak and confused.

Taking a seat opposite Gail, I reach for her hands. "Please tell me what is going on?"

Gail bursts into tears. My body and mind freeze as I prepare myself for horrible news.

Chapter 36: Stern

The sound of the lobby waterfall trickling into the pool is interrupted when the intercom on my desk crackles. I push the receiver button down. It's security calling from the lobby entrance desk; they basically act like my receptionists since Phyllis relocated to Apollo on First.

"Mr. Sterns, there is a lady here to see you. Miss Samantha Carson. She says it is important."

I am waiting for Gail to get back to me about what Brody Maitland told her when she contacted him in South Africa. Needless to say, I am not in the mood to see Samantha.

I can tell when a woman is more interested in dating my wallet than myself as a person, and she is at the top of that list. Okay, she is a hardcore horndog as well, always massaging whatever part of my body she can lay her hands on, but that's just the cherry on top of the enormous pile of money she sees whenever she looks at me.

Swearing under my breath, because I know that Samantha will be standing right there and able to listen to what I say, I tell the guy to send her up to the mezzanine level.

I get up and walk around to the front of my desk when she comes in. We shake hands awkwardly because she comes forward for an air kiss, but I manage to hold her off by sticking my hand straight out firmly.

"Stern! You've been so elusive lately. Why didn't I see you at the Spike Lee installation opening in Brooklyn? It was right up your alley."

"I was traveling, but thanks for the heads-up. I'll make sure to set aside an evening to go and see it."

We move to sit on the comfortable leather couches in the seated area. I hate playing host. That's one of the reasons why my penthouse is more of a retreat than a place for social gatherings. Growing up in the foster system—with eight kids all sharing a room meant for two—can make a man value his privacy.

"Can I get you a water, Sam? Coffee?" I point to the glass-fronted fridge opposite and then the espresso machine next to it.

"Do you have any room temperature water, Stern? Evian or Fiji?"

"No, because I am not a hotel. It's iced Ty Nant or nothing, I'm afraid."

I get up and move to the fridge, removing a cobalt blue Ty Nant water bottle from the top shelf and then hand it to Samantha. She thanks me and waits for a glass. I sit back down and wait for her to get to the point of this unsolicited meeting. She can drink out of the bottle if she's that thirsty.

"So, Sam. You said this was important?"

She seems to be choosing her words with care. Her fingers are nervous as she tucks a strand of hair behind her ear. "Yes, it is important, but not on my account, Stern. On yours."

Barely restraining an impatient eye roll, I try to frame my reply politely. "I will be the judge of what is or is not important when it relates to myself, thank you, Samantha. You must know that my loyalties are on the side of my best friend, Miles, when it comes right down to it. Your sister is out of the loop now."

A seductive smile tilts her heavily lip-glossed mouth. "Oh, believe me, Sternie. You are going to want to hear this."

Gritting my jaw to stop my impatience and intolerance from showing, I wait for her to get to the point.

Samantha seems to sense that I am rapidly reaching my limit, so she blurts it out. "Did you know that your cute little artist-in-residence has a kid? Carrie Maitland has a bastard living in South Africa."

To say that my world tips over on its axis would be an understatement. I must have gone white, because Samantha unscrews her water bottle and holds it out to me, saying, "Here, Stern. Drink some."

I have so many questions, the main one being this: why am I having this conversation with Samantha fucking Carson?

After drinking some water, I make some kind of recovery. "I don't believe you."

Samantha smirks. "Believe me. I was with Belinda and she overheard Gail talking about it. Straight from the horse's mouth too: Brody Maitland's wife, Alma."

Reaching for my phone, my mind turns circles as I think about who to call for confirmation, but Samantha grips my hand. "It's a secret, Sternie. They have all lied about it. Everyone except Miles, that is. The family kept it a secret from him too. They were sensitive about telling Miles because they know how much he wants kids."

"I have to speak to Carrie, Sam—"

"Listen to what I have to say first! She has been lying to you! She will continue to lie to you, Stern! She's only after your money!"

I shake my head because everything I know about Carrie is telling me that Samantha is lying. But everything Carrie has said to me in the past seems to confirm this. Pieces of the puzzle about Carrie's behavior and what she said are all falling into place. There is only one true question burning in my mind.

"Who is the father?"

"Some random guy who is no longer in the picture. Apparently, they only hooked up a couple of times. She leaves the kid with her parents most of the time. I suppose that is why she came over here, so the poor kid wouldn't cramp her style."

Those three little red-haired boys playing in the garden. Of course! Miles always said his brother Brody only had two small boys, but I never thought twice when I saw three boys playing together. The third kid is Carrie's! Three little redhead boys unwrapping presents.

No wonder she never wanted to introduce me to her family! Carrie must be ashamed of her poor fatherless kid....

Samantha is trying to read the expression on my face. "So, are you pleased that I brought this to your attention, Sternie? That's the sort of woman you have working for you. Maybe you should put some distance between yourself and Carrie Maitland now. She's a monster."

Moving quickly, I go and open my office door. "Thank you, Sam. It's always nice running into you."

She seems shocked. "You want me to leave? But I just told you something of vital importance!"

I just wait. Finally, she gets the message and stands up. "I guess you want to be alone to process this, Sternie. I'll go. Call me, okay? I promise that I can make you forget about this in the best possible way."

Closing the door quietly behind Samantha, I push a number on speed dial after taking my phone out of my back pocket. "Issac? Can you come to my office, please?"

I want to have a nice, long chat with my lawyer. My brain is firing like a rocket. I remember the smallest boy playing in the garden. He could not have been more than three years old, tops. Carrie's little boy is still a toddler. There is still time for us to get to know one another and bond.

Thinking back to all the cryptic things Carrie said to me over the last few weeks, they all start to make sense now. The importance of family. The need for her to make it here in Manhattan so that she can establish a home. Her insistence on visiting Simon's Town at every chance she gets. Her family's paranoia that it might happen again.

I have left the door open so that Issac can walk straight in, which is what he does. I feel restless, bursting with energy. It's time for Carrie to know that I know.

I don't care if she was embarrassed to tell me that she had an affair with some scoundrel who left her literally holding the baby on her own. But I need to explore my options. My thumbs fly over the keyboard as I shoot her a message on my phone.

"Do you mind if I change into sweats and work-out while we talk, Issac?" I'm already moving to the dressing room where I keep a small closet of casual clothes. "I am so amped up!"

Issac nods. "No probs, Stern. Just so long as you don't expect me to join you on the Peloton or anything."

Once I have the treadmill going at a steady rate that allows me to burn off my excess energy, I start talking. Issac sits on the weightlifting seat, taking notes on a yellow legal notepad.

"I want you to draft up a marriage contract for me, Issac. But I need it to include my future wife's first born kid in some way. How is that going to affect things, do you think? I want Carrie to know that I will look after both of them."

Issac is no longer scribbling on his notepad. He is gaping at me with goggling eyes. "You want to include your girlfriend's bastard in your prenup? Let me be clear, Stern. We're talking about Carrie Maitland."

The pace that I am running on the treadmill has got me working up a good sweat. "Yeah." Then I do a double take. "How did you know I want to ask Carrie to marry me?"

Issac shrugs. "Rumors, whispers, conjecture. Plus, it didn't help that you contacted some of Miles's old security buddies to help you clear up that mess you left behind in South Africa. They were on the phone to Miles a few days later, telling him that you were in South Africa with his sister."

Shit. "How did he take it?"

"Gail has made an appointment with me to discuss her legal options about dating a coworker. She told me over the phone that she has Miles well under control, so it looks like you might get away with it. Since Carrie Maitland came to work at the company, Boss, it seems like Sterns & Co. has turned into one gigantic fuckfest."

"How did Samantha Carson come to hear about this?"

Issac doesn't mince words. "Be careful of that woman, Stern. She's got you in her sights and won't let go. You're a wealthy man—don't be a fool now by listening to every bullshit story she tries feeding you. Hey, in the meantime, let me get these prenup contracts typed up so you can rest easy."

"Don't you worry, Issac. The only thing I need right now is for Carrie to say 'yes.'"

Chapter 37: Carrie

The door to Stern's office is open. I have an idea why he wants to see me. It might be about what Gail said to me in the coffee break room a few minutes ago.

When she saw me come in, she looked up, startled to see that it was me before bursting into tears.

"Oh, girl, I thought it was those Carsons coming to make trouble for me!" Gail was sobbing, "I don't know how to tell you this. Carrie—I know about your secret baby."

My stomach lurched. "Please don't tell Miles, Gail. We didn't tell him because he was going through so much stress with Belinda's refusal to have children. He would be heartbroken. You should have seen his face when he heard about Brody and Alma's second pregnancy."

Gail blew her nose with a small toot. "Why did you have to complicate it like this? Your brother has a right to know, for God's sake! Having a baby should never be treated like a big secret. They are a gift. A joy."

I hang my head. I feel ashamed for not being honest with my friend. "I know. That is how I have always thought of my son, Marcus. He is my very own precious little bundle of joy. But it broke my parents' hearts when they found out I was pregnant. They are super-conservative and strict. So, they told Miles I had been taken advantage of by some man, but nothing about the pregnancy. They said it was Miles's job to make sure I was never abused again when I came to work in New York."

Gail smacked the table with the palm of her hand. "So that is why your poor brother is halfway to going doolally worrying about you! It ain't right, girl!"

Sitting down opposite Gail, I take her hand. "I know. They were so worried about their own moral compasses that they gave my own moral compass no room to move! All I ever heard was "While you live under our roof, so you must abide by our rules!" I'm so sorry, but now that you are in our lives I promise we will do better. You have given my brother hope of a better, happier life. I can't thank you enough. I know my parents are thankful too."

Gail explained to me how Miles gave her my parents' number in South Africa. "I... I told Miles I wanted to introduce myself to your folks, Carrie. Seemed harmless enough. But it was Alma who answered the video call because she was on duty at the guesthouse... and we got talking. I saw three little boys, with red hair, and roughhousing in the background, so I asked all casual how many of the kids were hers. Alma said the eldest and youngest boys were her sons with Brody... and that the tallest boy was your son. I swear I nearly fainted from shock, Carrie! You should have told me. I am your friend."

All I could do was pat Gail's arm and apologize again. "I'm sorry, I'm sorry. I am so proud of my son. I never should have agreed to keep him a secret, but the pressure from my family was so intense. And I was too young, so I ended up listening to them instead of making up my own mind about what was best for me, Marcus, and…, Marcus's daddy."

Gail looks at me with a severe expression. "I get it, at least, I'm trying to. But Alma seemed fine telling me. You should have never agreed to let your family be the gatekeepers to your secrets, girl."

I try to explain. "I've been keeping secrets from everyone because my parents believed I should be ashamed. And I am ashamed, but not in the way they think I should be. I'm sad I didn't fight harder to tell the truth from the start. It made me hate and blame everyone else for the hole I dug."

Crossing her arms, Gail nods and says, "When was the last time you sat down with everyone involved in Marcus's life and communicated honestly with them, Carrie?"

All I can do is hang my head. "A lot of South African girls are coddled by their parents, Gail.

It's the by-product of all the crazy crime. It's really hard to break free of being coddled once it starts."

"Parenting is hard!" Gail says and then gives a chuckle. "But I get the feeling you haven't told me everything. I hope one day you do."

"It's not so much keeping a secret," I say in a confessional tone, "it's backtracking all the lies! Anyway, tell me what Alma said."

"We spoke for ages about the kids and what it was like in Simon's Town. Then we swapped contact deets and Alma emailed me." Gail brought her phone out and tapped the email app for it to open. "Alma says you were so brave raising Marcus on your own while working at the guesthouse as a maid to pay for his upkeep and studying for your art degree at the same time. She… she says you got so little sleep in the beginning, breastfeeding him for one year and still finding the time to be a good mom and all."

It made me smile to remember those stressful days raising my baby. "He was an angelic baby, Gail. Don't feel too bad for me. He hit all his milestones at least two months ahead of time.

Sitting up at four months. Pulling himself up to stand two months later. And walking at ten months. I left his baby book at home; when you go to visit with Miles, you must get my mom to show it to you."

Gail smiled mistily. "What a star. You make me proud to be your friend, Carrie. And now that's all out of the way, I have something to tell you too."

I acted cool, waving my hand. "Pfft, please. I know that you are moving in with Miles. When are the wedding bells going to start ringing?"

My friend blushed. "You don't think it's too soon?"

"No way. It's been over between Belinda and Miles for a year or more. You go, girl!" We laughed together, but then Gail got serious again.

"But honestly, I have to tell you, Carrie." Taking a big breath, Gail let it all out. "I've been reporting certain things to Stern. Only the stuff that concerns him, nothing private. That's why I called Alma—because Stern wanted to know why you are so against him meeting your family. He says he's getting mixed messages from you. Is that because you don't want him to know about Marcus?"

I did not have time to think about Stern wanting to meet my family. It doesn't take a rocket scientist to realize that I got it completely wrong about him almost right from the start. It's slowly dawning on me that I might have been misdirected by something- or someone.

I just remembered what I saw.

"Gail! Oh my God! I saw Belinda and Samantha snooping around your desk just now! I figured it was because Belinda got wind of you dating my brother. They were taking photos of your private email account." I tapped her phone. "Were Alma's emails on there?"

My friend bristled with anger. "Those bitches have been on at me about using the company phone to chat with Alma. But I couldn't tell Belinda that I was doing it with Stern's blessing. That is why I am so depressed, Carrie. There are too many secrets and lies flying around. Someone is going to get hurt, and I can promise you that Simon Sterns is not the kind of man who takes getting hurt lying down!"

My blood boiled when I heard that.

"I never kept the baby a secret from Stern! He knows. He just refuses to talk about it."

Gail looked at me all funny. "Are you sure about that, Carrie? That sounds crazy."

My memory churned backward to four months after I returned from my brother's Manhattan wedding.

To the love letter, I wrote to Simon Stern.

Dear Simon,

I am so sorry for not coming back that night. I still want to move in with you and be your girlfriend. I have to tell you the truth. My name isn't Caron Leslie. I'm Miles's little sister, Carrie. I'm not from Brussels. I was born in Texas but came here to South Africa when I was a baby.

I was a bridesmaid at the wedding, but it was my night to be so much more, and you helped me do that. That's why I love you so much.

I just have to finish my senior school exams here and then we can be together forever. I turned eighteen two months back, so you don't have to worry about me being underage.

Simon, I know we never got around to discussing contraception that night. And that has turned out to be a problem for me. You see, I haven't had my period since I came back home. That was four months ago now.

I remember you telling me about how much you wished for a family when you were in the foster home and how much you wished your mom had gotten her act together and made a home for you. I don't want that happening to our baby.

I'm pregnant. We are pregnant. I hope you are as happy and excited about this as I am! I haven't told anyone yet, only you. Please can you come over here and help me explain things to my folks? My sister-in-law, Alma, knows we hooked up for the most amazing one-night stand during the wedding reception.

She was not best pleased. She said that you would hire lawyers to escape any blame and that I must just get on with my life and forget about you. But I can't, Simon. Because I love you so much. And now we are going to be having a baby together!

I really need you beside me when I break the news to my parents. I am kind of scared.

Please email me back. My contact details are at the bottom. I can't wait to hear your voice, my darling, because I know that we were always meant to be together.

I love you with all my heart, Simon. See you soon,

Your darling,

Carrie M.

I put the letter into an envelope and marked it: IMPORTANT COMMUNICATION FROM CARON LESLIE at the back. Then I placed the envelope into a padded brown courier packet and labeled it: Attention Mr. Simon Stern, ℅ Mrs. Belinda Maitland, so that Belinda wouldn't think it was funny I had put the wrong name at the back of the envelope. I didn't realize that Simon had an S at the end of his surname. I was clueless.

When I never heard back from Simon, I started to panic. As a slim teenage girl, there was no way I could carry on hiding my pregnancy much beyond the first month of the second trimester. The baby was huge, already kicking me whenever they moved.

I loved to stroke my bulge, cooing down at my taut belly skin and saying comforting things in a whisper, but it was me who needed comforting.

Alma asked me why I was wearing baggy sweaters in the middle of summer when I was five months along in my pregnancy. I think she already knew. I made her promise to keep my secret about what I did at the wedding until I got the chance to write to Simon again.

This time, I could no longer pretend to be cool.

Dearest Simon,

Please please PLEASE contact me! I can't hide it anymore. I am scared. I have to tell my parents soon. I don't want to live here anymore because my mom will shout at me for being careless with my future.

But my future is with you, Simon. It has always been my destiny to be with you. Please don't let me down. Please help me.

Lots of love,

Carrie xxx

And that time, I mailed it directly to Belinda's home. There was no possibility of a courier-delivered packet getting lost if it was dropped off at my brother's house. Perhaps Belinda had opened my last packet and thrown it away when she saw the name at the back. I didn't want there to be any mix-up the next time.

Mrs. B. Maitland. There was no "℅ Simon Stern" on the front. At the back of the packet, I wrote very clearly. Belinda. This is the letter I need you to give to Simon, please. It's important. Thank you, Carrie.

I got a letter back one week later.

Alma brought it to me, turning the envelope around in her fingers before handing it over to me. "Who are you expecting a letter from in Manhattan, Carrie?"

Pushing her out of my room and slamming the door, I ripped the plain white envelope open. It looked official because the address and my name had been printed out on a sticker on the front.

Dear Ms. Maitland,

Mr. Sterns is aware of your attempts to contact him. He is, unfortunately, very busy right now. Whatever circumstances forced you to contact him are not important enough for Mr. Sterns to waste time on. There is no time in his life for insignificant additional problems.

Stop contacting Mrs. Belinda Maitland. Stop writing Mr. Sterns. And please may I remind you that there is a culture of strong work ethic at Sterns & Co. And that means there is no time here to waste on your pathetic family drama.

A word from the wise. It sounds as if you have lied to Mr. Sterns about many things. You should blame yourself for the situation in which you now find yourself.

Yours sincerely,

℅ Mr. S. Sterns's assistant's desk.

When I met Stern for the second time, I got the feeling from the way he behaved that his conscience was clear. Was he missing a piece of the puzzle that only I could provide? But the promise I made to my family stopped me from bringing up the subject so close to my heart.

In the coffee break room, I stood my ground. "I spilled my guts to Stern from the get-go, Gail. He just wasn't interested."

My phone beeps. Gail and I read the message.

Come to the mezzanine level office if you can, sweetheart. We have to talk. S.

"Well, it sure sounds as if he's interested now," Gail says in a gloomy voice.

That is what brought me to Simon Sterns's office. The door is open, so I go inside. The squeaking of a treadmill turning and the thumping sound of running shoes coming from Stern's private gym lets me know where he is. I hear a strange man's voice talking.

"Be careful of that woman, Stern. She's got you in her sights and won't let go. You're a wealthy man—don't be a fool now by listening to every bullshit story she tries feeding you. Hey, in the meantime, let me get these prenup contracts typed up so you can rest easy."

When I hear that, it's like I have reached my tipping point. Digging my nails into the palms of my hands to stop myself from screaming, I walk out of the office and walk out of the HQ building too.

I don't know where I am going, but I have to get away from Stern before he can mess with my heart more than he already has.

Chapter 38: Stern

It's been half an hour since I finished running on the treadmill and Carrie still hasn't arrived. Nor does she answer her phone.

I'm through ducking my head under the parapet as I negotiate Carrie's family's reaction to her being with me. The engagement ring arrived on my desk this morning and I can't wait to make us official.

After a quick shower and change of clothes, I head out to Heartbreak Hotel. That's what Carrie and I call the accommodation facility where she currently stays, because of all the divorced men living there. She has to be there because she's not at Apollo on First.

For the first time in my life, I put a little bit of thought into what I wear. After all, this is me, Simon Stern, asking a woman to be my wife forever and ever.

I go with a slim-fit Italian single-vent jacket, custom-made to sit smoothly over my shoulders, and matching pants. It's a navy wool-linen mix, perfect for fall weather. Add a light blue shirt and black tie, and I'm good to go.

Running my fingers through my hair, I can't seem to get that toddler with the bright red hair out of my mind. His father might be a deadbeat dad, but I will make that up to him. I want Carrie to know that we are in this together the moment she lets me slide this ring on her finger.

Gerry is waiting for me at the curb outside the HQ lobby. He knows the way to Heartbreak Hotel already. I'm not paranoid about carrying a gemstone worth millions of dollars in my pocket, but as a security expert, I am not about to take any chances.

"Drop you off outside the building. Is that okay, Stern?"

This is not the time for me to be thinking pessimistic thoughts. Of course, it will be okay for me to drop by Carrie's residence. Why wouldn't she be happy to see me?

"Sure, Gerry. But circle the block a few times before heading off. Carrie's phone is off, so I have no idea if she's really here."

Gerry tells me he'll keep his phone on for an update. I thank him and make my way to the foyer. A few middle-aged guys are sitting in the lounge area, chatting about whose divorce lawyer is best and swapping tips about how to hide assets offshore. Poor guys. I am positive such a thing would never happen to me.

The concierge uses the reception phone to call up to Carrie's room. "Ms. Maitland? There is a gentleman down here to—oh, you were expecting him. Fine, I will send him up."

He moves to open the elevator doors for me and then returns to his post. I have it all planned out. Knocking on Carrie's door, I get down on one knee and hold the ring box open in front of me. Corny, hell yes! But I'm only going to be doing this once.

I think Carrie goes into shock when she opens the door and sees me kneeling there in front of her. No, wait, she's in shock about the ring.

But she doesn't give me the reaction I was hoping for. "Aren't you going to shove a fucking legal agreement into my face first?" Leaving the door open, she turns and stomps back into her room. Slumping down on the couch, she folds her arms and stares blankly at the opposite wall.

Feeling foolish, I get up and walk inside, closing the door after me. "I thought you were expecting me? The concierge—"

"The world doesn't revolve around you, Stern. I am planning Miles and Gail's engagement party. I have hired Maurice and Dale. You remember them from five years ago. They were actually very sweet to me at that time. That's who I am expecting." The old mischievous smile plays on her pretty mouth. "Kind of as a way of saying 'fuck you' to Belinda."

I don't know what to say. "Yeah. Fuck Belinda. And fuck Samantha too. I can't stand either of those women. Sorry to change the subject, but what were you saying about legal agreements?"

Carrie sighs. Putting her bare feet up on the couch cushion, she huddles her arms around her knees. "I overheard you talking to Issac. He told you I was a gold digger, to be careful about me. He said I am feeding you some bullshit story about myself, Stern. But I'm not, I'm not."

Burying her face against her knees, Carrie lets her tears fall. I can't stand to see her in pain. Since the day we first met, all I have ever wanted to do is protect her from hurt and sorrow.

"We weren't talking about you, sweetheart." My need to comfort her is overwhelming. "I get the feeling you don't trust me to do the right thing by you." I tap her chest. "Let me in here, Carrie, please. What's the worst thing that can happen?"

Picking her up in my arms, I carry her through to the bedroom. She hides her face against my chest, weeping inconsolably. Laying her down on the bed, I stroke her hair back before handing her the white linen handkerchief from my pocket. I don't say anything about her son.

When the subject of Carrie's child comes up, it's got to be from Carrie's side.

"Issac was talking about Samantha Carson, Carrie. We were having a meeting about a prenup agreement and chatting about Sam trying to cause shit. It seems as though everyone at Sterns & Co. has been expecting news about our impending engagement except us!"

Carrie gives a sorrowful sigh and then sniffs. The color of her beautiful eyes is like silver pennies as she looks at me. Her hair looks like flames fanning around her heart-shaped face.

"What did Samantha tell you, Stern? Because the only time I ever lied to you was when we met." Looking shy, she blushes. "When I lied about my name and where I was from, but I only did it because you were the most amazing man I had ever seen! And I couldn't bear the thought of you walking away because I was Miles's kid sister."

Bending down, I kiss her. "To tell you the truth, I don't think that would have stopped me. I had to have you. And I really wanted to keep you too. Maybe it just wasn't our time."

I must know that Carrie is finally telling me the truth because that missing piece of the puzzle is really bugging me. "Carrie, when you returned home after Miles's wedding, did you try contacting me? Did you even know who your brother's best man was? Our time together was so rudely interrupted, I can't help wandering."

Carrie's face freezes and she gets pale. "You don't know that I tried to contact you...? My God, of course, I wrote you!"

Shaking my head, I give the surrender sign with my hands. "I never heard from you again, babe. Why do you think I've been such a grump for the last five years!"

Carrie seems frantic as all the words she wants to say fight to get out. "Forgive me, Stern. I'm in shock. I'm having to see you in a completely different light! You see, I was under the impression that you were ghosting me. After the wedding, I asked my parents who Miles's best man was. They only met you at the rehearsal dinner, but they approved of you. You know—ex-Navy SEAL, their eldest son's best friend, an up-and-coming security specialist for the rich and famous. What's not to like? That's how I found out your surname and how to contact you. So, I wrote you a couple of letters."

"I never got them." All those years we wasted over such a silly thing. "But does it really matter? We're together now. That is the most important thing."

She shakes her head. "No, Stern. That is not the most important thing. You see, th-the reason why I wrote to you is because I fell pregnant after that one wild night we had together. And I had our baby. You have a son. Marcus."

The world seems to shrink around me and then it suddenly gets larger and brighter. The future is so large and bright that this golden moment might last forever. It makes me forgive all the misunderstandings and anger Carrie and I have been feeling towards one another for the last five years.

"Carrie," when I say the words, my voice is hoarse with emotion, "all I need for you to make the happiest man in the world right now is for you to say yes. And then we're driving to Teterboro and going to see our son!"

Covering her face with her hands, Carrie gives a little scream of relief and joy. "Simon, I knew you would never turn your back on us. I was such a fool for believing that reply letter. Can you ever forgive me for thinking the worst of you?"

I hug her closely and growl in her ear. "Of course I forgive you. You poor girl. Believe me when I say that I am going to find out who poisoned your mind against me and make them pay... but in the meantime, I want to show you how much I love you."

Standing beside the bed, I begin to undress. This is what brings Carrie and me back together every time. The need for us to have sex. But now that we have a child together and are going to be married, the act of lovemaking is deeply meaningful.

Doing this has always been the best way to express our love for each other. After removing my jacket and tie and then my shirt.

Sitting on the edge of the bed, I hook off my socks. Then I stand up again to unbuckle my belt.

Carrie stretches like a cat as she watches me. "Stern, I'm so excited that we know the truth about one another, but I will never get tired of watching you drop trou. Oh God, the memory of you wearing that jockstrap during the wedding—!"

"I'm glad you remember me fondly, darling," I crawl onto the bed. "But I hope you are not disappointed with the boxer briefs."

That makes her laugh. "I could never be disappointed with you, Stern. I... I'm so glad you came. My crazy Manhattan life makes no sense without you."

Pushing herself up from the pillows, Carrie hooks her arms around my neck and pulls me down. Our kiss is sweet, lingering, and light as we feel our way around this emotional moment.

We kiss long and hard this time, Carrie's hand moves down to my briefs and begins to caress the rigid bulge in the pouch. I feel her finger pull the elastic band in the waist and free my throbbing cock.

She grips the shaft, but her fingers are too small to encircle it, so she massages my knob instead. The intensity of what we are doing never diminishes. I want her just as much now as I did that first time.

And now it's my turn to play. Slipping my hand under the hem of her dress, I pull the crotch of her panties aside. Her mound is so plump and soft. I love how naked her pussy feels after she shaves the labia. It lets me slide my fingers in the slit, playing with her clit and then going deep inside her.

It's so warm and wet there. I adore the way the tightness grips my finger. I can feel the sheath-like walls pulsing and gripping me, every time I stimulate her clit with my thumb. Her breath is coming in short gasps, which lets me know that her body is responding to my touch with rampant excitement.

I help Carrie sit up so that she can slip off her dress. As we kiss, our bodies undulating and pressing against each other in a frenzy of lust, I unhook her bra. Her pale breasts spill out of the lace cups, her nipples puckered, almost begging for me to lick them.

Carrie closes her eyes as my mouth fastens on her breast. But her eager hands are reaching for my cock. I know that she wants to guide me inside her, so I lift her and sit her on top of me.

"Just so you know our marriage will be an equal partnership, sweetheart."

Carrie smiles as her hair brushes my cheek. She bends to kiss me. "That's what you say now, Simon Stern, but I know you love to be the boss. And when it comes to sex, I am happy for you to ride me hard."

Oh God, I love it when she talks dirty to me. "Saddle me up, darling," I murmur deeply because I am fighting not to come, "because right now, you're the one doing the hard riding."

Tilting her hips forward, Carrie begins to slide her pussy up and down my cock. Her hands fondle her breasts and then slip downwards to cradle my balls. She gives them a gentle tug, stroking the smoothly groomed skin.

I grab her ass to grind her faster on top of me. She can feel I am close. Leaning forward so that her nipples are grazing my mouth, Carrie moans softly. "I'm coming, Simon, fuck me hard!"

When we cum, it is explosive. Carrie screams, biting her knuckle to stop it from being too loud. Arching my back to raise my hips, I shoot my load deep inside her.

We fall back onto the mattress, gasping for air. Slowly, we are aware of everything around us, because, for those few minutes, we were the only people in the world.

Pushing Carrie to one side, I bend over and pick up my jacket. When I lie back down again, I have the box in my hand.

Without saying a word, I remove the ring and wait. Carrie pushes the third finger of her left hand through the ring.

Then there is a knock on the door.

Chapter 39: Carrie

I am engaged to Simon Stern, and finally, finally, he knows about Marcus! Who could have ever been so cruel as to make me think Stern never cared for me and his son? What kind of twisted mind would do that? I think I must have felt something was wrong about that letter all along, I just couldn't put my finger on it because I was too young and inexperienced.

I knew his conscience was clear, especially after the innocent way Stern acted when I came back into his life.

I don't have too long to process the moment of my engagement because someone is calling me through the door.

"Yoohoo! Carrie. Why aren't you answering your phone?"

It's Maurice. I tell Stern who it is, but he recognizes the wedding planner's voice.

"Coming!" I call out in a loud voice, and then we both burst out laughing. My finger feels so strange having a big pink diamond engagement ring attached to it. It makes me feel like a fairy princess every time I look at my hand. It is my favorite color pink with very subtle mauve tones.

Pulling my dress down, I go and open the door. Everyone but the kitchen sink is standing in the hallway. Miles, Gail, Maurice, and Dale. Like the four horsemen of the Apocalypse. Well, that's what it feels like.

The six of us stand staring at each other for what seems like ages. Miles is the first to break the silence. "Well, aren't you going to invite us in? The jig is up, Carrie. Gail told me everything."

Maurice wastes no time in ushering us inside. "Forgive me, Carrie darling, but I still had Miles's phone number in my address book. I had to call him to find out if it was okay if I planned the engagement party. Bad memories about what happened last time and all that!"

Gail sits down, frowning at Stern as he casually buttons up his shirt. He's got his pants back on, but his shirt is untucked and hanging loose. "I said it was fine for Maurice and Dale to be here, Carrie because we have a lot to talk about."

"You're damn right about that," Miles mutters under his breath.

Maurice bounces up from the couch. "Carrie, Stern, I was there when you two first got together. I didn't realize it at the time—I thought you, Missy—" Maurice points to me. "—were sick because that's what you told your mother in the text. Mrs. Maitland came over to crap me out because she thought you were sick from the food! I remember that text, Carrie. Your mom showed it to me."

Maurice puts on a girly voice, "Hi Mom. Sorry, I feel sick and can't make the reception. The hotel is looking after me. Don't worry about me. They have given me a room to rest in. Love, C. All lies, wasn't it!?"

I hang my head. "Sorry, Maurice."

But the wedding planner is on a roll. "And I still didn't solve the mystery even though all the clues were staring me in the face! Miles told me he texted you, Stern, asking where you were with the champagne. Belinda was throwing a hissy fit about that. And then you come rabbiting into the reception, smelling of sex with a Cheshire cat grin on that handsome face of yours. You looked fucked, but you told the bride and groom you weren't feeling well."

"Blew me off to spend the night with my sister," Miles grumbles from the corner.

"Yahtzee!" Maurice points at Miles. "You got it in one, but five years too late. And then Little Miss High School here teeters up to the Great Ballroom, asking for Miles to come out and talk to her. Wearing a very crumpled white silk frock and reeking of sex. I didn't even recognize you, Carrie. You went from a little girl to a full-blown woman in a matter of hours. But when Dale tried to give Miles your message, your mom overheard him. That's why she came fuming out of the reception and dragged you home. Because, Girl—that dress! It was sex on legs and white. Your mom did the right thing. But I'm guessing Stern was expecting you to rejoin him in the bedroom?"

"Yes, I was." Stern interrupts. "And Carrie told me her name was Caron Leslie and that she was from Brussels."

Miles' hands bunch into fists. "Jesus H. Christ! You stood me up to go off and seduce my sister. I should punch you, Stern."

"He didn't know!" I shout at Miles. "I lied. But even if I hadn't, I still would have wanted to give Stern my V-card. Surely you of all people, Miles, can believe in love at first sight!?"

Gail and Miles hold hands and look lovingly at one another. "Yeah... I have to agree with you there, Sis," Miles admits to everyone.

Gail turns and nods to me. "Carrie, you're with friends here. Tell us what happened next...."

That lump comes back into my throat and I feel helpless. "It was all my fault. My parents dragged me home—they always treated me like their little girl—and I couldn't tell them what happened because Alma told me it would get Simon into trouble. So... so I called Belinda to ask her if she would deliver a letter to Simon. I told her Simon helped me get home when I felt sick at the wedding."

I have to break off and drink some of the bottled water Maurice is holding out to me before I can continue.

"But I never heard anything back! I was desperate. The next letter I sent to Belinda at home. That's how urgent it was—I didn't even care if Miles saw the letter. I had to let Simon know. Who I really was and why I had to leave. I didn't want him thinking I had run away from him."

Stern interjects. "And I had Miles threatening me on my side too whenever I tried to find out the name of the redhead bridesmaid."

"There were four redhead bridesmaids from my side of the family, Bru," Miles replies, "but you told me she was part of Belinda's entourage."

"Stop interrupting her!" Gail snaps before turning to me. "Please continue, Carrie."

"I got a reply to the second letter. From Mr. S. Sterns's Assistant's Desk." I go to sit next to Stern again, threading my fingers through his own. "I already told you about this. The letter I got back said that you were aware of me trying to contact you, but you were very busy. You didn't want me to waste your time... and that you had no place in your life for 'insignificant additional problems.' It ordered me to stop writing you and Belinda because Sterns & Co. was all about having a strong work ethic. And that I was trying to force my 'pathetic family drama' onto you."

Stern is gripping my hand so hard, he's cutting off the blood supply! I give him a quick hug to let him know how messed up it was before continuing.

"You see, Alma told me that would happen. That you would protect yourself from getting into trouble."

Stern shakes his head like he's waking up from a bad dream. "I never got any letter, Carrie. And you can call Phyllis right now if you want. She would never dare open my mail and take it upon herself to lecture you and scare you."

There is a break in conversation which Gail eventually fills. "I think we all know who is capable of doing something like that, don't you?"

She brings out her phone, presses a number, and then puts the phone on speaker so that everyone can hear.

"What do you want, Gail? You realize that I can still cause a lot of shit for you for making an international call from the office."

"Yes, Belinda, I know. I'm sorry. But that's not why I'm calling. Carrie saw Samantha and you hacking the password on my private email at work. Care to explain?"

"Not that it's any of your business, Gail, but Samantha has been suspicious about Carrie for a long time. You shouldn't listen to a word she says because that woman has her hooks in poor Stern."

"Really?" Gail pretends to be shocked. "What made Sam suspicious?"

"The silly little bitch was trying to get with Stern at my wedding five years ago. She asked me to pass along a letter to him, but when I opened the packet the envelope said it was from some other woman, Karen Leslie or something, so I binned it. Samantha says Carrie tried to get hold of Stern at my private home address too. My sister was staying with us at the time because her apartment block had bedbugs. She says the second letter was even more cringe-inducing and embarrassing. All about her not being able to hide it anymore, and that she loves him and was always destined to be with him. Stalker much?"

"Isn't it illegal to go opening other people's mail?" Gail manages to keep her cool.

"The idiot spelled his name wrong—Stern instead of Sterns—so technically, there is no such person. But seriously, Gail, be a team player. Don't listen to Carrie's lies. I swear we didn't go into your email—"

Gail disconnects the line. "Stern, there is something important Carrie was trying to tell you in those letters. She believed you received the second one because of that bogus letter Samantha sent her back."

Stern reaches for my hand and we stare lovingly into each other's eyes. I should have never doubted that my darling Simon was telling me the truth that first night we spent together. It was love at first sight, and I have a huge pink diamond engagement ring on my hand to prove it.

"Stern and I have a son together. Marcus. He is nearly four and a half years old and lives in Simon's Town with my family. Marcus knows Simon is his daddy because I made sure to show him photographs from the wedding every day of his life. Simon never knew, because Belinda Carson and her sister, Samantha, cut the communication between us. Pretending to be acting for Simon, Sam wrote to tell me he didn't want to be involved. I accepted it because I was a scared teenager. And because I lied about so much stuff when Simon and I got together for the first time. But I knew something was off when I saw Simon again and he never brought it up."

Stern stands up with his hands balled in fists. "I don't care what company rules say about firing someone, those two Carson crows better be gone by the time Carrie and I get back from South Africa!"

My brother rushes to hug his friend. "See, Stern? I told you how wonderful it is to have a kid! You're a daddy! How cool is that?"

The room is going crazy, everyone hugging everyone, laughing and crying, jumping up and down. Dale runs to the hotel fridge and grabs two miniature bottles of champagne off the shelf. We use the coffee cups to make a toast.

"To Miles and Gail!" Maurice cheers.

"To Stern and Carrie!" Dale shouts.

"Okay," Maurice wipes the corner of his eyes with a lace hankie, "shall we flip a coin to see who gets married first?"

Chapter 40: Family

Miles and Gail won the coin toss. They chose to have their honeymoon in South Africa so that we could all meet up in Simon's Town. The happy couple had a winter wedding. Gail looked absolutely divine in a high-necked gown with bell sleeves lined with white feathers.

I call my fiancé "Simon" now. To me, he will always be Simon in my heart. Stern belongs to other people and to his work, but Simon belongs to Marcus and me.

I don't see that much of my two boys during the mornings now. That's what I call my little family with Simon and Marcus—my two boys. Simon seems to have gotten younger over the last few months. He can't wait to get up in the mornings and have breakfast with Marcus. That is when they plan their activities for the day.

Simon is very generous with his time and attention. He includes Brody and Alma's little boys too. He's gone all-out buying the family lots of boy toys: jet skis, mini ATVs, bird-watching gear, camping equipment; you name it, Simon has bought it for his gang of little hangers-on.

Marcus always loved his daddy. He grew up speaking about Simon as if his daddy were waiting in the next room! But to have his daddy in his life full time has turned my son from being a mummy's boy into becoming a full-time daddy's boy twenty-four, seven!

My mom comes in. She's forgiven me for the lies, but most importantly, she's forgiven Simon. For so long, she begged me to tell her who Marcus's daddy was, but she respected my silence too. She supposed something bad had happened to me, but never forced me to confess until I was ready.

"Carrie, you have to tell Simon to stop spending so much money on the boys. They will get spoiled."

It's difficult for me to stop laughing nowadays. I am so happy, but my mom takes the cake when it comes to caution. "Ha! Mom, you're joking, right? He's a billionaire. I heard him on the phone to one of his famous Hollywood clients the other night, talking about bringing him to New York for Marcus's fifth birthday."

My mom clucks her tongue. "Simon tells me that he wants to buy us a yacht. Your dad was actually encouraging him. Who will pay the docking fees? That's what I want to know!"

"Honestly, Mom, I figure Simon will have that covered. He's a multitasker."

Rolling her eyes to the ceiling, my mom goes out muttering something about me not getting her point.

When my phone pings, I answer immediately. Simon made me promise that I would never stress him out again by not replying to his messages or calls. I blocked him out of my life and my heart for so long, I owe him that much.

Communication and the truth saved us in the end.

Only, it's not Simon calling.

"Hey, girlfriend," it's Maurice. He's my new BFF since Gail left me to concentrate on being Mrs. Miles Maitland!

"Hey, Maurice. How's Dale?"

"We good, darling, we good. Listen, I have a brilliant idea. What if we make your wedding theme one of those gorgeous Ndebele patterns? Those bright yellows, reds, blacks, and greens. I'm really feeling it, you know? And then we can have the reception at Apollo on First."

"How did you know that I finished the mural?"

"Didn't your handsome hubby-to-be tell you? He had a few New York art critics drop by while y'all were out of town. They are raving about the mural, Carrie! You are officially the talk of the town, and you are too far away to even enjoy it."

"Well, Marcus was homesick for his cousins, Maurice. I am going to have to set him up with a few play dates in Manhattan before we can make it through the month without him crying for South Africa."

"Well, I've seen the guest house in Simon's Town online, girl, so I can see the appeal. Even I want to trek up that dirt road to see the Admiral's Waterfall. It's divine."

"Maurice," I chuckle, "I would pay good money to see you do that in those shoes of yours! Listen, I love your idea for the Ndebele pattern and the reception. You are—as always—a genius."

"Thank you, darling. Coming from an art genius like you, that really means something. Bye. Mwah."

I look up when I hear the heavy tread of footsteps. I recognize that long, rangy stride. "Hey, Simon. Where's Marcus?"

He leans over to kiss me on the cheek before heading for the shower. It's fall in South Africa, but it's still hella hot outside. "I left him with Alma at reception. She's going to take the boys to Spur for supper."

There is a Spur Steakhouse restaurant in every South African town and suburb. They have a surefire recipe for success by including an extensive kiddies menu, while the moms and pops get to order steaks and schnitzels.

"Does that shower mean that you are in the mood for a little bit of Marcus-free time with your loving fiancée?"

He takes the hint. Coming out of the shower buck naked while toweling his hair roughly, Simon gives me a wink. "You must be a mind reader, darling."

We head for the bedroom after locking the door. Simon has booked out the guest house for the entire month, but we both promised ourselves that we never ever wanted to be interrupted in bed again!

I am wearing a bikini with a transparent beach wrap shirt over the top. Watching Simon lying on the bed watching me, I decide to put on a show for him.

Slipping my hands under the beach wrap shirt, I untie my bikini top. Never taking my eyes off his, I stroke my breasts. "Do you like what you see, Mr. Sterns?" Cupping my breasts and presenting them to him like an offering, I move closer to the bed. "Would you like to sample some? Have a lick?"

He tries to grab me, but I move away as though I am dancing. Turning my back on him, I bend over and begin to take off the bottom half of my bikini. I know that Simon craves my ass; he says it is nice and round like an apple, and it makes him want to bite it.

Jiggling my butt cheeks with my fingers, I dart him a sexy look over my shoulder. "How about now? See something you want to lick?"

Simon groans. "Come over here, you sweet little prick tease. I'm already hard as a rock."

He knows I love when he describes how rampant his cock is for me. "Ooh, Mr. Sterns, you are so wicked." I slide my fingers between my legs so he can see me getting busy with my slit.

This is too much for Simon to endure. In a flash, he is off the bed and lifting me into his arms. "Time for me to cash those checks that mouth of yours has been writing, Miss Maitland. Or is it Caron Leslie today?"

I can't stop giggling, but when Simon slides that delicious cock of his inside me, I get serious real quick.

My breath catches in my throat as I try telling him how good he makes me feel. "Remember the first time, Simon? When you took my V-card, I was dripping wet for you. It made the experience utterly sublime for me. You turn me on—you have always turned me on."

He rocks his shaft inside me, thrusting gently so that we last a bit longer. "I had to have you from the moment I saw you, Carrie. You belonged to me then, just as you do now."

Wrapping my legs around his waist, I push him into me deeper. His pulsing knob hits that perfect spot. My excitement begins to mount slowly, but surely. Simon can feel me get sopping wet. He grinds into me hard, allowing me to rub my clit against him as I search for my peak.

We have to kiss. I love the way he tastes, the scratch of his beard against my skin, the firm touch of his mouth as he explores my body.

"Do you want to cum, sweetheart?" Simon's deep voice and teasing tone just about drive me crazy with excitement. "Or is this going to be another one of our famous all-nighters?"

I give a little growl to show him I am displeased with his teasing. He can tell I am on the edge from the way I am digging my nails into his back. He watches my face contort from having to hold back my screams of ecstasy. Only when my spasms of pleasure are finished does Simon allow himself to cum.

After a while, we fall apart and lie in each other's arms for a spell. "I keep thinking it can't get better, darling," Simon growls, "but you make it better every time."

Snuggling up to him, I have a confession to make. "I think Miles is going to be pissed with us again, Simon."

That makes him laugh. "Miles is through being pissed. I've never seen my best friend so blissfully happy before. Did you know that they are already pregnant? Miles and Gail are going to have a honeymoon baby."

"They aren't the only ones, Simon...."

My first and only love sits up in bed, his face is full of joy. "Are you telling me you are also pregnant, Carrie?!"

"Second time's the charm."

Printed in Great Britain
by Amazon